The Silk Thief

Claire Buss

Published by CB Visions in 2021

Copyright © Claire Buss

First Edition

The author asserts the moral right under the
Copyright, Designs and Patents Act 1988 to be identified
as the author of this work.

All Right Reserved. No part of this publication may
be reproduced, stored in a retrieval system or
transmitted, in any form or by any means without the
prior consent of the author, nor be otherwise circulated
in any form of binding or cover other than that which it
is published and without a similar condition being
imposed on the subsequent purchaser.

This is a work of fiction. Names, characters, places,
and incidents either are the product of the author's
imagination or are used fictitiously. Any resemblance to
actual persons, living or dead, business, companies,
events, or locales is entirely coincidental.

www.clairebuss.co.uk

Cover artwork by Ian Bristow

Other works by Claire Buss:

The Roshaven Books
The Rose Thief
The Silk Thief

The Interspecies Poker Tournament – The Roshaven
Case Files No. 27
Ye Olde Magick Shoppe

The Gaia Collection
The Gaia Effect
The Gaia Project
The Gaia Solution
The Gaia Collection (Books 1-3)

Poetry
Little Book of Verse, Book 1 in the Little Book Series
Little Book of Spring, Book 2 in the Little Book Series
Little Book of Summer, Book 3 in the Little Book Series
Spooky Little Book, Book 4 in the Little Book Series
Little Book of Love, Book 5 in the Little Book Series
Little Book of Autumn, Book 6 in the Little Book Series
Little Book of Winter, Book 7 in the Little Book Series
Little Book of Christmas, Book 8 in the Little Book
Series

Short Story Collections
Tales from Suburbia
Tales from the Seaside
The Blue Serpent & other tales
Flashing Here & There

Anthologies
Underground Scratchings, Tales from the Underground anthology
Patient Data, The Quantum Soul anthology
A Badger Christmas Carol, The Sparkly Badgers' Christmas Anthology
Haunted, The Sparkly Badgers' Halloween Anthology
The Last Pirate, Tales from the Pirates Cove anthology

Chapter 1

It was Griff's funeral. Ned Spinks, Roshaven's Chief Thief-Catcher, watched from his elevated vantage point on the upper part of the shore as the crowd congregated by the water. He scanned the throng for any suspicious behaviour. A cool sea breeze carried some freshness his way, combating the aroma caused when you get lots of individuals gathering in one place. It gave him small comfort to see such a large turnout, his own grief was too raw.

'Yor not on the clock now, Boss,' Jenni the sprite remarked as she nodded a greeting at the Gingerbread folk. Wary of the water, they stood as far from the damaging liquid as they could without removing themselves from the ceremony.

'Yeah, well, you know, people,' muttered Ned.

'Fourteen's over there.'

Jenni pointed and they both stared at the elegant Imperial gazebo erected upon the Dead Pier. This was the other reason such a great crowd had assembled, and why the air hummed with animated chatter and gossip. The Emperor of Roshaven had recently revealed she was a woman, and this was her first formal event since that announcement. Unfortunate that it was a state funeral.

'Mhm.' Ned's reply was as nonchalant as he could make it. He hadn't seen Fourteen since they returned from their quest to save love and defeat the Rose Thief. After their triumphant return to the city, Fourteen had been immediately swept up by her administrators, the High Left and High Right. Every time Ned tried to get in to see her, the Highs cited important imperial duties that couldn't be disturbed. After several tries, Ned had resolved to leave it for a while. He wasn't certain if it were the Highs or Fourteen that were keeping him away.

'Sparkly dress,' commented Jenni.

Ned knew she was trying to get a response from him and his gaze flicked over again to where Fourteen stood, slightly apart from her retinue. Her short black hair framed her face and her silver gown was shining in the sun.

It relieved him when the opportunity came to change the subject as Momma K, Queen of the Fae, glided past bestowing regal smiles upon individual members of the crowd. Ned noticed he didn't receive one and Jenni had ignored hers.

'Things not going smoothly at home?' Ned inquired. Jenni was the eldest of Momma K's children, but she stayed with him in the city more often than not.

'S'complicated.' She was looking over at people on the pier again. 'Who's that talking to Norris?'

Ned decided not to push it, families were complicated, and his was no exception. Despite himself, he glanced over again at the dignitaries assembled on the pier. Fourteen was busy greeting some bureaucrat or other. There were representatives from all of Roshaven's trade partners and a few cities they had not yet connected with. He could make out Fat Norris, otherwise known as the Lower Circle, whose responsibility it was to maintain existing trade agreements and keep them running smoothly while working on establishing new ones. He was talking to a familiar looking man, dressed in blue. Ned squinted and then stiffened.

'It's Theo.'

'Wot, yor bruvver? Wot the 'ell is 'e doing 'ere?

Murderous scumbag!' Jenni took a couple of steps in the direction of the Dead Pier before Ned stopped her.

'Not now. He's probably here as a trading partner. I don't like it anymore than you do, but we've got a job to do. We can find out what Theo's up to later.' Ned tried very pointedly not to look at the people on the pier.

They had been escaping from Theo's clutches in Fidelia when Griff had helped them get away. That help had cost Griff his life. Both Ned and Jenni blamed Theo despite the fact the actual murderer was probably one of Theo's henchmen. When Ned had tried to find out using his official catcher authority, he'd been told that Fidelia had dealt with and executed the individual involved. Ned wasn't sure he believed it but he couldn't put his own city at risk, rocking the boat. Especially when Fourteen had just revealed her gender. She was the first official female Emperor. The slow wheels of progress, hampered by the brakes of tradition had not yet sanctioned the use of Empress.

Centuries ago, Roshaven had been the epicentre of a vast empire that spanned from coast to coast. It was that imperial lineage that Fourteen's forebears had clung to, downsizing yet keeping their Imperial Palace and fighting tooth and nail to keep their crucial trading position on the coastline of Efrana. Now Roshaven was a bustling commerce city. It might not be a centre of industry, but it facilitated the shipping of both essential and luxury items up and down the coast, in particular the fine silks that were coveted throughout Efrana. It also provided the perfect location for trading vessels to restock their supplies and gain additional crew. Many of Roshaven's trade agreements had been meticulously negotiated and arm twisted into place by Griff. Ned hadn't known that about his friend before he died, but it was the reason he was being honoured with a state funeral.

Ned winced. He had been trying not to think too much about the circumstances of Griff's death.

'It weren't yor fault, Boss.'

'Stay out of my head, Jenni.'

'I ain't reading yor fawts, I can't do that. It's plastered all over yor face.'

Ned sniffed and blinked. Damn sand was in his eye.

'If it wasn't my fault, then whose was it?'

Jenni hawked and spat.

'I can't ignore that Theo is my brother, no matter how much I want to. And if I don't take responsibility for his actions, who will? I cannot call myself innocent of any wrongdoing. It was my idea to appeal to Griff for help when we needed it on our quest. And it cost him. It cost him everything.'

'Family ain't blood,' replied Jenni.

'No, but he is my brother, and it's a debt I will never clear.' Ned stopped speaking as the funeral rites commenced.

Pristine white wrappings concealed Griff's body, and it lay upon a stack of firewood. There were blossoms and offerings of food pushed in-between the sticks and branches. Various runic symbols of protection and safe travels had been painted in gold around the decoratively carved canoe that held the pyre. Fourteen placed a single red rose on the torso and bowed her head in respect. She stepped backward and the many and various priests of Roshaven chanted a simple farewell prayer, each of them dedicating it to their own deity as well as chiming numerous bells.

Ned shivered as the chanting and chimes made the hairs on the back of his neck stand up.

Several druids came forward to push the canoe into the water. Ned spotted Kendra, the High-Priestess among them. Their druidic incantation danced across the breeze, and he heard snatches of their melodic prayers. A sudden swirl forced them to hasten back, allowing the canoe to be taken by a gossip of mermaids. Pearl's distinctive golden blond head bobbed above the water and Ned half-smiled to himself.

The harpies were next. They flew over the aquatic procession, scattering petals—a tender side to them Ned would never have expected. Fred, the young palace guard, led the Imperial Band in a farewell fanfare and Momma K sent a magnificent shower of silver stars shooting out across the harbour.

Ned took a deep breath. It was his turn now.

Dipping a pitch-tipped arrow into the bowl of flames nearby, it lit with a whoosh and, taking another steadying breath, he nocked and drew, mindful not to singe himself. He could sense all eyes on him with the heavy pressure of expectation, and his arms began quavering. Focusing on the body and canoe below, Ned shakily exhaled and released his flaming arrow. The crowd watched mesmerised as it arced high over the water before landing. The pyre had been doused with scented oils both to mask the stench of rotten flesh and also to serve as an accelerant.

For a long moment nothing happened and Ned half stretched out his hand to pick up a second arrow, but then the fire took and ran hungrily over the body. There was a collective stillness on the shore. Then the crowd began stirring, returning to their lives. Ned remained standing, watching the flames devour his friend as the canoe drifted further and further out to sea, his thoughts bleak.

'It was a grand send off,' said a gentle voice behind him.

Ned flinched in surprise as the spicy, warm perfume of Fourteen wafted to his nose. He had not expected to speak to her today.

'Are you allowed to be here?' The question came out harsher than he meant it to.

'I wanted to see you. Before this, I mean. But there were so many pressing matters to attend to...' She glanced back at her entourage before trailing off into silence.

Ned could tell Fourteen was attempting to reach out to him, to reconnect, but the fact that the Highs and other officials were so close meant she had to maintain her imperial persona. A quick check confirmed Theo was not among the retinue. He scuffed the ground with his smart boots, not caring if he dulled the patent leather. He could hear Fourteen breathing beside him, but for the life of him he couldn't think of anything to say that wouldn't come out snippy. And he didn't want to be like that. Not with her.

'Have you ever fired a funeral pyre before?' asked the Emperor.

'No, Your Eminence, I haven't.'

'You did a superb job, I'm very impressed.'

Ned turned to look at his Emperor but misjudged his footing and knocked over the fire bowl. He and Jenni spent several tense moments frantically stamping out the flames. Somewhat out of breath, Ned attempted to reclaim his cool.

'Perhaps I could visit soon. If you think it would be possible?' He smiled to soften the words. He wasn't trying to be argumentative, and he did want to spend some time with her.

A High cleared his throat and cast his eyes meaningfully towards the imperial coach that was waiting to take Fourteen back to the palace.

Fourteen didn't reply, but she touched one of Ned's hands briefly before returning to her retinue.

'That went well,' he murmured.

'It weren't that bad. At least she came and said allo. S'more than you've 'ad in a while,' Jenni said as she gathered up the bow, spare arrows and the now empty fire bowl which she handed to Ned. 'It takes two to wotsit but you gotta keep trying I reckon.'

Ned threw her a half-smile as they headed back into the city together.

'Thanks. Oh, and thanks for the assist by the way.'

'For wot?'

'The flaming arrow?'

'Nah, Boss. That weren't me and it weren't Momma K neiver. All youse.'

Ned tucked his chin in, trying to suppress a grin. He'd done it, he'd given his friend the tribute he deserved. He waved a hand over the virtually empty shoreline they were leaving.

'You don't think all this was too much?'

'For Griff?' Jenni scoffed. 'E would've wanted more, more, more, I reckon. You knew 'im better than me, wot do you fink?'

'I think you're right. He would have wanted a bit *more, more, more.*' They strolled on in silence for a few beats. 'Good turnout though, wasn't it?'

'Not bad. Wot we gonna do about Theo then?'

'We'll keep our eyes open, check out anything suspicious that we hear of. Hopefully he's already on his way out of Roshaven.' Ned hoped his brother wasn't planning to hang around.

'We ain't gonna arrest him?'

'Not today, Jenni. He hasn't committed a crime in Roshaven. Yet.'

'Hmm, if you say so, Boss. I reckon we could arrest 'im for summink if we looked 'ard enough.'

'You're probably right.' They had reached a crossroads. One way led to The Noose, Thief-Catcher HQ and disreputable tavern, the other towards Ned's home.

'Not going to the wake, Boss?' asked Jenni as Ned took a step away from The Noose.

'You can if you like. I'm gonna call it a day. Not been sleeping well.'

'Rightyoucha Boss.'

'Here, take this back to the office first with that other stuff.' Ned handed Jenni the fire bowl to go with the bow and arrows she was carrying. They kept their thief-catcher weaponry locked up at HQ.

'Awright Boss. Sees you later.' With half a wave Jenni peeled off, heading for The Noose and what would be a raucous wake.

Ned trudged on home, hoping that his nightmare would let him sleep tonight.

Chapter 2

'She wants payment upfront, Boss.'

Jenni was elbow deep in ocean and concentrating. Connecting to the entity that lived in the bay wasn't straightforward. The two fae spoke a distinct language and worked in different magics.

'And she ain't waiting much longer. We gotta pay 'er quick.'

Ned sighed. Payment for the Sea Witch. What would that be? He glanced around the wallowing skiff that carried him, Jenni and the rest of the catchers, tree nymph Willow and human Joe. Various bags and boxes were heaped in the centre. They were drifting neither forwards nor backwards and a pitiful wind tried ruffling Willow's leaves but refused to move them in any forward direction. On the shore Theo's men had now noticed the skiff, their spyglasses had confirmed the occupants, and heavily armed rowboats were being assembled. Desperate for a solution on how to evade his brother's clutches, Ned stared at the others for inspiration. Joe looked like he was about to throw up and Willow was matching Joe's greenness but as she was a tree nymph, Ned wouldn't expect anything less. She was, however, holding her tendrils as far away from the seawater as she could. Some paper was dancing in the slight breeze. Hang on, paper? Ned leant over and eased the note out from under two boxes, his heart thumping harder as he recognised the scrawl.

You'll have to pay the Witch. Look in the red bag, it's no one you know, eh!

Griff. Bloody Griff, saving their lives, again. Ned spotted a red bag sitting off to one side from the others, its wet base a darker rusty colour. There was a fair amount of heft to it. Something heavy lay within. In trepidation, Ned undid the ties and opened the bag. A coppery tang wafted out, and he peered inside. The head of his good friend and charismatic smuggler, Griff, stared back at him. The dead man's eyes snapped open, and the head began screaming.

Ned blinked. He sat bolt upright in his own bed, in his own house, in Roshaven. The screaming had been his. He wasn't on a skiff, Griff had been dead for a month, and they'd just had his funeral.

'Novver one, Boss?' asked Jenni.

Ned blinked in the gloomy light of his bedroom. It wasn't even morning yet. There was a lump at the foot of his bed. Was that Jenni or something else? He almost expected it to be Griff's body.

'Jenni? What are you doing here?'

Her hand thrust a glass of an unidentifiable liquid in front of Ned's face. It weaved back and forth a little, accompanied with the distinct smell of imbibed spirits. Jenni must have returned from the wake and come to check on him.

'Whatchoo lookin' at, Boss?' she asked.

Ned's tired brain was struggling to untangle itself from the nightmare. He groped to his left, where a compact power well had been plumbed into the wall. Gathering his highly scattered wits, Ned muttered under his breath, *Illumi.* Nothing happened.

Seeing what he was trying to do, Jenni clicked her fingers and nothing happened. Again.

Frowning now at the absence of magic, but reasoning Jenni's was down to her being drunk, Ned scrabbled for the book of matches he kept on the bedside table. A little further exploration unearthed a candle stub. The match flared and lit the wick, casting a small pool of candlelight. Blowing the match out, Ned regarded the lump at the foot of his bed. It was his coat. Nothing more. Jenni stood beside him. Ned let out a shaky breath. Griff was dead. Murdered for helping Ned and his team escape from Theo, Ned's brother. His body was sunk in the ocean and most definitely not at the bottom of Ned's bed.

'Drink it, Boss. It'll do you good,' said Jenni, waving the glass in front of Ned again. 'I got it from Kendra, in case.'

Relieved that the beverage was druidic and not one of Jenni's concoction, Ned took the glass and downed it.

'In case of what?' he asked belatedly.

'You know, stuffs.'

Ned silently thanked the Gods for Jenni. He wasn't sure what he'd done to deserve such a good second-in-command. She often waded far over the colleague line into guardian fae. And yes, there had been the potato incident, but that was a long time ago. That had been Ned's first case as a thief-catcher. Now he was the chief, and potatoes were banned from the office.

As his faculties regrouped, Ned's nose remembered Jenni stood very close to him. And she'd been drinking.

'A little space, please?' Her unique aroma was making Ned's eyes water.

The sprite huffed a bit but moved backwards.

'What time is it?' he asked.

'Two bells rang. S'not morning yet.'

Ned rubbed his eyes as tiredness washed over him again. His brain had finally caught up to the fact he was now awake, had just had a nightmare and Jenni was in his bedroom.

'Well then, there are a few more hours 'til we have to get up so why don't you go back to your room and get a bit of sleep. Hmm?' he said with a modicum of hope.

Jenni peered at him intently, as if she were attempting to look inside him.

'Yeah, I reckon,' she conceded. 'But 'ere. No more nightmares for you.' Dipping her hand into her coat pocket, she threw a handful of golden, glittering dream sand in his face.

'Jenni, nooooooooooo,' but Ned trailed off and sank into a deep sleep before he could chastise her any further.

Chapter 3

Jenni hawked, spat and whistled through her teeth. A glowing firefly twinkled into view. It was Sparks, another member of the thief-catcher team.

'Awright, Sparks. You watch 'im. Sound the alarm if 'e 'as anovver nightmare but 'e should be way under. No dreams down there. Nuffink to get 'im.'

The firefly responded with a complicated light show which meant *Yes, Sir—will do!* Jenni nodded in satisfaction and popped out of the room. She had business elsewhere.

Two hours later and Jenni had a numb bum from perching on top of The Noose's roof. She'd chosen Thief-Catcher headquarters for her vigil because of its proximity to the Black Narrows, and she figured that if there were any Nightmares galloping around, they would be here. So far, no luck. A light drizzle had decided to keep her company. Jenni sank lower into her red coat and contemplated her options.

Not getting hold of a Nightmare meant another day of a barely functional Ned, plus going into another night's sleep filled with horror. Putting all her apprehensions for her boss aside, she was bloody knackered as well. Fae could go longer than humans without sleep, but not that much more. Shifting again, to find a less numb spot, Jenni spotted movement from the corner of her eye.

Holding her breath, she slowly turned her head to see what it was.

Nothing.

There was, however, a somewhat smug looking gargoyle two rooftops over with a plethora of pigeon feathers around its feet so someone had just caught dinner.

Thinking that some wasp honey on toast might not be a bad idea, Jenni was about to call it a night when she heard hooves nearby. A Nightmare was trotting out of a bedroom window and heading towards her. Jenni clicked her fingers intending to magically pop from the roof to the back of the Nightmare, but it didn't work. A handful of blue stars fizzed from her fingertips, then disintegrated. The transparent Nightmare was almost level with her now, so she took a chance and jumped, landing on something solid.

Bouncing along like a rag doll and hanging upside down on one side, she had to swerve to avoid three chimney pots, but grabbing a fist full of insubstantial mane and pulling herself up got her in a better riding position on the beast. It was odd sitting astride smoke and shadow, but the gleaming teeth in the Nightmare's mouth that snapped back in Jenni's direction were nothing to be blasé about.

'Awright, take it easy. I just need a chat wiv yor boss, that's all. Will you take me to 'im?'

Jenni watched the Nightmare consider the fact that a sprite was clinging on for dear life. With a sinuous shake of its mane and a bone-chilling whinny, the Nightmare changed direction and began climbing towards a dark patch of sky.

It was the home of Barbas, the demon of fear and owner of the Nightmares. Jenni shivered. She might appear tough to the other catchers but she had her own share of fears, ones she wasn't keen on facing right now, but her worry for Ned had driven her here. She wanted to know why Barbas was attacking Ned and whether someone else was behind it. A powerful someone to get Barbas to do their bidding.

The temperature dipped as the Nightmare drew closer to the darkness, and once they were surrounded by pitch black, the horse stopped and whickered.

'Guess that means get off then,' muttered Jenni as she scrambled off the beast. She gave it a friendly pat on the rump. Just in case.

Looking around there wasn't much to see so rather than blunder about in the dark, Jenni began speaking.

'I'm 'ere to talk wiv Barbas and I ain't going 'till 'e listens to wot I gots to say.'

There was no response. Jenni changed tack. Muttering an incantation under her breath, she started poking her finger into bits of darkness, intending to create spots of light. Only one bright golden spot appeared, the others remained dark in various shades of black and grey. Jenni shook her finger, wondering why her magic was being so stubborn. It hadn't worked properly all day.

'I do wish you wouldn't try to change the décor. True pitch is so hard to maintain.'

The voice came from behind the sprite and whilst she hadn't jumped when it spoke, Jenni's heart was now beating ten to the dozen. Without turning around, she replied.

'You Barbas?'

'And whom am I speaking with?'

The voice glided past Jenni's shoulder and an ordinary looking man stood before her. She was disappointed. She'd expected something more nightmarish, bones or rotten flesh or snot or even just some horns at least. Instead it was a man in a pinstripe suit, white shirt, but no tie and salt and pepper hair that flopped to his shoulders.

'I'm Jenni. Got business wiv Barbas 'bout summink.'

The man inclined his head and waited for Jenni to say more.

'Right. That's you then, I guess. What it is, right, is me boss is getting nightmares. Ana I don't just mean little flippy floppy ones wot we all get. I means proper gut wrenching, making 'im ill ones, and s'not right. E ain't done nuffink wrong. So I'm 'ere to sort it out.'

She licked her lips, wishing she had some water for her dry mouth while she waited to see what Barbas would say.

The demon-shaped man watched Jenni with amusement dancing in his eyes.

'My, my. You came here, to confront me, over a mortal? Do you love him, little sprite?'

Jenni's sprite tail flicked despite herself. She did love Ned, but not like that.

'That ain't none of yor beeswax. You gotta leave 'im alone.'

'And what if I disagree?' Barbas made no movements, but the surrounding air grew darker and thicker, building up its inherent menace.

'If you don't, I'll 'ave a word with Momma K. I 'ear youse two 'ave got 'istory.' Jenni held her breath and waited. Most people had history of some sort with Momma K. You didn't get to be the longest serving fae queen without racking up favours and backstory with practically every other supernatural being. Jenni didn't enjoy using her mother's influence as leverage. It generally came back to bite her in the butt.

Barbas let out a short 'ha' of laughter and rubbed his

chin.

'Who is your boss?' he asked.

'Ned Spinks.'

The fear demon steepled his fingers and regarded Jenni for a moment. He sounded regretful when he spoke.

'The contract has been paid, there's nothing I can do. You understand. Rules are rules.'

Jenni's heart sank.

'Whose the contract wiv?' she asked. 'You can tell me that, right?'

But Barbas had begun to fade away.

'It's a blood contract,' he whispered before he and his realm disappeared.

Jenni had a partial answer to her question but now she was ten feet up in the air frozen in place as physics tried to decide what it was going to do with her. Gravity staked a claim and Jenni tried her magic once more, willing herself to pop while falling. She had aimed for landing neatly on her feet on the ground, but instead she popped inside the thief-catcher's office and hit the floor with a thump. A much better landing than her initial trajectory, which would have had her falling through its roof. Even so, she made Joe yelp in surprise at her abrupt entry.

'Jenni! Are you okay?'

'Yeah.' She rubbed her bottom. 'Wot you doing 'ere this early?'

Joe gestured at the many and various piles of paperwork.

'Thought I'd get a bit of filling done before the day starts. I'll be doing a breakfast run as soon as Willow gets here. You want anything?'

'Nah. Yor awright. I'll sees you later.' And she left

Joe to his filing as she went to tell Ned what she had
learnt.

Chapter 4

The powerful aroma of bean wafted into the thief-catchers' office, accompanied by the sleep-deprived Ned and a highly beaniated citizen. Ned's vision was wavering on the edge of blurry, but he couldn't decide if that resulted from being bone-tired or because of the powerful vapours coming from the strung out member of the public he had with him. The man had accosted Ned as he arrived for work, complaining that he'd been barred from *Headshot* for drinking too many beanspressos and that he wanted to file a formal complaint.

Beanspressos were new to Roshaven. As was the bean beverage. It had come into port on the last delivery from Griff's ships. The old smuggler had prepared ahead, securing a vacant shopfront and hiring a couple of preppy young things who'd travelled a bit and seen way more than they'd bargained for. He'd made them eager to front his latest scheme–Bean Shops, where people came to pay extra for a drink they could potentially make far cheaper at home.

Headshot was the name of the new shop. Or was it a bar? Ned wasn't clear. His experience of bars ran to *The Noose* because he ignored the advice of not drinking where you work. In fact, it would be bloody difficult to not drink where he worked, doing what he did.

'What have we got today, Boss?' Willow asked, her leaves fluttering. The bean was a new plant to Roshaven and once the tree nymph had recovered from the horror of learning that the beans were ritually roasted, ground and boiled alive, she'd taken on plant pride at how popular the beverage was becoming. That was until the trouble started. Highly beaniated individuals had been causing a ruckus when they'd drunk too much or too little bean so now Willow was in charge of all bean-related disturbances.

'This gentleman claims he was ejected with unnecessary force from *Headshot* on account of drinking too many beanspressos, He'd already had seventeen apparently,' said Ned. 'I brought him upstairs because he was starting to show tendencies.'

All the catchers had quickly become familiar with bean terminology and the associated tendencies. They included talking fast, acting manically, staying up working without sleeping, snapping aggressively at anyone who got between them and regular bean and creating a public disturbance when they couldn't get their bean.

'I just wanted a flat white. Although what's flat about it is anyone's guess. Always looks cup shaped to me.' The man spoke at breakneck speed, the result no doubt from the seventeen double shots he allegedly drunk. *Headshot* lined them up at the counter in little cups instead of shot glasses. They had more or less the same effect.

Willow glanced at the man's face, then did a double-take. His pupils were massively enlarged.

'Erm, are you feeling alright?' she asked.

The man nodded only once he started, he couldn't quit and his entire body started jerking. Ned guided him to a chair and got him to sit down. One knee continued to jig, causing the man's boot to tap tap tap on the floor, but with sitting down he'd manged to stop his head from nodding along.

Willow settled herself on the edge of the desk, leaves whispering and a couple of tendrils reaching out to touch but never making contact.

'Boss, what should we do with him? He can't stay here.'

Ned couldn't answer straight away as a giant yawn overcame him and his jaw cracked loudly.

'Sorry. Um, you'd better take him over to the Druid Grove. They can see about a tonic or a purge or something. Get him down enough to sleep it off.'

'No, no, no, no, no, no.' The man started talking again. 'The plan is to not sleep. Because without the sleep there are no dreams and without the dreams there is no screaming, so everyone wins because who wants to hear screaming, huh? Huh, huh, huh, nobody does, that's who, nobody does. Nobody. Nobody.' His face had cracked into a manic grin and he'd started tapping his fingers on the desk, doing a double-time rhythm with his toes.

Ned watched in fascination. His dreams were currently plagued with nightmares so he was getting very little sleep at the moment and doing his best to try and stay awake as much as possible. If what this man said was true, maybe bean was the answer to Ned's sleep problem.

'Where's everyone else? Shouldn't they be in by now?' Ned asked Willow.

'I'm the only one here. Sparks has a family day and Joe has nipped out. I thought Jenni was coming in with you.'

'No, she was gone when I got up. I thought she'd be here, to be honest,' replied Ned, not knowing that he and Jenni has just missed each other at the house that morning.

In her agitation, Willow was not paying attention to her spores and several new growths were latching into cracks in the floor, wall and ceiling and had began nestling themselves into the building. Unchecked, they would grow into a beautiful canopy.

Jenni banged open the office door, making Willow shed numerous leaves and the man in the chair jump.

'You've been told afore, tree-girl, no propagating,' said Jenni, pointing at the shoots. Then she noticed the beaniated man, who had stopped tapping his appendages in a jittery jig and was now staring blankly into space. Jenni clicked her fingers in front of him, but there was no reaction. 'What's going on wiv 'im?'

'I think he's had too much bean. He's been talking super fast, shuddering and shaking like a mad thing. I'm going to take him over to the Druids.' Willow glanced at Ned who was immersed in reading last night's reports. As she nipped her buds and shoots she whispered to Jenni. 'Did he get any sleep last night?'

Jenni checked to make sure Ned wasn't paying any attention to them. He wasn't.

'Nah. 'E's got a proper Nightmare on 'im. Paid for by blood.'

Willow turned sickly green and shuddered. A dull bark colour flashed over her skin. Every tree-nymph's fear was losing their power and becoming dead wood.

'Did you go see… *Barbas*?' she rustled.

'Yeah, ana fat lot o' good it did me. Bloody fear demon. 'E finks e's all that, but 'e ain't. 'E owes Momma K just like the rest o' the world.'

'So who put the curse on the boss?' Willow's thorns were flexing in numerous places as her fear and anger sparred with each other.

'Who do you fink? It's gotta be Theo.'

This time the thorns didn't disappear.

'I do not like that human. Not one bit,' said Willow.

'Yeah, join the massive queue.' Jenni sighed. 'But we gotta figure out why e's done it. Feels a bit late for the whole captured in his castle fing wot 'appened a while back. It can't be that. It's gotta be summink else.'

'What's got to be something else?' Ned was watching them curiously.

A clatter in the stairwell prevented Jenni from replying. It sounded like a helmet crashing to the floor, followed by lots of scrabbling noise.

'Oh 'ere we go,' muttered Jenni.

'Where are we going?' asked the beaniated man as Fred, the young palace guard, entered the thief-catcher office.

'Hello, Sir. Jenni. Willow. I'm ever so sorry to bother you. I was meant to be going up to Mother Wicklow for a poultice for our Brian, but then the message came down and they said it were very urgent. Couldn't wait for after me lunch break. That's when I was going over to Mother Wicklow's. In me lunch. Thought I could eat me cheese and pickle sandwich on the way, like. You know. Kill two birds and all that. Not actual birds, though.' Fred beamed at everyone in the room.

'The message?' prompted Jenni.

'Oooh yes, I do have one of those. Just a minute.' Fred began patting his left pocket to find the message. 'It's not here.' He checked the right pocket. 'Oh no, it's not here.' Then he looked in his inner pocket. 'Oh, oh, what have I done with it? I'm going to be in so much trouble. Corporal Hobbs still hasn't forgiven me for being off last Thursday and leaving him with the crest polishing. He doesn't like polishing.'

'Do you remember when you had it last, Fred?' Willow asked kindly, several tendrils patting him gently on the shoulder.

'I had it in me hand when I dropped me helmet in the hallway and then I was trying to pick the helmet up but it kept getting away from me and really you need two hands to grab them on account of the polish. I polish mine regular. I like polishing.' Fred held his helmet out for Willow to admire and she nodded politely, not being into buffing.

'So it's in the 'allway then, ain't it?' grumbled Jenni and she stomped outside to look.

'What's the message?' asked Ned, his tired thoughts feeling like they were pushing through treacle and the growing sense that as the person meant to be in charge he ought to be more alert.

'Fourteen wants you.' Jenni threw the message scroll at Fred, who caught it by dropping his helmet and shot a wounded look at the sprite.

'I'm supposed to announce it and everything. It's part of my role as a vital member of the palace guard,' said Fred.

'Vital member?' teased Jenni.

Fred puffed out his chest with pride. 'Yes. Ma Bowl told me mam that the palace guard seem to work twice as hard now they've got me on board. I've increased the workload. All by meself.'

The thief-catchers, although used to Fred's loveable yet dense nature, stood still for a moment in wonder at the naivety and simplicity that radiated out of the young lad.

'Yes, well. I've got the message now. I'll be along shortly. Just got to run through our own agenda for the day. Crime never stops. Busy, busy, busy.' Ned smiled his thanks at the palace guard.

'Great. Thanks Mr Spinks, Sir. I'll just have enough time to finish me cheese and pickle sandwich on the way to Mother Wicklow's and if I run back, I'll make it before me lunch break ends.' Picking up his helmet, Fred executed a smart salute that no-one was paying any attention to and marched out of the office.

The beaniated man stood up and started marching up and down the office, clearly inspired by Fred but never actually making it out of the door.

Jenni made a grab for his hand, pulling him down and peered into his eyes.

'What are you doing? Get off!' shouted the man.

'Way too much bean,' She tilted her hand and shut one eye as she considered the problem. Then waved her right wrist anti-clockwise and muttered under her breath.

'Is something meant to be happening?' asked Ned, half squinting, trying to see the magic.

Jenni scowled and repeated the spell, but still nothing happened.

'Snails!' she cursed before marching to the kitchen and grabbing a bottle from the box on the counter.

''Ere, drink this,' she said to the thoroughly confused man.

'What is it?' Ned asked.

'A tonic from Kendra. I made sure I got a bulk order in when we started getting these bean offenders.'

The man downed the druidic concoction and almost immediately his whole demeanour relaxed. He brought a hand to his head.

'No more bean, mate. It ain't doing you no good,' said Jenni.

'It keeps me awake. Keeps the dreams away,' muttered the man.

Ned watched with interest. If drinking bean stopped you dreaming then maybe it could get rid of his nightmares so he could get some decent sleep. He sighed, first he had to go see Fourteen. Then he could investigate the bean effect.

'Right, looks like I'm headed to the palace. Willow, after you've taken this chap to the druids, can you continue investigating the theft of Marrick's pig, please? I'm pretty confident it's the boggart down the road, but we need to be certain so take Sparks and question it thoroughly. Where is Sparks?'

'He took a family day,' Willow reminded him.

'Oh yeah, right, well, take Joe with you then.' Ned looked around the office. 'Where's Joe?'

'Um, he went out for…' but before she could finish, the door opened and the potent aroma of bean wafted in from the two cups Joe was holding further enriched by the intoxicating smell coming from a bag of freshly made doughnuts he held under his arm.

'Giv us one,' said Jenni as she snagged the bag and stole a doughnut.

'Want one, Boss?' asked Joe, but Ned ignored him. He was too busy keeping hold of the beaniated man who had lunged towards Joe as he came in.

'Have I done something wrong?' whispered Joe to Willow, but she just shook her fronds and took the bag of doughnuts from Jenni.

Ned hurriedly pushed the man towards the door and encouraged him to leave the office, Jenni following behind.

Chapter 5

Ned stalked all the way to the palace, Jenni hurrying to keep up with him.

'Boss? I gotta tell you summink.'

'Not now, Jenni.' Ned was focused on trying to figure out whatever it might be the Emperor had summoned him for. He could hear Jenni tutting but they'd arrived at the palace. Whatever she wanted to tell him could wait.

Palace guards waved Ned through, directing them to the third best meeting room. Fourteen stood waiting for them, her elegantly manicured hands clasped together.

'Fourteen,' Ned said by way of a greeting.

There was a sharp intake of breath from one of the Highs in the far corner of the room. He looked like he was busying himself with a clipboard, yet it was obvious from the outraged gasp he was listening and felt Ned shouldn't presume to call the Emperor by name.

Ned sighed. His highly sleep deprived state couldn't handle court intrigue right now. He tried again.

'Your Eminence.'

A pair of perfectly kohled brown eyes regarded Ned.

'Thank you for coming. There is someone who wishes to speak with both of us.' Fourteen gave nothing else away.

Ned's heart was thumping at being close to her after so many weeks. He wondered if hers was doing the same. There was a faint air of resignation in her mannerisms which Ned knew was down to Fourteen having to perform her official role in public. If they'd been in private, perhaps they would have had a proper conversation. Instead, she glided over to where a table and three empty chairs stood waiting for their occupants.

'Looks like she's gotta bee in 'er bonnet 'bout summink, Boss,' whispered Jenni.

Before he could ask what she meant, another person entered. It was Mr Simms, the undead solicitor Ned had last faced across a poker table.

'Good morning, Your Eminence. May you live for ever and ever,' intoned the zombie.

'Why are you here?' asked Ned.

Fourteen took her place at the head of the table in the more ornate of the three chairs, leaving Mr Simms and Ned to decide whether to sit on her left or right-hand side.

'I'll sort meself out,' grumbled Jenni, clicking her fingers. A toadstool appeared which she looked taken aback by, but she still sat atop it, grinning, waiting to find out what this was all about.

'You have both been summoned here today to witness the reading of the last will and testament of one Griffin Bartholomew the Third, Duke of Kinglass and proprietor of WGI Emporium with over one-hundred and fifty purchasing venues this side of the Great Sea,' intoned Mr Simms leaving polite greetings to those with a pulse.

Ned sat motionless in his chair, echoes of nightmarish screams ringing in his ears. Griff. It was Griff's will. Fourteen was attentive and even Jenni was listening and not making any wisecracks. A trickle of uncertainty ran down Ned's spine.

'Did you say Duke of Kinglass?' he asked. He hadn't known Griff was gentry.

Mr Simms ignored the interruption.

'You, Mr Edmund de Silverthorpe, Chief Thief-Catcher of Roshaven, are appointed the sole executor of Griffin Bartholomew the Third, Duke of Kinglass and…'

'Just call him Griff.' Ned's voice was hoarse.

'… the sole executor of *Griff*'s will. There are several magical items listed in the will that require careful handling and delivery to their recipients. These items will appear at the office of Barnaby and Simms at a predetermined time. Once arrived, I shall deliver the item to you, Mr Spinks. It is the express desire of the Duke of Kinglass that you be the individual responsible for delivering each magical item. Each delivery comes with a preset time frame and failure to deliver an item to the correct person within the specified time frame will result in dire consequences that the Duke of Kinglass has stated that you, Mr Spinks, will comprehend and adhere to. There is no further information as to the dire nature of these consequences however, we at Barnaby and Simms accept no responsibility for loss of income, limb or life. Once every item has been delivered, the sum of one million gold bits will be paid into the account of Mr Edmund de Silverthorpe.'

Ned knew Mr Simms was telling him important details, but the words weren't making any sense. He was feeling too big for his body, hot and prickly all over his skin. That Griff had left a will wasn't surprising. The man had been organised, he was a smuggler after all. But the fact he trusted Ned enough to be the sole executor of his will just hammered home if Griff hadn't known Ned, he wouldn't be dead. Even the thought of one million gold bits, ample to buy himself actual status in the world, was not enough to dispel the bleakness he felt at Griff's death.

He glanced at the others for their reactions. Jenni was bouncing up and down in excitement. But then this had all the makings of a quest, and she enjoyed a good quest. Ned could understand that. Usually there were posh biscuits. Plus, he knew she found it interesting to see what mortals thought were magical items. Nine times out of ten they were just everyday things with a small glamour on them, designed to trick the average person into thinking the item was something special. But from the way she was reacting, Ned suspected Jenni was hoping some of Griff's things would be truly magical.

'Dire consequences?' Ned asked as his brain caught up with Mr Simms spiel.

'Of which the Duke of Kinglass is confident you already know the outcome. He left no further information.'

Mr Simms tilted his head towards Ned, as if encouraging him to share what he thought the dire consequences might be but Ned was unforthcoming. To be honest, he wasn't entirely sure. He just knew that if one of these magical items turned up, he wasn't going to hang about in delivering it.

Fourteen also sat in silent reflection. Ned sensed her empathy and knew she understood some of his personal conflict and how he was feeling. After they'd visited Griff in Fidelia, Ned remembered her telling him that Griff was a friend of her father's and had come to court occasionally. She'd said he had always brought the best gifts.

Ned knew in his heart Griff had been a good man, smuggler or not. And as for the one million gold bits… if he earned all of those, then the imperial court wouldn't be able to look down upon him as a suitor for the empire.

Mr Simms had stopped speaking, realising that no one was paying any attention to him.

'Ahem,' he said,

'AHEM!'

'Yes? What?' Ned pulled himself together, as much as he could do while running on no sleep and being plagued by nightmares.

'As I was saying, Your Eminence,' Mr Simms looked at them all in disapproval. 'Each item will be issued to you with instructions on who it should be delivered to. The first item is due in three days' time.'

'I gotta question.' Jenni spat to one side, making Fourteen twitch. 'Who is doin' the original deliverin' and the payin' and stuffs? And why isn't they doing the bequeefing an'all?'

'It appears Griff made extensive magical arrangements for his will. I'm afraid I am not party to the mystical machinations. Perhaps if you spoke to your mother, I believe she had a hand in the execution,' replied Mr Simms.

'Corse she did,' muttered Jenni. She was in no hurry to see Momma K so she'd just have to wait for the magics to spring into action.

'It seems like a lot of trouble to go to. Why not have the items sent directly to the individuals they were intended for?' asked Fourteen.

'I'm afraid I do not have the answer to that question, Your Eminence. Perhaps it was a humorous endeavour by the deceased. Here at Barnaby and Simms, we see all kinds of unusual things.'

'Why was I brought to the palace to be told about Griff's will?' Ned asked. 'You could have easily done this at the Thief-Catchers office.'

'A caveat of the will stated it must be read, and I

quote, "in the presence of my two favourite people". We thought inviting you to the Imperial Palace would be a more suitable locale than have our Emperor, may you live for ever and ever, visit the Thief-Catcher establishment,' explained Mr Simms.

He looked smug and waited for more questions. He was disappointed.

'Right. Well, that's that then. Anything else?' Ned pushed himself to standing and hoped he was only swaying that much on the inside.

'You need to sign your agreement as executor with the Emperor, may you live for ever and ever, as your witness.' Mr Simms glanced at Fourteen. 'I must say, it surprised us that your eminence was included in such a trivial matter.'

'Griff was a friend of the family. Not trivial at all,' replied Fourteen softly.

Ned tried to curb his impatience. He wanted out of the palace and back to his office where he might be able to catch forty winks. His brain was calling out for rest, and the wicked pressure building behind his eyes was promising to behave if he had some sleep. Grabbing the proffered quill, he dashed off his signature. He began walking towards the door while Fourteen was signing. He heard her speak when she thought he was out of earshot.

'Jenni?'

'Yeah?'

'Look after him, please.'

'I always do.' She scampered after her boss.

Chapter 6

After finding out about Griff being a lord, being rich and leaving it all to him if he completed these crazy magical deliveries, Ned decided he needed to take his mind off that bombshell.

'Jenni? Wasn't there something you wanted to tell me?' he asked.

'Yeah, but…'

Ned didn't slow his pace, but his stomach dropped. Jenni being reluctant to tell him something had never turned out well before.

'Go on.'

'It's 'bout your nightmares,' she said.

'I told you not to worry about them. They've got nothing to do with you.'

'Yeah, wotever. You've got a proper Nightmare on you. One of them 'orses wot brings the worst dreams and cos of that yor not casting spells, yor not sleeping an Fourteen tol' me to keep an eye on you, so tough bums.'

Ned felt both gratitude and irritation at Fourteen trying to look after him.

'So, what did you do about this Nightmare then? Catch it? Use it as your own personal steed? Eat it?' he asked.

'Boss, I ain't gonna eat a Nightmare,' Jenni retorted in disgust. 'I went to see Barbas.'

'Barbas?' Ned's fourth eye prickled. He thought he ought to know who that was.

'Yeah, Barbas. The fear demon. 'E said it weren't nuffink to do wiv 'im, sorta. 'E said it were a contract paid for in blood so it were out of 'is 'ands to do anyfink about it. I fink it were yor bruvver wot took out the contract.'

'Jenni, why are you sticking up for Barbas? Couldn't you have sat on him or got Momma K to threaten him and make him lift the contract?' Ned was unsurprised at who Jenni thought had paid for the Nightmare. There was only one person he knew who would do something like that. His brother Theo was a nasty piece of work.

'There weren't nuffink I could do. 'Im and Momma K already got summink going on, and I weren't getting in the middle of that. And anyways, I don't fink you should go pick a fight wiv a fear demon. S'not like 'e can be killed, right?'

Spotting *Headshot* in the distance, Ned made lots of reassuring noises and picked up his pace. He'd made a decision to give this bean stuff a try.

'Whatchoo gonna do about it, Boss? You gonna talk to Theo?'

'No. If he thinks a few nightmares are enough to stop me from doing my job, he needs to try harder. Do you want anything?' Ned gestured towards the bean shop and Jenni shook her head. Bean didn't agree with her.

'Jus the one though, Boss, yeah?' She cautioned him. They'd seen too many people have extreme reactions to bean and with Ned being so sleep deprived, she wasn't sure what it would do to him.

Ned waved agreement at her as he entered the café, breathing in the aroma.

'Anna I don't fink we should ignore Theo eivver,' grumbled Jenni under her breath, kicking at pebbles as she waited for Ned to come back. After about ten minutes of beating nearby weeds and gravel into submission, Jenni tutted in annoyance and ventured inside to retrieve her boss.

He sat on a stool, eight empty beanspresso cups lined up in front of him.

'Keep 'em coming,' he called out to the beanista.

'Boss! I don't fink you should be drinking bean like that. Can't you jus do normal shots like every ovver person?' She shot a deadly glare at the pimply young server approaching who smartly veered off in a different direction with the two beanspressos she had in her hands.

'Got to be awake, Jenni. Got to keep the nightmares away. Got to be awake for the task Griff is sending us. Got to be ready. Ready for Griff. We got to do this. Got to. Got. Got. Got.' Ned's fingers were tapping out a rapid staccato on the counter top.

'Bloody 'ell. It's made you go doolally. We're gonna see Kendra. I ain't got time for this.' Jenni scowled at everything as she pulled her boss off the stool he was perched on. Fae magic didn't work that well on these sorts of things.

Various nervous tics had developed on Ned's body and he spasmed as Jenni frog-marched him to the Druid Grove. The druids would have something suitably purging. They were good at that. Everyone thought they were only good at dancing naked, but purging was also high on the list.

Chapter 7

The druid grove was bustling.

Ever since Sister Eustacia had joined the grove it had developed into a more eclectic religious space. It had always been a unique grove with a strong female druid complement. A phenomenon that had encouraged healthy public attendances to the midnight rituals where everybody was required to go sky-clad and frolic. Nothing like a spot of frolicking to bring a community together.

Jenni surveyed the crowd with interest. She could feel the power prickling in-between her toes. It wasn't magics she could use, but it was still a healthy magical place. A harassed-looking druid hurried over to them.

'I'm afraid we are all booked up for tonight's ritual. You'll have to come back next week and try the Thursday one. It has a few spaces. But it's first come, first served.'

'I wanna see Kendra,' Jenni announced.

The druid adjusted her robes and looked down at the sprite, who stood as tall as her hips. Jenni was about the size of a six-year-old human.

'The High Priestess is not receiving anyone. She is in sacred preparation for tonight's ritual. If you leave behind your name and request with me, I shall enter it into the book of hope and if you are lucky, we will pray for you.'

'S'alright. I know the way.' Jenni pushed past and keeping a firm grip of Ned's sleeve, towed him after her into the inner sanctum. They'd been to see Kendra before when love was dying and Willow lost her mojo. Jenni was also familiar with where the kitchen and the baths were. Being able to get free food was a given, but the sprite didn't bath regularly. It was more of a knowing where your danger areas were located thing.

'But, but…' The welcoming committee druid stammered after them, but her attention was soon taken by a group of newbies who were already blushing furiously.

Jenni sniggered. The druids didn't mind visitors, they wouldn't get in trouble for going to find Kendra. At least, not much anyway.

'Should we be here? I'm not sure we should be here. Should we ask someone if we should be here? Do you think we should be here? Here, here, here, here!' Ned's voice was echoing down the corridor.

Jenni glanced at him and saw a stupid, happy grin on his face, the result of excess beanage. She rolled her eyes and made certain her grip was secure. Not bothering to knock, she went straight into Kendra's private quarters.

'I said no disturbances!' It was Kendra, but it was not her usual serene manner. A flying slipper missed Jenni but ricocheted off Ned's shoulder.

'Hey! That's assault, that is. Assault with a flying slipper. Assaulting an officer of the law with footwear cannot be ignored. It cannot. Jenni? Make a note.'

'Yeah, corse.' Jenni said, then ignored him. 'Look, Kendra, I gotta problem. He ain't sleeping and he's not wiv it. I just caught 'im drinking loads of bean and I needs 'im sorted out. 'E's no good to no one like this. E's 'ad some of that potion wot you gave me for sleeping, but 'e 'ad annover nightmare and he's just not getting any sleep. I needs your help. And yor magic. Mine's not working right.'

Kendra blinked at Jenni in surprise.

'What's wrong with your magic?' she asked.

Jenni shrugged.

'I dunno but I gotta sort 'im out first. Then I'll figure that out.'

Kendra began walking around Ned, who was bouncing up and down on the balls of his feet, unable to keep still.

'Hmmm, it's a fascinating reaction. The sleep deprivation seems to have ramped up the effect of the bean.'

'Yeah, it's a bloody marvel but the fing is, Kendra, 'e's not 'imself. 'E ain't told me off once since I dragged him 'ere and 'e let me drag him 'ere. Wot if summink 'appens to 'im when I'm not around? 'E could get 'imself in all sorts of trouble.'

Kendra put a comforting hand on Jenni's shoulder. A small silver spark leapt from the sprite to the druid making them both jump.

'Jenni? How long had your magic been playing up? You're not a hundred yet, are you?'

'No, I ain't. It's been fritzing the last couple of days, why?'

'I think it's almost time for your coming of age ceremony but you are a little young. Must be something to do with how powerful you are.'

Jenni gaped at Kendra.

'Yor kidding, right? I ain't got time for that.'

'It's an important moment in every fae's life and it's not something you can ignore. You should be so excited to be finally choosing your major arcana.'

'Wot?' But Jenni's heart wasn't in her question. She was thinking about all the spells that had been going wrong or not working at all. Short-lived relief bloomed now that she knew it had been happening for a reason, but she wasn't ready for her coming of age ceremony. She wasn't that old. And she hadn't prepared.

Kendra was not paying attention to Jenni's inner turmoil. She was peering into Ned's eyes.

'How much bean did you say he's had?' asked the druid.

'Um, I dunno 'zactly but 'e were doin' shots before we got 'ere and there wos at least eight cups in front of 'im.'

Ned blinked twice and seemed to register where he was and who he was with.

'Kendra! How have you been? How did I get here? What's going on? Is that for me?' He pointed to a steaming cup on the mantle. 'It's bean, isn't it? Did you go for a regular or something with a bit of jazz to it? Did you know you can eat them raw? Isn't it amazing? And all from a little bean!'

Kendra side stepped Ned and made sure she was in the way of him and her cup of hot tea.

'I don't think you should have any of my tea. In fact, I think maybe we should get you down to the kitchen for something else. I hear Sister Eustacia has been making honey cakes. Would you like one, Ned?'

Ned nodded enthusiastically and his neck took on a life of its own, bobbing his head up and down at a startling pace.

'Okay then, here we go. Let's turn out of here and down the corridor.' Kendra shepherded Ned towards the kitchen with Jenni stomping along behind them.

There was no one around when they got there, but it was warm and welcoming with the glorious smell of freshly baked honey cakes. A plate of them stood on the worktop and Ned eagerly helped himself to two, then three.

'Just keep an eye on him for a moment, please,' Kendra asked Jenni as she moved over to the supplies store.

'Wot you gonna make?'

'I think something to purge the bean and then send him to sleep so he can get through the initial withdrawal,' Kendra replied as she chose her ingredients. 'This isn't the first bean reaction we've seen, it takes a while for the body to shake all the effects, depending on the individual.'

'Yeah? 'Ow many you seen then?'

'I don't want to speak ill of him and I know he was Ned's friend, but that smuggler Griff didn't do Roshaven any good when he arranged shipment of bean here.' Kendra paused for a moment in her work and looked at Jenni. 'What's going to happen when we run out?'

Jenni shrugged. She hadn't thought about it.

'People will 'ave to find the next summink.' A burning sensation was prickling Jenni's back. She viciously scratched what she could reach. 'Do I need to be 'ere for the purging or can you manage wiv 'im?'

Kendra waved her away having gathered all her ingredients. 'I've got this. Send Sparks to check in with us later if you like and I'll give him an update.' She glanced at Ned, who was now on his fifth honey cake and showing no signs of slowing down. 'It'll be a while before the bean is out of his system.'

Jenni nodded and grabbed two honey cakes for herself before leaving.

'Good luck at your ceremony,' said Kendra with a smile.

'Fanks.' Jenni walked over to Ned making sure she caught his eye. 'I'll see you later, Boss,'

He nodded and made a start on a sixth honey cake.

Once she was it outside the druid grove, Jenni clicked her fingers to pop back to HQ. Only nothing happened. She tried again and a few silver stars spurted out, but still no pop.

'This ain't no fun,' she muttered as she changed her mind about returning to HQ and began walking towards the small patch of greenery in the centre of Roshaven that led to the fae realm. 'I s'pose I gotta find out wot's going on. This better not be one of 'er fings.' A mini thundercloud gathered above her head in keeping with her mood. 'You can bog off an' all,' she said, flicking her fingers at the apparition. It was time for Jenni to visit her mum.

Chapter 8

Ned thrashed in his sleep, as the Nightmare above him trampled through his subconscious with wild abandon and sharp hooves.

The sound of hurrying footsteps brought Kendra to her feet, and she half-waved as Sister Eustacia entered the recovery room. The large yet nimble nun traversed the floor, avoiding the other patients and various randomly placed visitor chairs.

'Thank you for coming, Sister.' Kendra cleared her throat, feeling foolish at what she was about to ask. 'I...'

'A Nightmare, eh? What have you tried so far?'

Relieved that Sister Eustacia had gone straight to the problem, Kendra reeled off six potions, a poultice, and three chants that she'd already used on Ned after he'd eaten a dozen honey cakes and crashed out.

'And there's been no change?' asked the Sister.

'Nothing at all.'

'Have you prayed to the gods?'

'Which one? That's more your area of expertise than mine,' replied Kendra. 'Who would you recommend?'

Sister Eustacia pursed her lips whilst she thought. She walked all the way around Ned's bed and observed the Nightmare from every angle.

'I propose we do all of them. Just to be on the safe side.'

Kendra nodded in agreement but was overwhelmed. There were an abundance of deities to factor in, so this could take a long time. She hesitated at where to begin.

'Shall I lead?' the nun offered.

'Yes, please, if you don't mind?'

'Not at all, my dear, not at all.' Sister Eustacia pulled out the necklace that was hanging around her neck. The chain was long and thick. At the bottom hung a dozen or more deity signs. There was the standard oval for the one-god, the sister's own chosen faith, and the three stars for the three sisters. A triquetra for the pagans, a pentacle for the wiccans and the moon for the druids. Kendra also glimpsed clasped hands, five feathers, what looked like a pair of socks and one copper bit before Sister Eustacia closed her fingers around all the trinkets and bowed her head in prayer.

'Oh gods, goddesses, deities, minor and major, spirits of the earth, we call to thee. Bless this man, for he is weak and troubled. Lift him up above the poison that threatens his soul, we beg of thee...'

Kendra coughed. 'Um, perhaps we should be more specific about the Nightmare? I'm already treating the poisoning. Bean overload.'

Sister Eustacia clucked in annoyance and picked up her rhythm.

'We beg of thee that you surround him in your love, your light and your protection, keeping him in your circle of safety so he may escape the evil that has been bestowed upon him. In your names, we pray. In your power, we are not worthy. In your greatness we are mere specks before thee. Amen.' Nothing happened. 'Blessed be.' Still nothing. 'Namaste?' Sister Eustacia offered. A cricket sang in the silence.

Sister Eustacia muttered under her breath and tried again.

'Spirits above and below, I call thee...'

'Tut, tut, tut. Interfering in matters that don't concern you?' The soft voice made both women whirl around. Barbas stood with his arms wide, palms up, one eyebrow raised and a sardonic smirk on his face. 'You cannot take away this man's fear. A blood contract has been paid.'

Sister Eustacia paled as her own worst fear tickled her brain while Kendra's hand shook as her fear of deadly spiders began creeping up her spine. With an effort, Kendra tried to ignore the feeling and gripped her hands together.

'Can you at least tell us who put the contract out?' she asked, trying to keep her knees still, which were doing their best to knock.

Barbas steepled his fingers and regarded her. The Nightmare finished tormenting Ned and trotted over to his side, whickering.

'I already told the sprite, more or less,' he replied before fading in front of their eyes.

Ned stopped thrashing from the Nightmare and was now sweating and groaning in his sleep because of the detox.

'Wasn't Jenni here earlier?' asked Sister Eustacia. 'She might have mentioned Barbas was involved. Demonology involves chicken feet. Everyone knows that.'

'She was, but she is very close to her coming of age. It's a very distracting rite of passage.'

'Coming of age?'

'It's a fae thing. Young fae have wide power bases, some of them are strong at everything, like Jenni. Others show proficiency in particular areas, but when they come of age, they undergo a sacred ceremony which locks their powers down. Most come away less powerful than they were before.' Kendra gave the nun an odd look. 'But you're part-fae, aren't you? Surely you know about the coming of age ceremony.'

'I'm only one-sixteenth on my Father's side, several generations removed. How did you know?' Sister Eustacia was fiddling with her necklace of religious icons.

'Ned told me you were unaffected when love was dying. Said it was something to do with your fae ancestry. Don't worry, the grove is accepting to all.' Kendra smiled at her.

'I know.' Sister Eustacia patted Kendra's arm in thanks before another question occurred to her. 'Why on earth would they give young fae more power than older ones? Sounds backwards if you ask me.'

Kendra mopped Ned's brow before answering.

'It is odd, but it's how they manage their magical system. When you come of age, you pay for the magics you've used in one way or another. Some lose features like wings, some age, some lose power. They don't believe in telling you everything about the ceremony when you're young. A child should be free to be a child.'

They were leaving Ned's bed and the recovery room, walking towards the corridor that split to their own separate chambers.

'How do you know so much about fae power?' asked Sister Eustacia, intrigued.

Kendra lifted the hair away from the side of her face to reveal a slight point to her ear. She smiled faintly at the nun and nodded her thanks before retiring for the night. She would pray for Jenni to have a swift ceremony so they could find out who had the fear contract on Ned.

Chapter 9

Ned woke up, leaned over the side of the bed and vomited. Fortunately, one druid had sufficient presence of mind to put a sick bucket in the correct place. Unfortunately, the correct place on the opposite side to the one Ned had chosen. The splatter of expelled bean left a noxious odour and had Ned's stomach clenching further. He was shivery and cold, but after pulling up the blanket to his chin he was quickly too hot. The room was buzzing at the edges and he felt as if he hadn't had a drink in forever.

'Help,' he struggled to call out. It came out as more of a 'Nnngh' and had little volume about it. There were no druids in the recovery room, just another patient who appeared to be in a deep, heavy sleep. The kind Ned wanted to fall into after feeling like he'd been awake for a week straight.

He resolved to go find a mop. He swung his legs over the edge of the bed, or at least he tried to, but his body was not paying any attention to his brain and all he managed was a twitch of his eyebrows. That wouldn't do. Ned contemplated that he would need to scream and scream and scream his lungs out until someone came, and he wasn't convinced he had the breath to do that, when the swish-swish-swish whisper of robes sounded from the doorway.

'In here! Help!' cried Ned faintly.

The owner of the swishy skirt didn't hear his cry, but she did come in. Ned watched Kendra recoil as she entered. The acrid stink of vomit was doing its best to

"

permeate the entire atmosphere of the room.

Kendra rang the bell located by the entrance to the recovery room. It was the general dear-gods-help-me alarm and soon many swishy skirts came dashing in assistance. Before long mops were mopping, windows were opened and sage was burning as cleansing rituals were performed. Ned himself had been stripped, washed, redressed and now sat upright with a cup of Ma Bowl's homemade chicken soup in his hands. The aroma was glorious.

'How are you feeling?' Kendra sounded solicitous and wore a slight frown as she checked his brow with the back of her hand.

'Very much like I've been druid-handled.' He smelt the soup again. 'Was a sponge bath really necessary?'

Kendra looked as if she was trying to hide a grin, but failed miserably.

'Some of the girls have taken quite a shine to you, after what happened at the last moon ritual you attended.' Her smile faded, and she touched Ned's arm. 'Thank you again, for avenging the High Priestess.'

'Just doing my job.' Ned began slurping the soup. 'This is wonderful.'

'We always keep some on standby for special cases. Ma Bowl will only make a batch for us once a month, so you're lucky there's some left.'

'What's the verdict then?' Ned asked between slurps.

Kendra pursed her lips as she regarded him.

'You are massively sleep deprived, that much you know. And drinking all that bean wasn't a good idea, it will take a while to come out of your system completely. It's a tricky little substance. Seems so innocuous and yet most people are drinking several cups a day to avoid withdrawal headaches. We have a couple more purges set up for you, they seem to do the trick. But you're likely to experience some cravings for at least a week. You need to stay off the bean and you need to get some decent rest.'

'It won't keep the Nightmare away, will it?'

'No, I'm afraid not.' Kendra felt sympathy for Ned as she looked at his crestfallen face. 'I heard we are not getting another consignment of bean anyway, so temptation won't be too much of a problem. Apparently, Griff had only arranged the one shipment before, well, you know.'

'He named me executor of his will. There are some magical items that I'm supposed to hand out to specific people at a specific time. As if I didn't have enough on my plate,' grumbled Ned.

'Mmm. Barbas.'

Ned leant forward. 'Who told you about Barbas?'

Kendra flinched. In the clean up, they had neglected to brush Ned's teeth. She passed him a couple of mint leaves from the pouch at her waist.

'He appeared while Sister Eustacia and I attempted to ease your inner turmoil. We were unsuccessful because Barbas has a Nightmare tethered to you. He says it's a blood contract, and that Jenni knows all about it.' Kendra gave Ned a flat look. 'It would have been nice if Jenni had told us all about it.'

Struggling to swallow mint leaves, Ned spluttered. 'Where is Jenni?'

'She's been called to her coming of age ceremony. Didn't you know?'

Ned shook his head. He knew fae had them, but he hadn't realised Jenni's was due.

'When did she go?' he asked.

'Just after she brought you here. It might take a few days for her to pass through the ceremony, but I'm sure she'll return to the thief-catchers afterwards. Everyone knows...' Kendra tailed off.

'Knows what?'

'Everyone knows Jenni loves being a thief-catcher. Magic or no magic, I'm sure that's what she'll want to choose.'

Ned had the overwhelming urge to jump out of bed and run down the street to *Headshot* and drown his sorrows in bean. It was an odd craving considering he'd only just had his first bean experience. A dangerous beverage.

'How long do I have to stay here?' he asked instead.

'We'd never keep you without your consent. You're free to leave at any time, but I would recommend you stay the night. Go through these next twelve hours with us. We've got some herbal teas that will help with any cravings.'

Ned was tempted, and without Jenni at home or work, he didn't fancy being on his own. If a magical item turned up, it would just have to wait. He looked down at the empty mug and sighed.

'I can check if there's any soup left, if you like?' offered Kendra.

'And a cheese sandwich?' Ned pushed his luck, handing the mug over.

Kendra laughed. 'I'll see what I can do.'

Chapter 10

'Congratulations, Jenni!'

'What are you going to choose?'

'Have you decided yet?'

'Good luck!'

Jenni nodded at all the well wishes directed her way as she entered the fae realm and Momma K's kingdom. The prickling in-between her shoulder blades was becoming worse and now burned like mad. She couldn't quite reach it, so she stopped at a nearby oak tree and got bear-scratching.

There was a loud tearing noise. Jenni took off her trademark red coat and looked at the back.

'Ripped! This is me favourite coat. This is me only coat. Wot's going on wiv me back?' Jenni wore a cream tunic and shorts, standard fae clothing but she felt naked in just those so she glumly put her torn clothing back on.

'Daughta. Is time.' Momma K had appeared and was extending one delicate arm to her left.

'Time for wot? 'Ave you seen this? Look at me coat. Me back's all itchy. Is summink on it?'

Momma K wrinkled her nose at the grimy article of clothing and stared at her daughter, then tilted her head to the left, making her beaded dreadlocks swing and clack together.

'Awright, awright, I'm goin' left. Wot am I goin' to?' Jenni looked up at Momma K who glided alongside her daughter flapping her silver and black patterned slender wings.

'Ya come a' age. Is time fo' ya magics ta settle in ya

bones. Time ta see if ya wings come. Time ta choose.'

'To choose wot? Wot you going on 'bout?'

Momma K glowered. 'If ya didna' miss so much in ya world, ya'd know more wat comin'. Is time for ya power ta choose ya direction. No more spell everyting. Strength in one ting. Power in one ting.' She fluttered her wings in annoyance. 'Young fae get all de power to test and change and explore. All de time ya magic is deciding how ya fit, wat ya goin' be. Ya ceremony is 'ere. Ya magic is choosing.'

'But I don't wanna choose. I likes doin' everyfink.'

'Tsk. Is not ya choice ta make. Magic come wi' a price. Is time ta pay. Me 'ope fo' ya sake chil', ya ready fo' wat come.'

Jenni's skin goose bumped as she recalled her fae school lessons. She was only seventy-four. Surely it was too soon for her power to settle. She had always figured she would have at least until she was a hundred to prepare. But now the magics would decide if she'd become a winged-fae like her ma or whether she'd stay sprite-formed. The ceremony would determine how her magic would be used. Jenni gulped. Even worse, if the magics found her lacking, she would be turned mortal.

'Wot 'bout everyfink I've already spent?'

'Da magics will weigh. Right fo' wrong. Good fo' bad. Ya will be measured.' Momma K looked down at her daughter. 'Me 'ope ya done right. For all our sakes.'

The two fae were silent as they entered the sacred space in the middle of Momma K's kingdom. The drooping purple blooms of wisteria grew in a loose circle, the boughs of the trees entwining above, encircling the magical heart of the kingdom in a soft canopy of blossom. Jenni staggered at the weight of raw power concentrated in one place.

'Wot do I do?' she whispered to Momma K.

Momma K pointed to the very centre of the grove where a silver light was revolving, getting brighter and bigger.

'I jus' walk into that?'

Momma K didn't reply so Jenni shrugged her ruined coat to the floor and wiggled her still itchy, burning shoulders as she walked towards the light.

Chapter 11

Jenni had stepped through the twinkling light and now stood in gloom. She wiggled her toes and felt grass beneath them. The scent of wisteria hung in the air. She was standing within the inner sanctum of the sacred grove. Three large chairs were arrayed before her. The sides of the sanctum stretched into darkness, and a quick check confirmed the gateway had vanished. She was on her own.

She stood for a moment waiting for something to happen, but it didn't. So she started humming. Still nothing. Then there was a slight rustling from behind the chairs.

'Ello?'

There was some frenzied whispering and despite straining her hearing, Jenni couldn't make out what they were saying.

'Just a minute, please,' called out a voice. The whispering continued and the sound of scuttling legs came closer and closer.

'I'm sorry. The larva wouldn't settle and Janine has been having terrible trouble with the grubs. You know how it is,' said a voice. There was more rustling. 'Are they here yet? Did I make it in time?'

Jenni chuckled to herself. She didn't feel so nervous as she listened to the voices, they sounded normal enough.

Finally, after another bout of rustling and whispering, a giant caterpillar, a powerfully built black dog and what looked like a walking tree appeared from behind the large chairs in a semi-stately fashion and seated themselves.

'Welcome, Jenevieve Babet, daughter of Kimona Ducayet and… erm…' The caterpillar peered at the piece of paper in front of him, squinting through his pince-nez. Flustered, he passed the paper along his many legs to the black dog sitting in the chair next to him.

The beast's golden eyes glowed as the paper hung before him. He spoke gruffly in Jenni's direction.

'Child, do you know your father?'

'I ain't never met 'im. And it's just Jenni, not all that ovver malarky.'

The living twig, complete with green luminous eyes, regarded her. Then it uttered a series of clicks.

'I agree,' growled the dog, and the paperwork returned to the caterpillar.

'Ahem. Jenevieve Babet, known as Jenni, daughter of Kimona Ducayet and unknown. You are here today to pass into adulthood. We, the Fae Elders, will guide you through your coming of age ceremony. I am Greg, this is Amos and QuiQuo the Imp.' The caterpillar extended a leg towards the dog and the giant stick. 'We are here to celebrate your childlike feats of magic and settle your gift in strength. To be tested, place your hand on the globe.'

Jenni was about to ask what globe when an electric blue orb materialised in front of her. Without hesitation she touched it and the entire chamber was bathed in a flash of blinding white light.

'Argh!' Jenni let go. The orb had turned red and was blazing hot. It fell to the floor, making the grass sizzle as it crisped and died where the orb touched the ground.

'Incredible!' 'Most unusual.' 'Click click click whistle click click.' Each of the fae elders expressed their amazement.

'Wot was that? Wots going on? Why'd it go all 'ot like that?' demanded Jenni.

'We delved your magic usage, and it seems you have used everything you were given, young Jenni. Plus a great deal besides,' explained Amos. 'Though how that was possible, we don't know. We've never seen anything like it before.'

'Many young fae use considerable amounts of magic, but we've never encountered someone who burned through all they were given and yet was able to generate more,' Greg added. He sounded part in awe and part disbelieving. 'It must be some kind of self-perpetuating loop or perhaps an unknown divinity spike?' He started muttering other ideas under his breath, which Jenni couldn't make out.

Jenni's stomach churned. If she'd burnt through all her magic, was she to be made mortal? She took a half a step toward the smouldering ball.

'We have much to discuss. Please sit and try to relax.' The caterpillar waved an appendage and a small couch appeared next to Jenni.

She could see the beings in front of her talking, but she couldn't hear anything. They'd spelled her out of the conversation. Huffing, she slumped on the couch and glared suspiciously at the Elders. What did they mean—used all her magics and been able to make more? She had always been the most powerful fae in Roshaven, besides Momma K of course. What else had they expected?

Chapter 12

The Fae Elders were in a quandary.

'How has this young sprite used above and beyond her allocation?' asked Greg, the caterpillar, shooting a concerned glance at Jenni. 'That's a whole heck of a lot of power. She should be a burnt-out husk.'

QuiQuo the imp clicked, clacked and clucked.

'What do you mean we haven't tested her magics properly?' spluttered Greg, looking to Amos next to him for moral support. 'Finding out who her father is, surely that's more pressing? Not more tests?'

'It is true we have only considered what she has spent. We have not yet determined what she has left.' The giant black dog nodded his agreement with the imp. 'We already know her lineage is elevated, because of her mother. Finding out the father would be useful, but that is not something we can achieve here now. It could be months before we are able to find him and we cannot leave this young sprite awaiting the end of her ceremony until then. I say we test her further and ask if she wishes to find him.'

'But Amos...'

'Greg, clearly we have a unique case. It calls for a unique response.'

Greg waved several legs in the air before surrendering with a shrug. Amos dissolved the privacy bubble.

'So wot's gonna 'appen to me now?' asked Jenni.

'We'd like to test your future magic ability,' replied Greg but the sour look on Jenni's face startled him.

'Please…?'

'I ain't touching no more balls,' Jenni stated flatly.

QuiQuo the imp unfolded its giant stick-like body and strode over to the sprite. Before she could move away, it pressed one gnarled finger to the middle of her forehead. A humming filled the chamber as the magic left in Jenni resonated. The hum became a high-pitched whine that threatened ear drums and was abruptly replaced by deafening silence as the pressure in the room grew and grew. Greg cried out first, his soft caterpillar body unable to cope, but Amos wasn't far behind, his canine ears responding to sound at only a pitch he could hear.

'Stop! Stop!' They both exclaimed.

QuiQuo was blasted across the chamber as Jenni arched her back, screamed, and a second blast of blinding white light flashed, turning everyone momentarily blind. Blinking furiously, the three elders of fae magic warded themselves and the inner sanctum and each other and then themselves again.

Jenni knelt one knee on the floor, one up, her hands resting on that while she took several deep shuddering breaths.

'Wot were that?'

'That, my dear, was a power gauge. Despite your excessive usage prior to your coming of age ceremony, it looks like you still have plenty more magic at your disposal. Far too much for one fae alone.'

All three elders fixed Jenni with a stare.

'Wot 'appens now?' she asked.

'Usually, a youngling decides on their directional magic and gains additional features accordingly,' began Amos.

'I like all me spells,' interrupted Jenni.

'Yes. I'm sure you do but as an adult fae you will find some spells easier than others, depending on your magical preference chosen here today.'

'There is the matter of wings…' interjected Greg. 'Did you want wings? You have the magic to pay for them.'

'Why would I want wings when I can pop?' scoffed Jenni. 'All I want is to get out of 'ere and go back to work.'

QuiQuo clicked aggressively.

'Jenni, it's not that simple. We must seek advice from the Source. From what we've seen here today, your magic is incredibly powerful, and one being cannot wield that much. Fae law is very clear. Too much power in one fae would cause division in the realm and beyond. Factions would spring up demanding your strength for themselves. We'd have fae riots. It's happened before and we cannot allow it to happen again. And as for your mother…' Greg trailed off and shivered.

'If I'm meant to be all powerful n' stuffs then 'ow are youse gonna stop me from using me magic?' Jenni cracked her knuckles.

QuiQuo chittered and gestured one twig-like arm in her direction.

Jenni smirked and clicked her fingers, intending to turn the imp into a festive tree complete with the pointy star on top. Nothing happened. There wasn't even a spurt of stars at the attempt. Jenni frowned and shook her fingers, then tried again. And again and again. Still nothing happened. She stopped visualising her intent and began muttering incantations under her breath. Not one worked and nothing left any magical residue.

'Wot you done to me?'

'This place is sacred.' Amos scratched his left ear

with his right leg. 'Upon entering the inner sanctum, your magical power was stoppered and will remain so until you complete your coming of age ceremony.'

'I could jus' leave,' suggested Jenni.

'You could try,' growled Amos, lowering the atmosphere of the grove from mostly confusing to gently threatening.

'I think communing with the Source is your best option, my dear,' Greg waved various legs at Jenni in an encouraging way. 'It can answer any questions you might have and help balance your power for you.'

'Right, so that's me only choice then? Doing that will get me out of 'ere with as much power as I'm allowed so I can do me job?'

'And which job is that?' asked Greg, still feeling a little discombobulated from being almost squished to death.

'Thief-catcher.' Jenni didn't bother to elaborate.

The council of three looked at one other. Greg shrugged his many legs, while QuiQuo rustled leaves. Amos nodded and stared at Jenni.

'You're not interested in the throne?' he asked.

Jenni thought about it for a nanosecond. 'Nah.'

'Then step through the arch, my dear,' gestured Greg with four legs.

'Wot... oh.' Jenni looked around and saw a stone archway had appeared from nowhere and now stood behind her. It was black, and the stone was etched with a multitude of magical symbols, some Jenni recognised but most she'd never seen before. There was an air of severity about the archway in its harsh construction, as if it had been hacked into shape. As she drew closer, the stone hummed like a warning alarm. It both repelled her and lured her towards it.

'Should we tell her what happens next?' asked Greg with a nervous body roll.

'She is already under the influence of the Source. Now we wait,' replied Amos, watching the sprite walk between the arch and disappear.

Chapter 13

Walking through the arch made Jenni disappear.

She panicked at first when she couldn't see or sense her body, but the panic died down as she was bathed in pure magic. Pulses of light shot through pinky purple clouds that weren't really clouds. Flashes of silver and gold came and went, as did shoals of multicoloured stars. Everything was flowing free form yet somehow connected and inter-related. The place thrummed.

'Jenni, nice to see you again,' spoke a disembodied voice, neither male nor female.

'Er, fanks.' Jenni tried to look around, forgetting she didn't have a body or eyes. 'Ave I met you afore?'

'I connected you at birth with your link to fae magic.'

'Oh. Right. And you are?'

'I am the Source of all fae magic.'

'Yor a lot pinker than I 'spected,' offered Jenni, not sure what she ought to say to the Source of all magic.

'I'm not the Source of *all* magic, just fae magic. And I'm pink because you expect me to be. The mind truly is an ingenious creation.'

'And you read minds too.'

'I do.' The Source laughed, or at least amusement infused the space their consciousnesses were inhabiting.

'You gonna s'plain fings then?' Jenni asked, wanting to get down to business.

'Let me see… the Elders sent you to me because you are a magical anomaly. They happen every so often. As a child, not only have you spent a lot of magical energy, you also self-generate your power. That's why when the Elders delved you, it reacted so powerfully. Magic is flamboyant that way.'

As if in agreement with the voice, shooting stars began wheeling across the vista, their tails made up of black sparkles and when they collided, rainbows of the wrong colour rained downwards.

'Why can't I keep generating?' Jenni wished she had arms to cross or a foot to tap.

'It will upset the balance. This entire universe exists on the fundamental concept that balance in all things must exist. Light for dark, good for evil, magic for non magic–you get the general idea. As the Source of all fae magic, I can correct your flow…'

Jenni interrupted.

'So there is summink wrong wiv me then.'

'Not wrong, different, and it's a difference that could have catastrophic consequences.'

'Yeah, the elders said summink about wars and stuff.'

Jenni felt the Source enclose her a little tighter. It wasn't uncomfortable, but she was highly aware of being enveloped in every direction.

'If I leave you with untapped power, war will follow. I've seen it before, it is inevitable no matter the purity of the individual. Ultimate power corrupts ultimately. Do you understand?'

Jenni scratched her head. Or at least tried to.

'I guess…'

'Yes, go on.' The Source was encouraging Jenni to speculate further out of the box.

'I s'pose I'd wanna 'elp wiv fings and that. It would be for good to start wiv but, the power would take over.' Jenni's tone turned shrewd. 'I knows what you mean. I seen it too. When some people get a taste of power, it goes to their 'ead and fings start going bad. Why does it never go good?'

'It's a matter of balance. Very rarely does a single individual achieve the karmic state of pure balance. There is nearly always a pull to one side or the other, and these pulls can be the tiniest of motions. Most people oscillate about a central margin of acceptability.'

Jenni's brain was starting to hurt and she couldn't even feel her head.

'So 'ow did I get like this? Shouldn't you 'ave noticed I was using magic like water? Upsetting the balance and all that.'

'All fae children are encouraged to develop and grow naturally. To explore and test their magical limits and boundaries in order to discover where they stand upon the balance. It is why we have the coming of age ceremony. To catch and correct these anomalies and to nudge those that need nudging. This is the way.'

'Will it 'urt?'

'No, Jenni. I shall merely pinch your conduit to me. You will still be able to do magic, but you must learn how to balance your gift with what energy is available. It may take time to adjust, but trust your new abilities. Once you get to grips with the changes, you have the potential to emerge as a powerful adult fae.'

Jenni thought for a moment.

''Ow come you ain't the Source of *all* magic?'

'Some gain their magic from natural sources, like the elementals and some pay for their magic with pieces of their soul, like witches. Fae magic is your sacred birthright and stretches back generations, to well before man conquered these lands.'

'Wot about me Dad? Is it 'is fault I'm anomalising?'

'Your father is magically indistinct. What makes you special is you, Jenni, nothing else. Would you like me to tell you who your father is?'

Jenni shrugged and this time the cotton candy pink clouds moved fractionally. She was acclimatising to her surroundings.

'I don't fink it matters. E's not been interested afore, so why would 'e be interested now?'

Calmness and serenity flowed from the Source through to Jenni's consciousness.

'Ow long will it take? To pinch me I mean?'

'It will be completed when you return through the arch.'

Jenni was about to complain that there was no arch when the black stone tore its way into view, the pink cloud dissolving as the stone touched it.

'I better get going. Fanks for the chat.'

'You are welcome, Jenni.'

Jenni felt the Source give her a gentle mental nudge, and she moved closer to the stone arch. It tingled as the physicality of the structure caught her essence and drew her back through to the real world.

Chapter 14

The journey back through the arch took longer than passing into it. Jenni could hear the elders talking as she travelled.

'Do you want something to eat?' asked Amos. 'Curry?'

'Will we have time?' replied Greg.

'Remember how long Momma K spent in the arch?'

'Ah. Let's…' but before the giant caterpillar could declare his take-away meal of choice, the archway shuddered and Jenni stomped back out.

'Can I get outta 'ere now?' She scowled at the elders, arms crossed, one foot tapping.

'Delve her,' Amos ordered QuiQuo.

The imp once more unfolded its stick-like body and once more touched a gnarled finger to Jenni's brow. This time the sprite glowed pure white, and this time a pleasant humming noise filled the air. QuiQuo clicked in appreciation.

Jenni shook her head, breaking the connection and looked past the imp at the others. 'So, can I go?'

'Aren't you going to tell us what happened, child?' asked Greg, who sat forward eagerly.

'Nah. I gots magic, it'll work somehow. And I ain't yor child.'

'Very well,' Amos barked the enchantment that re-opened the sacred chamber and the entrance appeared.

Without a backward glance at anyone, Jenni stalked out. She felt prickly all over, like her skin was too tight for her body.

***

'What did the Source do, QuiQuo?' asked Greg.

There followed a complex series of clicks, clacks and clucks. Greg and Amos nodded along in fascination as the imp explained how Jenni's power had been modulated by the Source.

'What about Momma K? Won't she be disappointed that Jenni turned down the throne?' Greg waggled his legs in worry.

QuiQuo chittered.

'That is not our fault. There was no coercion involved on our part.' Amos flexed the claws on his paws. 'It is a matter for Momma K and Jenni to discuss. Decisions made in the heat of youth are often reconsidered later. If we are done for the day, I shall get back to my studies.'

'Yes, yes, I have grubs to tend. Until next time, gentlemen.'

***

Momma K floated up to greet her daughter as she returned, her beautiful wings effortlessly lifting her.

'Chil', ya back quick.' She craned her neck to see past Jenni's back. 'Where ya wings?'

'I didn't want 'em.'

'But... wings is wat make us who we are. Ya can't be queen wi' no wings.'

'Guess I ain't being queen then, am I?'

Momma K regarded her wayward daughter suspiciously.

'Chil'? Wha' ya choose?'

Jenni regarded her mother for a moment, then clicked her fingers to pop herself out of the grove. Nothing happened. A faint sense of unease prickled at the end of her tail, but she tried not to show it in front of her mother.

'I gotta go back to work. I'll see ya.'

Momma K watched Jenni stomp away, towards the portal out of her kingdom and back to the city of Roshaven.

'Oh chil', wat ya done?' she murmured.

***

Once she had feet on the cobbles of Roshaven streets, Jenni tried popping again, but it still didn't work. Unease had travelled up the length of her tail and was now dancing at the back of her ears, making her want to turn around all the time as if someone was there. She pretended to ignore it and started walking to HQ. The Source had said it might take a while for her magic to start working again. Maybe that's all it was. A reset.

Then she remembered Ned. Switching directions, Jenni headed over to the Druid Grove and hoped that her boss at least was having a better day.

***

Ned wanted a cup of bean. And it wasn't that *oh let's have a cuppa* feeling. This was deep down in his bones, a desperate need that he'd never felt before. The addiction response was kicking in, just like Kendra had said it would. He drummed his fingers on the side of the bed. He was sitting, fully dressed, boots on and ready to go, feeling much better after several purges and Ma Bowl's soup but Kendra had told him he ought to try and get some sleep before he left the grove.

'Maybe I could learn to brew myself,' murmured Ned as his mind danced away with the notion of having a little bean machine in the office, brewing away all day. He inhaled deeply, the tantalising aroma tickling his tastebuds. Miraculously, a cup of bean materialised in front of him. It hung in mid-air. Cautiously Ned reached out but when his fingers touched the cup it disappeared into pale grey smoke and there was a soft whicker behind him. He sighed. The Nightmare was back, and he wasn't even asleep.

He swung his legs onto the mattress and flopped down. The Nightmare shook its wispy mane and began trotting around the bed. Ned tried to ignore it but it's quite difficult to ignore equestrian-based phantoms. They tend to be large and clip-cloppy.

***

'It's getting worse,' Kendra told Sister Eustacia. They were catching up over honey cakes. The Druid Grove ran itself. Organised religion is just that, organised. New recruits have a certain zeal for following routine.

'Is he still vomiting?' asked Sister Eustacia.

'No, but now he's seeing the Nightmare while awake.' Kendra had been observing Ned earlier.

Sister Eustacia grimaced. That wasn't a good sign.

'We need the sprite,' she said.

'We really do.'

'Wot you want me for?'

'Jenni! You're back. How was the ceremony?' Kendra whirled to see the sprite and considered giving her a hug but quashed her natural instinct at the thunderous look on Jenni's face.

'I don't wanna talk about it. Where is 'e?'

'I'll take you,' replied Kendra, flashing a concerned glance at the Sister.

They walked down the corridor in silence and Kendra paused before entering the recovery room.

'It can be rough, going through the coming of age ceremony. I've been through it, if you ever want to talk about it.'

'Yeah, mebbe.' Jenni pushed the door open to the recovery room.

Ned was lying very still on his bed, eyes wide and fists clenched. There was a sheen of sweat across his skin and his focus was riveted directly above his head.

'Alright, Boss?'

There was no answer.

'It's 'ere, innit?' Jenni asked Kendra.

'I think so. We summoned Barbas earlier to get him to remove the Nightmare, but he said it was a blood-debt and you knew all about it. What's going on, Jenni?'

'I fink it's Theo. That's the only person wot would summon summink like this.'

'Who's Theo?'

'His bruvver.'

Chapter 15

Ned scowled at the way the druid hovered beside his bed.

'Are you sure you want to leave? The bean may still have a hold of you and the Nightmare…' Kendra fussed with his pillow.

'The Nightmare is my problem. I'll deal with it.' Ned replied gruffly as he stood up, then felt guilty. Kendra had shown him nothing but kindness. 'My brother set up the contract. He obviously wants something, and this is his way of getting my attention.'

'Couldn't he just have sent a note?'

'That's not his style.' Ned smiled at the druid. 'I appreciate your help.'

She returned the smile and put a small paper bag in his hands.

'These are from Sister Eustacia. Sugar snails. She says they help with the cravings. Stay off the bean.'

Ned nodded and strode out, Jenni meeting him in the outer courtyard of the grove where she had been waiting for him. They strolled along in silence. Ned's boots wanted to go towards *Headshot,* but he ignored them and headed for HQ instead.

'What's up?' he asked Jenni.

'Stuff.'

'Stuff? What does that mean?'

Jenni kicked at the path as she walked along, trying to pick her words.

'I growed up.'

Ned frowned, then realisation dawned.

'You had your Coming of Age ceremony, didn't you?'

'Yep.'

They went a bit further.

'How did it go?'

'Dunno.'

Ned scratched his head.

'That bad, huh?' He looked at her more closely, finally realising what was so different about her. 'What happened to your coat? It's got a bloody great big tear in it.'

Jenni shrugged. Ned stopped walking.

'Jenni, come on. It's me. Talk to me.'

She rubbed her eyes and tried to stop the prickling feeling in her nose.

'They said I ain't got all me magic no more an' I can't do everfink like wot I used to. An' I tore me coat. That's me only coat. And they asked if I wanted wings. Wings! When do I ever want wings?' Jenni paused for breath, but Ned didn't have time to get a word in. 'Wot am I? Some kind of fairy or summink? The Elders delved me and said that I got too much and it weren't allowed so they sent me off to see the Source and it reduced it.' She kicked a small stone hard and watched as it ricocheted off a wall. 'I didn't even know I was supposed to be doin' me coming of age already. I fawt I were too young.'

Ned waited to hear if there was any more, but it seemed Jenni had said all she wanted to.

'Growing up is… what I mean to say is… you know what, Jenni? Life sucks sometimes, and we just have to do the best we can with what we're given. And you've got me and all the Catchers. You'll always have a roof over your head as long as I live. We're family.'

There was a lengthy silence because both parties could not speak due to dust in their eyes. Strange how dust shows up like that.

'Wot we gonna do about Theo, Boss?' Jenni was the first to recover.

'It's a bit odd, isn't it? I receive this weird gig from Griff to go hand out some powerful magical objects at the same time that I'm being hounded by a bloody smoke monster. Maybe he knew about Griff's will somehow.'

'You fink e's afta summink then?'

'He's always after something, Jenni. Always.'

They continued down Slingshot Row until The Noose came into view.

'We haven't had any details through yet, have we?'

'For wot?'

'For our first mystery item. From Griff.'

'Nah. Least, not since I've been growing and you've been 'urling.'

Ned smiled. He could count on Jenni to cut right to the chase on anything. He held the inn door open for her as they entered and headed for the rickety stairs at the back of the room. If he was lucky, he'd have time to put his feet up before the next disaster fell in his lap. They both heard the shouting as they reached the top of the stairwell.

'Why did you bring it here?' demanded Willow.

'I couldn't leave it there!' replied Joe.

'The Boss is going to kill us. We can't have that, that thing here. This is an inn.'

Ned braced himself for what he was going to find as he entered the room. It revealed itself to be a small pig nosing around the artfully arranged stack of paperwork in the far corner. The filing was wobbling alarmingly.

Willow and Joe were standing nose to nose, fists on hips, glaring at each other.

'Wot's going on? We 'aving bacon sarnies?' Jenni leered at the pig, licking her lips.

'No!' Willow bristled thornily and stepped in front of the animal protectively.

'She's just kidding,' Ned reassured Willow whilst simultaneously scowling at Jenni. 'What is a pig doing here, anyway?'

'It's Merrick's. You told us to solve the case of the missing pig. I found it.' Willow bloomed with pride.

'Yeah, but only after I figured out one of Jimmy Fingers' lads had taken it on a dare,' countered Joe.

'And it's here because…' Ned looked from one earnest thief-catcher to the other.

'Well… it was late once we'd finished investigating, and the pig was a bit scared so I brought it back here, figuring we would return it this morning,' explained Joe.

'Right,' Ned rolled his eyes. 'Two questions. Is the pig housebroken and did anyone think to get Merrick to come pick it up?'

They both shook their heads.

'Right, well get Sparks… where is Sparks?'

''E was on a family day yesterday. Should be back by now.' Jenni wiggled a finger in her ear and inspected the find.

'I need a drink,' muttered Ned, sitting down at his desk. There was a mostly clean cup perched on a pile of reports. Ned reached into the desk drawer and pulled out a bottle of scumble.

'Bit early, ain't it, Boss?'

'Let a man have one vice,' Ned replied, uncorking the bottle. The aroma of fermented apple percolated through the room.

The pig stopped eating paper and trotted over to Ned with hope in its eyes.

'Yeah, this isn't for you.' Ned swigged from the bottle, cleansing his palate that was yearning for bean more than he'd care to admit. He recorked the scumble and shoved it back in the desk drawer. 'Willow and Joe, get hold of the pig and return it to Merrick. Tell him Fingers' boy was charged... you did charge him, didn't you?'

'I spoke very sternly to him, Boss,' replied Willow.

'I bet he were shaking in 'is boots at that,' snarked Jenni, giving the pig a good scratch in between the ears. The little piggy snorted in delight.

Ned tried to hide his grin.

'Just take it back. The Thief-Catcher's HQ is no place for a pig,' ordered Ned.

'Yes, Boss.' Willow wove a thin vine into a collar for the animal and led it out of the office, Joe trailing behind.

Ned sniffed the air. Something unsavoury was wafting from somewhere, and he didn't think it was him.

'Jenni, would you check for er... droppings, please? In case of accidents.'

The sprite clicked her fingers. Nothing happened. She muttered the words of the spell under her breath. Still nothing.

'What's wrong?' asked Ned.

'It's nuffink.'

Ned snorted. 'I'm fairly certain that making sure there is no pig poo in the office is pretty important.'

'That's not wot I mean,' retorted Jenni as she checked the cupboard for a broom. Miraculously, there was one. She started half-heartedly moving it around the floor.

'What are you doing? Why don't you just disappear the poop?'

Jenni threw the broom handle on the floor with a clatter. 'Cos I ain't got proper access to me magic no more, 'ave I! And it ain't come frew yet, like the Source said it would,' she shouted and clenched for a pop. She did not pop. 'Argh! I can't even pop nowhere no more! I can't make nuffink work. They never said it would be this rubbish.' She stalked out of the room, slamming the door behind her.

Chapter 16

It had been two days since the funeral and Fourteen couldn't get Griff out of her mind. She knew why she had wanted to honour Griff with a state affair. He had been an old friend of her father's and instrumental in setting up many of the trade routes in and out of Roshaven. The *Silk Road,* he'd called it, claiming that dresses and other women's finery were the root of all successful business decisions. And he had been a very successful man. But she hadn't realised how close Ned and Griff were, or why Ned had insisted on being the one to fire the arrow at the funeral.

As the imperial carriage clattered along on her morning constitutional, Fourteen thought it was odd that Ned knew Griff so well, but he had never mentioned the relationship to her before. Strange too that Griff and Ned's paths hadn't crossed at the palace before she'd gone with Ned on that quest to capture the Rose Thief. Then again, Fourteen had been just another numbered offspring at the time of her memories of Griff and not the Emperor of Roshaven, so there was no reason for Griff to tell her anything personal. And Ned - Ned must have been in Fidelia then. Doing whatever it was he did before he moved to Roshaven and became Chief Thief-Catcher.

A breath caught in Fourteen's throat as she realised she knew next to nothing about the man she loved, and the breath threatened to turn into a sob as she remembered how upset he had seemed at the funeral. She hadn't meant to keep him at arms-length for so long.

Things had been busy since they'd got back from saving love and catching the Rose Thief. There was always so much paperwork to go through, and the Highs kept her occupied with numerous important duties as well as numerous unimportant ones.

Wishing the coach would slow down a little before returning her to the palace, Fourteen sighed. It was only mid morning. If she were lucky she would get away with only one or two meetings. The horses clattered into the palace courtyard and Fourteen wiped her face of personality, becoming the mask of authority she had to portray. It didn't do to smile at the servants. It made them nervous.

As anticipated, the High Right stood in the courtyard, his fingers tapping on a sheaf on paper he was holding.

'Your Eminence. We have a distinguished visitor waiting for you.'

'Which meeting room?' asked Fourteen. This was an important question. The answer dictated how much time she would have to spend on the meeting and whether she could delay it.

'Second-best. And Fat Norris is waiting for you in the third. But he can wait…'

'Actually no, I will see Fat Norris first. I'll take tea.' Fourteen strode down the corridor, keen to get these two meetings over and done with. 'Who is the other visitor?'

'The new Lord of Fidelia.'

'I didn't know Fidelia had a lord. Who is it?' Fourteen asked. The last time she'd been to Fidelia, the man in charge had been Ned's brother Theo and he was definitely no lord.

'His full name is Theodore Michel de Silverthorpe,' replied the High Right.

Fourteen stopped abruptly.

'No. I will not see him. Remove him from my palace immediately.' Her voice was tight with fury.

'With respect, Your Eminence, the Lord of Fidelia has travelled many miles. It would be rude not to receive him.'

'I don't care. He is not welcome here.' She rounded on the High. 'You do realise who he is, don't you?' She didn't wait for an answer. 'He is the Chief of T.A.R.T.S. I will not hold court with someone in charge of thieves, arsonists, raconteurs, tarts and solicitors. I won't do it.'

The High Right bustled and fiddled with the sheaf of paper he held.

'My Emperor, Griff's death has rippled throughout the trading ports of Efrana with negotiations unravelling and upstarts attempting to gain a piece of the pie. Maintaining peaceful, unbroken trade is of the utmost importance. As you know, we are a trading city, Your Eminence, it's our lifeblood. If the Lord of Fidelia is here, it may mean he has come to broker a new treaty.' The High softened his tone a little. 'Regardless of how he came to his title, he now holds considerable power and influence. You owe him your time and respect.'

'I owe him nothing!' hissed Fourteen furiously. 'He killed Griff. I want him out of my palace. NOW!'

The High Right was still spluttering when they arrived at the third best meeting room. Fourteen put her hand on the door and took a steadying breath.

'Bring cake. With my tea.' Then she glided into the room, her emperor smile plastered on her face.

'Norris, this is an unexpected pleasure. I did not think we would see each other so soon.' Fourteen had last stood with her advisors at Griff's funeral. Fat Norris, the Lower Circle, and Madame Silk, The Stalls, were both instrumental in keeping the cogs of Roshaven moving.

'My Emperor, may you live for ever and ever.' Norris inclined his head as far as his triple chins would allow. It may have been that he bowed and bent a leg, but his bulk made it hard to tell. 'I come with dire news.'

Great, thought Fourteen as she took the Emperor's chair at the table. *I hope they bring plenty of cake.*

Waiting for Norris to lever himself into a seat, she nodded in what she hoped was an encouraging way for him to explain why he was there but they spent the next few minutes discussing the weather, Fourteen's gown and of course, Griff's funeral. This seemed to lead Norris to his actual reason for meeting with her.

'It was Griff I wanted to talk to you about,' he said nervously with a small laugh. 'It was him who actually ran the trade routes in and out of Roshaven, specifically the lucrative silk trade and…'

'I thought he just facilitated the set-up?'

'No, my Emperor, my you live for ever and…'

'My liege is quicker, if you prefer,' Fourteen gave Norris a brief personal smile to let him know it was alright. Her father had been a stickler for honorifics and strict with decapitating those who didn't comply.

'My liege.' Norris returned the smile with gratitude. 'Griff ran the trade routes. He shared some of the players but not all of them, and I have not been able to re-establish all the links. We are trading maybe one third of our usual cargo, which is beginning to affect, well, everything. With so few buying or selling in Roshaven, traders are looking elsewhere. We only had three ships this month. Just three. Our city's own supplies are running low and the bean situation is critical.'

'The bean situation? I thought we had a huge

shipment. Griff planned for its popularity. He knew it would be a hit.'

'Well, my liege, it has been a tremendous hit. Too tremendous. We can't keep up with demand, especially as there is no more supply. There have been a few bean *incidents* where customers unable to get their fix have been trashing tea shops in vain. When it's leaf versus bean, there's no comparison. Apparently. I don't care for bean myself.'

'But you have Griff's notes or contacts, something surely that can help you renegotiate the trade agreements? I can't believe it isn't in the best interest of our trading partners to reconnect with us. Surely they must be losing money as well?'

Fat Norris's third chin wobbled, and that's when Fourteen realised the man in front of her was scared. A faint sheen of sweat lay upon his face and his hand trembled.

'What is it you are not telling me?' she asked gently, trying to put him at ease.

'My liege, there is a... um... new player in town. Well, not our town, but several towns over. I think you know it, you returned from there recently. It's er... the place where um... Griff passed. Ahem.' Norris took a handkerchief to his brow and avoided eye contact with Fourteen.

'Fidelia? They're taking over our trade routes? Why?'

'Some of them my liege, yes. I am not without any contacts, but it takes time to get in touch with people and organise meetings. Fidelia have moved swiftly, decisively, and apparently they've offered excellent rats.'

'You mean rates.'

'Yes, those too.'

Fourteen was incensed at the gall of bloody Theo and her anger grew. She tried not to let it show and instead asked the obvious question.

'Why are excellent rats important?'

'Ships' cats and dwarves. Rats are a very important sweetener for any trade agreement.'

Fourteen nodded, pretending to understand.

'So if I have this right, Griff set up our trade routes, held all the contacts, contracts and agreements and didn't share any information with anyone. He probably gave you ten per cent off the top and handled all the paperwork, leaving you with an easy life running the warehouses. When he was brutally murdered in Fidelia, Theo had spies with their fingers in all the right pies and more or less wrenched the entire system out from under us before we even knew what had happened. Is that about the gist of it?'

Fat Norris nodded miserably and whispered something Fourteen couldn't quite catch.

'Pardon?'

'It was seven and a half percent, my liege.'

Fourteen snorted. Her Lower Circle couldn't even get a good deal for someone else doing his job. And that slimey, murderous, trade stealer of a person was sat waiting for her in the second-best meeting room.

At that moment the tea arrived with a couple of slices of Ma Bowl's wonderfully sticky and citrusy lemon cake. Fourteen fixed Fat Norris with an icy stare as his hand lifted towards a slice. She didn't feel inclined to share cake with someone who had a hand in destroying her city's entire economy.

The High Right had followed in on the heels of the tea trolley.

'Ahem, I am sorry to interrupt, Your Eminence, but the Lord of Fidelia is wondering how much longer he will have to wait before an audience. Apparently, he has lots of trade meetings with our Guild heads planned and only came here first as a professional courtesy.' The High Right quailed under the fierce look on Fourteen's face. 'His words, Your Eminence.'

'Very well. Let's hear the words of a murderous snake, shall we?' And she stalked out of the meeting room, leaving a relieved Fat Norris, an agitated High Right and two delicious slices of lemon cake.

Chapter 17

Fourteen smiled to herself at the young palace guard, Fred, who swept a low bow at her arrival and managed to hang on to his helmet. He was improving. Fred opened one of the main doors and was about to announce her presence when Fourteen arched an eyebrow at him.

She watched as panic flashed across Fred's face and she could almost see the cogs turning. He was casting around for an indication of what he'd done wrong. Fourteen took pity on him and flicked her fingers towards the second door. Flushing, Fred opened it and in a high-pitched squeak announced the Emperor of Roshaven.

Theo was sprawled on the Emperor's chair, one leg hooked over the ornately carved arm of walnut wood, muddy boots dangling carelessly.

Fourteen narrowed her eyes and waited for the High Right to catch up. He trotted in a moment later, surreptitiously wiping lemony fingers on his robe. The High Left joined the room as well with fresh paper and pen, ready to take notes.

Theo sprang out of the chair at the arrival of the bureaucrats and flourished a flamboyant bow in Fourteen's direction. She tried to hide her shudder of disgust as his excessive cologne washed over her.

'What do you want?' she snapped.

'Your Grace, I am honoured that you found time to speak with me today. I'm sure matters of state are… pressing.'

'Lord Theo, if you would please join us for refreshments?' The High Right gestured to where a table and chairs had been set up with what looked like more lemon cake.

Fourteen was annoyed. Not only did she have to meet with this scum, now she was expected to make polite conversation and share her cake. She held her tongue until they had poured the tea and served the cake, then asked her question again.

'Why are you here?'

'Do you not drink bean, Your Grace?'

'The correct honorific is Your Eminence,' replied Fourteen tightly.

'Of course. My mistake.' Theo took a slurp of his tea and took the largest slice of cake, making Fourteen bristle even more.

Silence stretched on. Fourteen refusing to ask again, the two Highs not sure whether they ought to intervene and Theo clearly loving every second. Finally, he wiped his mouth on a napkin and leaned back in his chair.

'I'm here to discuss our trade border.' Theo paused. 'Your Eminence.'

'We don't share a border.'

'That's what I thought until I discovered an ancient scroll in my extensive historical library. The scholars there were quite excited. In times past, Roshaven and Fidelia shared a trade treaty across the ocean in an agreement cemented by marriage, specifically trading in silks and other high-end goods. Instead of fighting for individual trade agreements, both cities benefitted from dividing the costs and expenses, sharing their protection and wealth.'

Fourteen's insides clenched, and she went cold.

'It has come to my attention that a disreputable

criminal has been managing your trade routes for his own benefit, and now that he has been executed, you are left with a problem. Fortunately, as Lord of Fidelia, I have been able to use my extensive powers of persuasion to gather many of those former trade route contracts under my jurisdiction but alas, without a port in which to resupply here in Roshaven, the journey to distant shores is too far for some and those wishing to trade their exotic items are disinclined to risk the voyage without safe harbour here. The mermaids, you understand.'

That piece of information clicked something in Fourteen's brain. She had wondered why the mermaids had insisted on a role at Griff's funeral, now she knew. He had them involved in his trade agreements. It made sense, really. They were blood thirsty but loyal and had obviously acted as protectors in the waters, preventing piracy and possibly even had some agreement to not attack particular boats. Presumably, all of that was defunct now, but she made a mental note to try to send word to Pearl, the mermaid she'd met when she travelled under the sea with Ned, to see if she were agreeable to continue the arrangement.

'I am willing to extend access to these trade routes to you and revive prosperity in Roshaven, which I'm sure you are aware has been lacking of late. I only ask that you seal the contract in the spirit of the ancient scroll.' Theo licked his lips and smirked at Fourteen.

'I'm sorry, my Lord, are you asking for the Emperor's hand in marriage?' The High Left had stopped taking notes.

Theo sat back in his chair with a smug look on his face. He steepled his fingers and looked at Fourteen and her advisors over them.

'It seems like the best option, don't you think?'

Theo leered at her. 'Your Eminence.'

Fourteen held up one finger, pre-empting either High from answering.

'Thank you for your gracious offer, we will give it the utmost consideration. I do hope you brought a copy of the ancient scroll with you. For our own historians to peruse. Purely academic. Roshaven would never slur a prospective trade partner.'

The two Highs gulped back anything they were going to say and exchanged glances.

Theo patted his jacket pocket and pulled out a rather crumpled piece of paper. He passed it to Fourteen, but she gestured for the High Right to take it in her stead.

Rising gracefully, Fourteen plastered the most imperial smile she had on her face and dipped her head ever so slightly in Theo's direction.

'We thank you for your visit and wish you safe travels.' She turned to leave, flashing warning glares at the two Highs to follow her, immediately.

'Oh, I'm not leaving the city. I have other business to attend to here in Roshaven, and then there's your official coronation. I can't miss that.'

Again Fourteen's insides froze but she did not deign to turn around.

Outside the meeting room, Fourteen balled her fists and took a deep breath before jerking her head towards her study. The Highs followed, for once in complete silence. Fourteen had time to sit down at her desk and ring for more tea before they began speaking.

'Emperor, we must consider this generous offer.'

'It could be the solution to all our trade problems.'

'Have you read the scroll?' asked Fourteen, stopping them in their tracks.

'Well, no but...'

'Let's hear what it has to say.'

The High Right unfurled the paper and scanned it before reading snatches out to the others.

'It says here that whilst Fidelia and Roshaven do not share a physical border… the Lord of Fidelia has conquest rights should a female Emperor arise… ancient agreement made centuries ago between the rival founders… there's a caveat… mhm ah…'

'What? What does it say?' Fourteen was on the verge of snatching the paper for herself.

'It says that an unnamed Emperor has no recourse whatsoever and the marriage would result in all imperial rights passing to the Lord of Fidelia *in summa*.'

'What does unnamed mean, exactly?'

'It means an Emperor that has not been officially coronated with a formal imperial name,' replied the High Left in a soft voice.

Fourteen felt like someone had punched her in the gut. Her city had lost its trade lifeblood thanks to Theo yet he would restore the all important trade links if she married him. But, if she did that, then the slimy maggot who killed Griff would then have the legal right to her empire.

'Fear not, Emperor. There is always hope.'

Fourteen laughed bitterly.

'What hope is there here?'

'The ancient scroll is quite specific. The Emperor must be female, unnamed and uncrowned for a certain period in order for a Lord of Fidelia to stake his claim.'

Fourteen felt the first ray of light. Her coronation was set for two months' time.

'We may still make it out of this pickle, Your Eminence. If that's what you want to do.'

Fourteen couldn't help but smile at the High Right's

use of the word pickle. She would've called the whole thing a hot mess of despair, but pickle lent a certain lightness to things.

'Why does it say if the Emperor is female? Have there been many female emperors?'

The High Right tutted fondly.

'You never did pay attention to your history lessons. There have in fact been many female emperors during your family's imperial lineage.'

'But they've never married anyone from Fidelia,' broke in the High Left.

Fourteen smiled grimly. She wasn't about to let it happen now either.

Chapter 18

The tea arrived, giving Fourteen time to marshal her thoughts and to finally drink a cup. It seemed she had uncovered another subject which the Highs either thought she knew about and didn't bother to elaborate on, or a topic they hoped she didn't know about so they could avoid explaining.

'Let me get this straight. There has always been an Emperor in Roshaven, yet some of those have been women. Why not call them Empress?' asked Fourteen, although she could guess what the answer would be.

'Tradition,' replied the High Left.

'It's against the law, Your Eminence,' huffed the High Right. 'It would be unheard of. A radical move. There is no need to break with tradition in these matters. Tradition is the backbone of your empire.'

'Yet I am Emperor.'

'Exactly!' The High Right clapped his hands together. 'May you live forever and ever.'

Deciding to leave that historical revelation to one side, Fourteen picked up another.

'How did these female Emperors have children?'

The High Left sighed theatrically.

'Are you sure you didn't cover this in your studies? I seem to remember there was a scientist professor fellow employed for a short time.'

Fourteen flushed.

'I don't mean the mechanics. I understand the biology. I meant who were the fathers? And why has this never been explained to me before?'

'Well, the Emperor has always been encouraged to sow his seed amongst his concubines as freely as he wanted to. So when the Emperor was a woman, they would just be male concubines.'

'And false eunuchs,' piped up the High Right.

'False eunuchs?' Fourteen was bewildered. 'But what if I were to marry? Everyone would see me, a woman, marry a man.'

'Well… it's slightly more complex than that. Upon marriage, the female emperor gives away their imperial rights to their husband because Roshaven has always had an Emperor.'

'I can't believe what I'm hearing. This is ridiculous! Why wasn't I informed?'

'It was need to know,' replied the High Left.

'Pretty sure I needed to know!'

'Well, now you do,' said the High Right quickly. 'And it's the way the Roshaven Empire has run for hundreds of years so…'

'If you're about to say it's how things will be run for hundreds more, you can go throw yourself into the snake pit. I've never heard anything so backwards in all my life.' Fourteen drummed her fingers on the arm of her chair angrily as she tried to think. 'When exactly were you going to check that I knew this?'

The High Left looked to the High Right for support.

'We thought you already did…' he trailed off under Fourteen's glare.

'That is sloppy guidance. Both of you should be ashamed of yourselves. Allowing me to rule in ignorance is… is… blindingly unfair. How long were you going to let it go on for?'

Both Highs shuffled their feet, and the Left muttered under his breath.

'I can't hear you.'

'The Emperor said he would explain it to you but then he died, and you had already accepted the role of Upper Circle to maintain your female cover, so we thought you were fully cognizant of the situation.'

'Well, I wasn't,' Fourteen replied flatly. As the oldest surviving child of the previous emperor, it had been her court duty to take on a role, and she had chosen the Upper Circle to give her the chance to interact with her city and its people. After the death of her father and the transition of emperorship from him to her, that role had allowed Fourteen the opportunity to meet Ned and go with him on the Rose Thief quest. It had been a lengthy crossover period and she had been loath to lose all her freedoms hence her last hurrah as the Upper Circle. It was also the reason why her coronation had been delayed.

'Do you still have that paper?' asked Fourteen.

'Yes, Your Eminence.'

'Then take this down. I decree that from this moment on, the ruling monarch of Roshaven will be Emperor or Empress depending on the sex of the individual. I declare that husbands and wives will only have the power given to them in ratified pre-nup agreements and that the throne will be inherited parent to child.'

'But you can't just make laws...' stammered the High Left, casting a desperate glance at the High Right for support.

Fourteen stood to her feet and put her most imperial look on her face.

'I am your Emperor, am I not?'

'Yes, of course, but the committee will need to approve any new rule making.'

Fourteen continued to stare imperiously down her nose at her two advisors.

'The imperial committee that will of course be meeting tomorrow and voting on the amendments to imperial law. A vote that I'm sure will be carried through in your favour, Your Eminence,' chipped in the High Right.

Partially satisfied, Fourteen sat back down.

'At my coronation, they shall crown me Empress of Roshaven and my coronation will happen as soon as possible.'

'Well, yes, Your Eminence. Almost everything has already been planned. I'm sure we could pull it forwards.'

'How quickly?' asked Fourteen.

The Highs looked at each other and one of them held up four fingers, the other nodded in agreement.

'The earliest we could do is four days' time. That shouldn't upset anyone and give most guests ample time to arrive in Roshaven. As long as we send out the invitation today.' Right looked to Left for confirmation.

'It's a possibility but we're still waiting for your imperial name, Your Eminence. Unfortunately, numbers are not officially recognised.' The High Left bobbed his head slightly, knowing this was a touchy subject.

Fourteen scowled. Choosing a name was indeed a sore spot and something she was struggling with.

Chapter 19

The High Right was droning on.

'Ahem.' He cleared his throat to make sure Fourteen was listening. 'Then there is the matter of the Upper Circle.'

That caught her attention. 'What about it?'

'We have three suitable candidates. I've created a report on each for you to read and decide on your replacement. Our preference is for the second one but it is as the Emperor decrees.'

'Of course,' murmured Fourteen. She'd known that declaring herself officially as Emperor would mean changes to her roles, but she hadn't considered all the implications. Being Upper Circle had been so much fun. Apart from the headdress. She wouldn't miss that at all.

'The Lower Circle and the Stalls will be required to sign off on the choice as well, in the interest of partial democracy. What the Emperor decrees is, of course, the law.'

'Quite.' Then she realised what he'd said. 'Partial democracy?'

'Yes, Your Eminence. The illusion that people of title have some power. A long-standing tradition, I'm sure you'll agree.'

Fourteen smiled wryly.

'Going back to choosing your name, Your Eminence, we must make a decision.'

She shifted in her chair. For once, it wasn't an uncomfortable one. They were in her study, the only space they had given her permission to decorate, so consequently it looked nothing like the rest of the Imperial Palace. There was absolutely no gold lacquer.

'As Emperor, it is customary to take a name from the Imperial Record.' He pointed to the enormous book on the table. 'Within are listed every ruler of Roshaven, their official wives and recognised children.'

'Am I in there?'

The High Right cleared his throat and opened the book with reverence. He turned to the final page with writing and lifted the tome so Fourteen could read it.

'No other name, just my number,' she murmured.

'It was tradition to number offspring. One never knew which would survive to adulthood and the imperial family believed numbers to be less emotional.' He looked at Fourteen with a small smile on his face. 'I happen to know that your predecessor had a fondness for the number fourteen.'

Again she smiled, this time with a little more warmth.

'I think I need a bit of time to have a look through the book and decide on a suitable name. I never thought I'd be anything other than my number. It's a huge decision.'

'Indeed it is, Your Eminence. But we will need to know by four o'clock. For the official invitations.'

Fourteen sighed. That gave her a couple of hours to choose a name for herself for the rest of her life.

'If there's nothing else?' she asked and the High Right took the hint, gathered up his papers and bowed himself out of the study, the High Left behind him.

Fourteen drifted over to the window and stared out at the beautiful, immaculate and intricately designed rose garden her father had commissioned. There were roses of every colour in gloriously arranged flower beds.

She'd undone all the magic on the individual blooms after the debacle with the red rose of love. She didn't want any more thieves trying to disrupt her kingdom.

'After all,' she whispered to herself. 'What's in a name, anyway.'

Turning resolutely away from the window, she picked up the book and began flipping through. *Alberta, Brasalita, Cassandra.* None of them had the dignity she was looking for, and they all ended with an 'a'. An Emperor ought to have an impressive name or at least one they liked. *Maybe a spell will help me,* she thought. Fourteen was an accomplished spellcaster, and it had been her magic that had almost caught the Rose Thief when it was entangled in Joe's mind. She didn't use her magic often but made sure she wore a power well, for cases of emergency. Fourteen mentally reached for her power and considered what she was looking for.

It always helped to be as specific as possible when casting magic. It was a powerful force, but it was also terribly literal.

Powers of the earth, powers of the sky
Powers of water, powers of fire
I beseech you to hear my plea
And help provide a name for me

Fourteen waited. And waited. But other than the slight flicker of a lit candle on the table, nothing happened. *So much for the powers that be,* thought Fourteen. *I guess my name isn't that important in the grand scheme of things.*

The clock on the mantle chimed midday. Fourteen pushed herself to standing and decided to visit the library. Perhaps there would be more inspiration for a name there.

*****

As Fourteen left the room, there was an elemental rustle.

Why can't we help her?

Because. It's thing. Interfering. We don't do that.

I'm pretty sure we do.

Yes, well. Not this time. The Emperor must choose her own name without any help from us. Or anyone else, for that matter.

Yes, but...

But what?

Why not? We're great at names. We named everything in the natural world, after all.

True, but she is not one of ours. The magics flow in her a little, but her humanity rules her heart.

Okay... we could leave some suggestions out for her.

You are free to try but beware, most humans can't read elemental.

I have faith in this one.

There was the sound of wind laughing and the candle in the room snuffed out, then reappeared with a furious pop. Fire was going to leave some clues whether Air liked it or not.

*****

A few hours later, a rather dejected Fourteen returned to her study. The library had been a waste of time. Far too many books for her to go through them with any accuracy and spot checking had just delivered more names she didn't like. The candle she'd left in the room had sputtered and now there was wax in unusual blobs across the surface of her desk and some ash which was odd as the flame was still burning. There was something about the pattern that drew Fourteen closer. Her eyes partially unfocused and her brain seemed to be on the edge of grasping something wonderful when there was a loud knocking on the door and the High Right entered.

'We need that name, Your Eminence. For the invites.' He prompted gently.

Fourteen came to a decision.

'I don't have one. Just put down on the invite, the where, the when and the what. I shall reveal my name at the ceremony.' She caught a brief frown pass across the High's face. 'This is my prerogative. A name, after all, is a very serious thing.' Fourteen tilted her chin, ready to defend her position if needed, but the High Right bowed his head.

'As you decree, Your Eminence.'

'And can you send someone to clean this desk, please? The candle has made a terrible mess.'

*****

Fire sparked in annoyance, then brightened. It looked like it had more time to get the hint across. The Emperor would have a name.

Chapter 20

Fourteen felt like crying–how would she figure a way out of this mess? She was sure this ancient scroll must be bogus, but she had no idea how to prove it. It was unlikely that there existed a legal arrangement between Roshaven and Fidelia that the two Highs knew nothing about. Theo's reputation as Chief of T.A.R.T.S meant she didn't trust a single word he said, and the fact that he had killed Griff cemented her loathing. Yet with Theo bleeding Roshaven's trade routes dry, she couldn't wait too long before taking action. Her city's future depended on it.

Why couldn't she just marry for love? She knew why. It was rhetorical. But still her heart ached. If only Ned was nobility. Fourteen frowned. If Theo was now the Lord of Fidelia and Ned was his brother, then that meant he had to be a noble of some sort or another as well. If she had to, she would discover her own ancient scroll. Feeling slightly less despairing, she considered her options.

If she said yes to Theo's proposal to buy more time and partially revive the trade routes into Roshaven, she could try to find a loophole getting her out of the ancient scroll, figure out the trade agreements Roshaven needed and be officially crowned as Empress with the right to marry whoever she wanted.

It seemed like a lot, but Fourteen felt a spark of hope. All she needed now was someone she could completely trust. Ringing bells for a messenger and the Highs, Fourteen wiped her cheeks dry, vowing there would be no more tears. She had a solution. She hoped.

The Highs arrived first. They appeared so quickly, Fourteen was sure they had been lurking, waiting to be called back. She saw a spark of pride in their demeanour as she told them she was prepared to accept the Lord of Fidelia's hand in marriage. Clearly they thought it was the right thing to do for the sake of the empire.

'I do have some caveats,' she added.

'And what would those caveats be, Your Eminence?' asked the High Right.

'I will marry after my coronation, and I want Fat Norris to have all the trade agreement details in triplicate. I want every deal scrutinised by our lawyers and where possible, I want contacts confirmed and approached individually. I would prefer direct lines of communication.'

The Highs nodded sagely.

'I imagine it will take time for Lord Theo to gather together this information. It may mean delaying the coronation...' began the High Left.

Fourteen cut him off.

'No! I will not delay the coronation. And I have a suspicion that Theo brought everything with him. He expected victory and would have planned accordingly. Let's get those trading meetings set up and tell Fat Norris that I want him at every single one, on pain of death.'

'Death, Your Eminence?'

Fourteen nodded. Fat Norris liked to delegate. He had groomed several young deputies to attend meetings on his behalf, each one had perfect recall yet none of them could read. Which was one reason why Fat Norris still had his role. However, these trade meetings would require Norris's full attendance. Not only would that ensure he got all the right information, but there would also be delays, as Norris would do almost anything to get out of attending meetings. She would use his reticence to help buy her some more time.

'I will take your offer to the Lord of Fidelia at once, Your Eminence.' The High Left made to leave, but Fourteen stopped him.

'Tomorrow morning will be soon enough. Let's not be too hasty to seal my fate, shall we?'

The Highs laughed nervously and bid the Emperor good night. There was a light knock on the door after they had left. It was Fourteen's requested messenger.

Actually, it was Fred, the palace guard. Fourteen had heard he was doing a bit of extra overtime so he must be standing in for Messenger Phil tonight because Phil had a hot date with that new girl in accounting. Fourteen's maid was a fount of palace gossip.

'Good evening, Fred.'

'Yes, my Emperor, may you live for ever and ever.'

Fourteen stifled a sigh.

'I want you to take this note to the thief-catchers, but it must be handed to Jenni, please.'

'Not Mr Spinks, my Emperor, may you live for ever and ever?'

'No. It must be Jenni.' Fourteen paused and thought she might as well try. 'And you don't have to use the live for ever bit every time you speak to me, Fred.' *It's archaic and one of things I intend to get rid of,* she added to herself.

'Yes, my Emperor.' There was a pause and Fred's lips moved minutely for nine syllables. 'I will hand the message to Jenni and no-one else. You can count on me.' He gave a sharp salute and smartly about turned.

Left to her own devices, Fourteen considered

heading down to the kitchens. Ma Bowl would be glad to see her, but it unsettled the kitchen girls, and she wasn't sure she had the energy for wide-eyed adoration right now. No, an early night would be the best option. She would need to be sharp witted and clear-headed tomorrow. Sitting down with Theo to hash out the trade agreements would be like wrestling an alligator with one hand tied behind your back whilst blindfolded. She couldn't risk giving anything else away. Hopefully Jenni would be able to come up with something.

Chapter 21

Jenni swayed. At least she thought she was swaying. It could have been the room. That's what happened when she tried to keep up with dwarves. Those short arses could drink! She hiccupped and her vision doubled for a brief while.

Deciding to call it a night, Jenni staggered to her feet and tottered out of The Noose. She was navigating a wibbly wobbly route back home to Ned's when she saw a plume she recognised.

'Plumey!'

'Miss Jenni, are you alright?' asked a concerned Fred.

'I'marvellous,' she slurred, trying to decide which Fred was the real one. 'S'up?'

'I've got an urgent missive from the Emperor for you. Did you know she said I didn't have to say the honorific anymore? That's because I'm a trusted member of the household and she values my work. It's not everyone who's allowed to not say it although I'll always say it in me head because it's only polite and after all's said and done she is my Emperor.'

'You sure it's for me?' Jenni scratched an armpit, dislodging a couple of sozzled mites.

'Absolutely. The Emperor was very specific. I don't know what it could be about. I don't read my missives, unlike some messengers at the palace. You know, that Howard, the one who came over from the Guild of Amusing Shaped Vegetables, well he reads everything with not so much as a by-your-leave and the worst of it is that everyone knows he does so they only use him for the really boring stuff which he says is fine by him because he doesn't really like being a messenger and actually just wants to be a greengrocer. Something to do with mangoes.' Fred beamed at Jenni, who was trying and failing to keep up with the conversation.

'Jus' put it in my pocket, yeah. I'll read it laters.'

'Of course, Miss Jenni.' Fred carefully tucked the note into her coat pocket, ensuring he buttoned it up to prevent it from falling out by accident. 'Can I help you get home? You seem a little worse for wear and our mam always says you should look out for those in a poorer state than you are and our Brian says they shouldn't get in that position in the first place but he never drinks a drop on account of his gout.'

'Home?' Jenni spun around a few times trying to get her bearings, then looked up at Fred with what she thought was a winning smile. It was actually an incredibly alcoholic breath of air into his unsuspecting face, which made his eyes water.

'Let me help you, Miss Jenni. This way.' And Fred took hold of one of the drunken sprite's arms, leading her towards the crooked house she called home with Ned.

It took twice as long as normal to get there because Jenni's sense of up and down was a little skewered, so it was with some relief that they arrived and Fred knocked on the front door.

'I got… I got… I got keys. Somewhere. I fink.' Jenni hiccupped. She didn't know if Ned was home.

'I think this way will be faster, Miss Jenni,' replied Fred.

Eventually footsteps could be heard clattering down the hallway and Fred adjusted the now comatose Jenni into what he hoped was a more comfortable position.

'What the blazes… oh, it's you, Fred. Bring her in. She didn't cause too much trouble, did she?'

'No, Mr Spinks, Sir. I was coming to deliver a message when she was leaving The Noose, so I thought I'd give her a hand home cos me mam always says you should help those in need.'

'Quite right, Fred, quite right.' Ned took the other half of Jenni from a relieved Fred and half swung her onto the sofa. There were plenty of cushions to break her fall.

'Have you got the message?'

'No, Mr Spinks, Sir.'

'Well, did you deliver the message?'

'Yes, Mr Spinks, Sir.'

'Huh. So it was just for Jenni, then?'

'Yes, Mr Spinks, Sir.'

'And it came from the Emperor?'

'Yes, Mr Spinks, Sir.' Fred paled. 'I weren't meant to tell you anything.'

Smelling a rat, Ned went in.

'What makes you say that, lad?' His tone was kindly, yet his eyes were sharp as they weighed the young man in front of them.

'It was just a private message, you see, and the Emperor, she says I don't need to use the honorific anymore because I'm such a trusted member of the household, well she said that it needed to be handed to Jenni and not to anyone else and that was all of it really so I suppose it doesn't matter that you know a message was sent just that you don't read the message. After all, you're not Howard.' Fred finished with a smile while Ned tried to put the pieces together. He was getting used to talking with the young palace guard.

'Fourteen sent a private message to Jenni?' he mused to himself, wondering what it could be about. 'Alright then, thank you Fred. You've done a sterling civic duty. I'll be sure to fill in a satisfaction survey next time I see one.'

Fred puffed out his chest proudly and ripped off a sharp salute before marching out the door, whistling a cheerful tune.

Ned regarded the drunkenness before him and wondered whether he could risk rummaging through Jenni's pockets for the message. Deciding that he didn't want the two women in his life talking about him behind his back, he went for it. A gentle pat down the body revealed one of Jenni's pockets was buttoned up, which was unusual. She preferred easy access. Aha, there it was. Sealed. *Dammit*. Ned weighed up the odds of Jenni remembering that Fred had given her a message and whether she'd think she'd read it or not. He plumped for her having no memory.

Breaking the seal, Ned took a seat in his easy chair and read the note. He turned it over. Turned it back and read it again, then folded it back up and replaced it in Jenni's pocket. Which he also rebuttoned.

Pulling out his pipe, he filled it with fresh tobacco, lit, and puffed a while thinking, doing a great job at ignoring the Nightmare which was hanging about ready for Ned to fall asleep. He stayed awake and didn't move until dawn broke. Then he stood to make some tea.

Whilst clattering in the kitchen, he heard a loud groan from the sofa and called out,

'Do you want tea?'

'Do dwarves drink too much?' came the sarcastic yet pained reply.

Ned half-smiled to himself and swirled three spoons

of sugar into a strong black cup of tea.

'How was your evening?' he asked, passing Jenni her cup.

'Yeah, it were awright. Busy. Seemed like there were everyone there. Trolls, fae, dwarfs, gnomes, even a few druids but they didn't last long cos of the inny fingies.'

Ned translated in his head. Innuendos.

'Sounds like I missed a good night.'

'People was still talking 'bout you and yor arrow. Said it were and I quote 'a bloody good shot'.'

'Really?' Ned was pleased and smothered a smile by drinking his own hot tea. Jenni seemed to have recovered from her outburst yesterday.

'You did good, Boss.' Jenni slurped her tea loudly, dribbling it down her front. She wiped at the wet patch and saw that her pocket was buttoned. Patting her pocket, she looked as if she was trying to summon a memory of how she got home.

'Ow did I get 'ere? Where's the plume?'

'Fred helped you home.' Ned paused. 'He said he had a message. For you.' He waited to see how Jenni would react.

She opened her pocket and pulled out the note.

'Bloody 'ell, it's from the Emperor. I weren't supposed to go see 'er, was I?'

Ned shrugged as she opened the message.

'Huh.'

'What?'

'Bin opened.' Jenni cast a sceptical look at Ned, who shifted on his chair slightly. 'You fink 'e opened it?'

Ned shook his head quickly.

'Not Fred, he's no Howard.'

'Who's 'Oward?'

'It doesn't matter. What does the note say?'

Jenni opened the note and read it, then crumpled it up and threw it in the grate, sending a few sparks after it to set it alight.

'Your magic seems to be finally working,' observed Ned, disappointed that she hadn't let him read the note.

'Yeah, I'm learning the ebb and flow of fings. S'about balance and stuff. Sorry about yer fern.'

The half-dead plant on the window-sill was now all the way dead. Ned wasn't bothered. It had been a gift from someone or other for a solved case. He wasn't the green-fingered type anyway.

'Wot you fink, then?' asked Jenni.

Ned was caught out taking a mouthful of tea. He coughed and spluttered.

'About what?'

'Come off it, Boss. I ain't stoopid. I knows you read it'

The backs of Ned's ear coloured slightly as he considered his answer. His insides squirmed with anger, misery, and unrequited love.

'I think… I think we should do everything we can to help her. She can't marry him. He's a monster.'

'Agreed.' Jenni yawned so widely her jaw cracked. Smacking her lips, she got to her feet. 'I fink we need breakfast and then a plan. Seems like yor pal Griff dropped the ball on this, big time.'

'Looks like it,' agreed Ned sadly. It wasn't like Griff at all. There should be meticulous records somewhere. 'We haven't got long.'

'When's the big day?'

'According to your message, the coronation is in three days' time. We'd better get a move on. After another cuppa.'

'Do we have time for that, Boss?'

'I didn't sleep last night. Gotta stay awake somehow and be vigilant, especially if Theo's in town and this thing is clattering around my head.' Ned pointed to the Nightmare Jenni couldn't see and felt bleak. There was no doubt in his mind that his brother would be up to no good and now it looked like Roshaven would either lose all their trade, livelihood and income, or Fourteen would have to marry his murderous, deranged brother. Neither option was great, but he'd die first rather than let her marry Theo. Not his Fourteen. Echoes of their burgeoning romance bubbled up through his despair and he set his jaw. 'Come on, let's get cracking. We've got this.'

Chapter 22

Fourteen dressed with care. She had requested the most ornate imperial robes to be laid out for her. These were the traditional vestments, so she lost all femininity when she wore them, but for once she did not mind not looking like a woman. She did not want to do anything to encourage Theo in any way. The Highs had suggested she accept his proposal formally, so they had sent a summons for that morning. Her acceptance was merely a ploy to give her more time to find an alternative solution.

The androgynous golden mask of the emperor was placed over her face by her maid and carefully held in place with hair grips and ties. It was uncomfortable, but Fourteen needed every tool at her disposal, especially as she didn't think she would be able to hide her reluctance for what lay ahead.

With imperial sceptre in hand, Fourteen walked slowly to the second-best meeting room. She had refused to make this deal in the grand hall but had agreed to show a little respect after the pleading of both Highs. She couldn't walk any faster. Both robes and sceptre were heavy, and she was beginning to think she'd made a mistake. But finally the meeting room doors appeared.

She smiled warmly as she saw Fred, forgetting that he couldn't see her face at all. Fred stood ram-rod straight and executed a perfect salute before bowing low as he opened one door.

'Mick!' he hissed at his counterpart, who hadn't been quite so sharp, deferential or quick. The second door opened and a loud gong sounded as Fourteen glided into the room.

This time Theo stood waiting, dressed in his own finery. Soft red leather calf boots held muscular legs in tight fitting dark brown trousers. A red silk shirt was cinched with a simple leather belt and huge gold buckle with an ornate scabbard hanging down on one side. It was empty–no weapons in the emperor's presence. His shirt was open several buttons, revealing a black hairy chest and some kind of golden pendant. Jewelled rings flashed on his fingers and he had a black cape. An actual cape! A wide-brimmed hat complete with a large red feather sat on a nearby table.

Fourteen was grateful for the mask as she stifled laughter at this peacock display in front of her. She glided to her throne, and using the sceptre to steady herself, sat down. Imperial robes didn't bend easily.

The gong sounded again, and she waited. One of the Highs stationed behind Theo leaned over and whispered in his ear. He nodded and strode forwards. With a flourish, he swept the cape and scabbard backwards as he bent one knee to the floor.

'My Emperor. I, Theodore Michel de Silverthorpe, Lord of Fidelia, come before you to offer my hand in marriage. What say you?'

Fourteen blanched. *What say you?* It wasn't exactly the romantic proposal she dreamed of.

The gong sounded again and the High Left, who stood on her right holding an impressive six-foot, wooden talking stick, intoned in a solemn voice.

'The Emperor of Roshaven accepts your proposal.'

Theo's face broke into a broad grin.

'With caveats.' The High finished speaking.

Theo's grin faltered slightly, and he wobbled on the

one knee.

'Caveats?'

'The Emperor, may they live for ever and ever, wishes to be crowned before being wedded.' The High Left thumped the talking stick he was holding for added effect. It made Theo jump. 'The Emperor, may they live for ever and ever, requests direct communication with all trading parties and to have established trade routes in place before being wedded.' The stick thumped again, and Theo had definitely turned a somewhat chalky colour. 'The Emperor, may they live for ever and ever, wishes to have their Lower Circle draw up every new trade agreement in triplicate and have them agreed, signed and witnessed before being wedded.' The stick thumped for a final time.

A tense silence filled the meeting room. This was the moment Fourteen had been dreading - whether Theo would agree. And whether he would throw in any caveats himself, although he really didn't have grounds, seeing as she was sure his 'ancient scroll' was a work of fiction. She was also touched by what the High Left had said. He had used ambiguous gender phrases. It wasn't as good as him saying Empress and may *she* live forever and ever, but for the first time in her reign, he hadn't referred to her as 'he'. He'd also avoided stating a wedding with named parties. Fourteen wanted as much wiggle room as possible.

The High Right coughed quietly, trying to prompt Theo to respond.

He seemed surprised at her requests. Did he see the hidden agenda behind her demands, or did he just believe she was desperate to save her trading routes? From what Ned had told her of Theo, greed and the desire for power fuelled his brother, and right now he was looking hungrily at Fourteen.

No, not at me, she realised. He was entirely focused on her imperial mask.

'My love, I agree, of course. You will announce the betrothal at your coronation, I'm sure.' Theo rose to his feet. 'I will gather the necessary paperwork to begin organising the new trade agreements. Shall we reconvene tomorrow? I trust that is acceptable for you?' All attempts at using the emperor's honorific had gone. Theo's mind was clearly full of the wealth he would amass and the power he assumed he would be gaining.

The gong sounded again and the High Right whispered to Theo again. He made an elaborate bow, snatched his hat from the table and strode out of the meeting room.

Fourteen sagged back into her chair and motioned for one of her ladies-in-waiting to hurry over. She wanted to get the mask off. Finally free, Fourteen took a few deep breaths.

'Thank you,' she said warmly to the High Left, who blustered about only doing his duty.

'If I may, Your Eminence, I have been thinking about Fat Norris and I wonder… should we perhaps install him here at the palace for the duration of these meetings? I know you said you wanted to delay proceedings as much as possible, but it won't take long for the Lord of Fidelia to realise we have duped him if we leave him to his own devices.'

Fourteen had a sinking feeling that the High was right. At the moment, Theo was semi-blinded by his greed, but that wouldn't last, and she needed to make sure she'd done everything in her power to secure the trading routes before breaking off the engagement. Besides, she would have to hope that Jenni could come through with something.

'A good idea. See to it.' Fourteen stood, using the sceptre to help unfold her from her seated position. 'I'm going to change. If the Thief-Catchers request an audience, make sure they are brought to me as soon as possible.'

'Yes, Your Eminence. And… don't forget about choosing a name. For the sake of the empire,' pleaded the High Right.

Fourteen's semi-good mood evaporated. All this fuss about a name. It wasn't like they meant anything, it was just a series of letters in an order that was pleasing to somebody else. If she wasn't balancing the future of her city, its trade lifeblood and her hand in marriage, she'd be tempted to push back, but there were more important things happening than deciding on what her name was going to be.

Chapter 23

The sun was glaring through the window. This was a problem because Ned was so tired the light was hurting his eyes. It also seemed to be hurting his entire face and making his ears tingle. And he couldn't shut the blind because Sparks hadn't turned up for work yet. He wasn't late, but he wasn't early either and Ned could feel his anger swirling and building. His annoying Nightmare shadow wasn't helping his mood either.

Joe and Willow had their heads together in the corner, whispering about something or other. Jenni was making tea. *Probably tastes like feet,* thought Ned unkindly as Sparks buzzed into work.

'Finally,' barked Ned, causing everyone to jump as he leapt up and slammed the window shut, closing the blind behind it. He sank back into his chair and glowered at the other thief-catchers.

'Ere drink this,' Jenni thrust a cup of hot tea in front of him. 'It's a Kendra special. You want 'oney?'

Ned nodded. Kendra's teas could be loamy, but they worked.

'Did night-watch leave anything for us?' he asked Willow. He was keen to get on with the thorny problem of figuring out what Theo was up to, but he didn't want to neglect their thief-catcher duties.

She shook her tendrils.

'Anything new in the box, Joe?'

The box had been a suggestion from Fourteen, back when they were talking like friends who might end up as lovers. She'd thought it would be a great way for people to anonymously report crime in case they were frightened to speak to a thief-catcher. It had worked, sort of. They got a lot more neighbour complaints and a lot of accusatory notes, but with no names. Still, it helped keep a temperature on the city and know what people were up in arms about on that particular day.

'We've got something from Old Mrs Goggins, she says…'

Ned sat up in his chair and interrupted.

'Old Mrs Goggins? Are you sure?'

Joe double-checked the note and nodded. 'Or it might be Goffins, the writing is very spidery.'

'Old Ma Goffins is a spider,' offered Jenni helpfully.

Ned sank down, frowning. Old Mrs Goggins had been one of Griff's many aliases. But he was dead, so why would he be sending a message? Ned tuned back into what Joe was saying.

'… and then someone deliberately broke the northwestern connecting thread… uh, it goes on to say some swearwords.' Joe looked up. 'You don't want me to read those, do you?'

'No. You two go check it out. If it's a case of broken webbing, offer your help to fix it,' ordered Ned.

'But I can't fix spider web,' replied Joe in alarm.

'Yeah, but if you offer, Ma Goffins will be well pleased and say nice fings about us, right?' explained Jenni.

Understanding bloomed on Joe's face. He helped Willow to her feet and the two of them left the office, heads bent together, whispering again.

'What the bloody hell are they whispering about?' muttered Ned grumpily.

Sparks flashed half a dozen times in Jenni's direction.

'Yeah, e's inna foul mood. Don't worry about it, mate.'

Ned scowled at them both and was about to make a nasty retort when a polite yet firm knocking on the office door stopped him. He focused a spell from his power well, just in case. People seldom knocked on the thief-catchers door.

'Come in.'

It was Mr Simms, the undead lawyer from Barnaby & Simms. Ned relaxed the spell and without thinking took a sip of his tea. It was vile even with the honey and he pulled a face.

'Good morning. I see you are as pleased to see me as I am to be here.' Mr Simms looked around in distaste at the rough-and-ready ambience in the thief-catcher's office. There was no point in having anything of value in there. The rooms were above The Noose, a pub notorious for dodgy dealings, situated on the edge of the Black Narrows, the entrance to Roshaven's criminal underbelly. The perfect place for law enforcement.

'No, I… er… it was the tea, very bitter.'

Mr Simms sniffed and declined Ned's gesture to sit. Instead, he unclipped his briefcase and pulled out a cup. It was a reddish-brown colour and seemed to be made out of clay, yet someone had spent a lot of time and love on smoothing the inside and outside. An intricately twisted handle blended into the sides of the cup. A fine piece of craftsmanship.

'This is the first item from Griffin Bartholomew the Third, Duke of Kinglass's will, the Cup of Good Luck.'

'Ow did you get it?' asked Jenni.

'We have several magically sealed boxes in our safe which appeared upon the death of Griffin Bartholomew the Third, Duke of Kinglass. As soon as they activate and open, Barnaby & Simms are bound by contract to bring the item to you, Mr Spinks, in order for the completion of Griffin Bartholomew the Third, Duke of Kinglass's wishes.'

'Just Griff,' muttered Ned. He held his hand out for the cup and Mr Simms placed it carefully down on his palm. It was warm and seemed to hum. 'You hear that?' Ned asked, but Mr Simms and Jenni shook their heads. Only Sparks was affected. He was pulsing brightly and zipping in tight little circles.

'You have two hours to get this cup to its rightful owner, as per the will's instructions.' Mr Simms sounded like he was smiling, but his face was impassive.

'And who would that owner be?' Ned asked.

'Why, our Emperor, may they live for ever and ever.'

'They?' Ned frowned. He'd never heard the honorific using they.

Mr Simms shut his briefcase with a clack. 'Don't you know? At the coronation we shall invest our first Empress. How times change. Good day.'

Ned couldn't help but smile. It sounded like Fourteen was firmly asserting herself. Good for her. He stared at the cup, wondering exactly how it was lucky.

'I'll take it if you like, gotta go talk to 'er anyway 'bout that ovver stuff.'

'I dunno, Jenni. I imagine the magical rules are strict. But we can go to the palace together and see if Fourteen has any further information on what Theo's up to. Feels as if we're there every five minutes as it is. We should have our own rooms.'

'We can 'ope,' murmured Jenni too low for Ned to hear her.

'Sparks, stay here and keep an eye on things.'

The firefly buzzed angrily. He wanted to remain with the cup.

'Fine. You can come with us as far as the palace, and then it's back to HQ for you. You still haven't written up your report on Mr Edderly's missing shoe.'

Sparks flashed sulkily. It took him ten times longer than anyone else to write up reports because he had to jump on each typewriter key individually and it was exhausting.

'C'mon, let's go.'

'You just gonna carry it like that, Boss?' Jenni asked, prompting Ned to consider his clumsiness record.

He cast around for something to put the cup in, but nothing seemed quite right. Whilst patting the pockets of his overcoat to see if they were hiding a bag, Ned realised it would fit in there and he could cradle it with one hand at the same time. He didn't want to stop touching the cup for some reason.

He smiled triumphantly at Jenni.

'It is a good luck cup, what's the worst that can happen?'

Jenni snorted.

'Now that you've said that, bloody everyfink I reckon,' she replied.

They left the office and traipsed down the stairs, through the taproom and out of The Noose.

'Why do you fink Griff wanted youse to give this to the Emperor? Ain't he like a nuncle or summink?'

'I think he was friendly with the old Emperor. I know he didn't get on with Fat Norris, that's for sure. Said he was lazy.'

Sparks flashed a complicated pattern. Jenni translated.

''E wants to know if 'e's that lazy why is 'e the

Lower Circle?'

'He's a very good delegator. If you want a job done, Fat Norris will get it done. He just won't do anything himself. It's masterful. You can learn a lot about people management watching Norris in action. It used to be a required training unit for membership to the thief-catchers,' replied Ned.

'Oh yeah, I remember you telling me about that. You wos one of the last ones to do it, weren't yer?'

Ned smiled fondly at his memories of being a trainee. He soon lost his smile as they passed by *Headshot*. Several people had taken affront to the fact that the café was closed. There were broken eggs and rotten tomatoes on the windows, and someone had scrawled *YOU SUCK!* on the door.

Ned lengthened his stride. Despite it being the morning, the streets were unusually quiet.

'Isn't it market day today?' Ned felt certain it was market day every day, except for the day he went shopping for something. Then he couldn't find anything.

'Yeah, but wiv less coming in there ain't much to buy and I reckon a few traders have already moved on. No point in setting up shop 'ere if there ain't nuffink to put in it.'

The group's mood was sombre as they arrived at the palace. The Commoners entrance was open for petitioners to enter, so Ned sent Sparks back to the office and went in that way. He didn't want to have to finagle past guards today.

One of the Highs, who was overseeing the petitions, looked up and spotted them. He hurried over from where he'd been working and addressed Jenni.

'The Emperor, may they live for ever and ever, will see you immediately.'

Ned followed on behind until they got to a series of corridors he didn't recognise. The High had stopped and was looking Ned up and down.

'She said nothing about you. Wait here,' he ordered before ushering Jenni further up the hallway and slipping her into a side room.

Chapter 24

Ned cast his eyes up and down, looking for a chair or suitable alcove where he could sit. There was one close to the place Jenni had vanished. Without intending to eavesdrop, Ned sat down and found that through some fluke of architecture and wotnot, he could hear every word. Jenni must be in Fourteen's study.

'Jenni, anything?' Fourteen wasted no time on niceties.

'Nuffink yet. Yor note wos a bit… vague?'

Ned heard Fourteen huff and imagined her crossing her arms.

'I don't see how. There's an ancient scroll claiming that Fidelia has the right of conquest over Roshaven if the Emperor is unmarried, unnamed and uncrowned by their twenty-fifth birthday. I need a loophole.'

'Ave you got the scroll?'

'Not the original, Theo kept that. I do have a copy, if that's any good?'

Ned felt a twinge of disappointment. If Fourteen had the original scroll, they might have been able to use a spell of divination on it to find the source. A copy only gave them the wording.

'We'll 'ave the copy. I got someone whose good wiv linguistics 'n stuff. See wot they get out of it.'

Ned wondered who Jenni was talking about, then realised with a chuckle that she meant Jimmy Fingers, the best forger in Roshaven.

'What was that?' asked Fourteen, and Ned inwardly cursed for having laughed out loud.

'Dunno. Let's look at the un's. You ain't married yet, right?'

'No, but… I had to accept Theo's proposal in order to gain us some time.'

Ned's insides turned to ice.

'Ow do you mean?' asked Jenni. 'You didn't sign nuffink, did you?'

'No. We came to an accord. I said I will marry him once they have crowned me and all the trade routes have been re-established with face to face meetings and new contracts.'

'Smart. I like it. 'Ow you gonna get Fat Norris to do that?'

'We have invited him to stay here for the duration of the negotiations. I guessed Theo would have all the trade agreement information with him. We've gained a little time. Not much, but a little.'

'And 'e agreed to it all, yeah?'

Ned couldn't hear anything, so he assumed Fourteen was nodding.

'Sure you don't wanna 'ave a quickie marriage on the side wiv someone else?'

'Jenni!'

Ned could feel his ears burning and his heart thumped in his chest. He held his breath and strained his hearing in order to catch every word.

'If Ned were to ask… I mean… it's not unknown for emperors to marry commoners. Not that I think Ned is common but you know, the look of things.'

''E might be a Lord or Earl or summink too, right?'

Ned winced. He tried very hard to keep the details of his family name buried. Like their father before him, Theo had been Chief of T.A.R.T.S before his mysterious elevation to Lord of Fidelia. Ned felt sure that title resulted from his brother's own machinations rather than anything else.

'Well, I assumed there might be something when we first met Theo in Fidelia, but I wasn't sure and I haven't checked into the lineages.'

Even Ned could tell Fourteen was lying and he wasn't looking at her.

'Mhm. Well, mebbe youse two can sort that out after this, eh? Wot about the unnamed? Anyfink there?'

'No, not yet. I will have to find one soon.'

'Owcome you don't 'ave one yet?'

'My father named us numerically so as not to show favouritism and in case of death. I'll reveal my name at the coronation.'

'Yeah, 'ow does that all work? You've been Emperor for like, wot, six months already?'

Ned leaned in. He did not know how it worked either.

'The coronation is a ceremonial acknowledgment. They bring the imperial crown out of storage. Apparently it's very heavy - I've not even seen it yet. I am officially presented to the people of Roshaven, and I swear an oath to uphold the law and obey the gods…'

'Which ones?' interrupted Jenni.

'All of them, it's a very lengthy process. After that, they crown me and present me to the city.'

'And that's when we 'ave the party.'

'Sort of. We actually have a formal party two days before and a celebratory dinner the day before,' said Fourteen with a light laugh.

'Fair do's. Looks like you've got it all sorted—wot do you need me for?'

'I need you to discredit this scroll of Theo's. To shred any authenticity it seems to have and make sure

there are no additional loopholes that Theo hasn't
shared. He accepted my terms way too easily, and it
makes me nervous. The man is greedy for wealth and
power, but he's not stupid.'

Ned nodded in agreement. Unfortunately, his brother
was both cruel and clever.

'I fink I've gotcha. These fings wot you're sorting
could go wrong. The trade agreements might 'appen
super quick and then bish, bash, bosh and yor in a
wedding dress wiv no way out. And we don't want that.'

'No, we absolutely do not.' There was a rustling
sound. 'Here is the copy of the so-called ancient scroll.
Do you think you'll be able to figure out where it came
from? I've asked the palace scholars to use their
knowledge and check historical records, but something
tells me this scroll has more of a criminal origin.'

'Corse. We'll get to the bottom of it.'

There was a long pause.

'We?'

Ned imagined Jenni muttering curses under her
breath. Knowing her, she'd own it.

'E read the note. When Fred found me, I was seven
sheets to the wind and in no fit state to do owt. Fred
didn't do nuffink wrong though, so don't 'ave a go. 'E
saw me 'ome. Fine lad is Fred, fine lad. I fink Ned read
it while I was out of it.' Jenni's tone got stern. 'You
should'da gone to 'im in the first place. Ain't nuffink 'e
wouldn't do for you, you know?'

Ned couldn't hear anything apart from the faintest
swishing noise. He guessed Fourteen was pacing.

'I thought… I thought he might take it badly. That I
accepted his brother's hand in marriage when we were…
well, when we were just beginning, I guess. I know the
two of them didn't get on before and then…' Fourteen

sighed and Ned felt her sorrow.

'And then my brother killed Griff,' he whispered.

'E's 'ere, you know. Got a fing for you.'

'Jenni!'

The sprite cackled.

'Naw, I mean e's got an actual fing for you. From Griff.'

'Where is he?' asked Fourteen.

'Aanging about outside, probably. One of the 'igh's tol' 'im to stay put.'

Ned didn't hang about to hear anymore. He darted out of the alcove and tried to look nonchalant, leaning on the wall, opposite to the door of Fourteen's study, but in his haste, he knocked over a large vase that stood in the hallway. It didn't break but rolled to the doorway and stopped at Fourteen's feet.

'I uh…' Ned's ears burned.

'You better come in,' replied Fourteen in an amused voice.

Ned debated stepping over the vase, but common sense took over and he picked it up, manoeuvring it back into place. Slightly out of breath, he crossed the threshold into Fourteen's study and was immediately charmed.

There were two round chairs by a fireplace. Books lined one wall whilst French windows looked out into the rose gardens. There was an ornately carved desk and chair with a less fancy footstool that Jenni sat cross-legged upon.

'I'll ring for more tea, if you like?' offered Fourteen, the faintest blush across her cheeks.

'Yes, tea would be nice. Thank you.'

There was a brief silence as he watched her pull the call rope and they waited for a servant to respond. After placing her request, Fourteen drifted over to one of the round chairs, leaving Ned standing uncomfortably in the middle of the room.

'Youse two,' sighed Jenni. 'Show 'er wot you've got, Boss.'

'Oh right, yes, of course.' Ned reached into his overcoat pocket and pulled out the red clay cup. He presented it to Fourteen. 'This is the Cup of Good Luck. It's from Griff.'

Fourteen politely took the cup and gasped.

'It's warm! And it's humming, can you hear that?'

Ned nodded enthusiastically and began humming a few bars. Fourteen joined in while Jenni looked at the pair of them like they'd gone mad.

'And it brings good luck, you say?' Fourteen asked.

'Apparently. You know Griff, it could be a highly magical object or it could just be one of his clever tricks,' replied Ned. 'Here, Jenni, you hold it. See what you think.'

Jenni hopped off the stool and eagerly took the cup in her hands. She looked up at the other two and shook her head.

'Nuffink. S'not humming or anyfink. Dunno wot you mean about warm.' She peered inside the cup. 'Beats me wot makes it so special.'

She tossed it in Ned's direction. Fourteen gasped.

'Jenni!' Ned yelled as he fumbled to catch the flying cup and managed to snatch it from the air.

'Well, I think it's wonderful.' Fourteen was interrupted from saying anything further as a maid entered with a tea trolley.

'Shall we toast Griff, do you think?' asked Fourteen. 'I'll be mother.'

'Whose mother?' asked Jenni.

Fourteen grinned and poured a little milk into the cup of good luck. She swirled the teapot and elegantly poured the tea.

'Sugar?' she asked Ned, looking up at him through her eyelashes. His heart did a double-take and he shook his head mutely.

Picking up a delicate silver spoon, she stirred the tea and passed it to him, her hands on the cup. Ned reached out to collect it from her, his hands covering hers, and they caught their breath.

Jenni huffed to herself.

'Make me own bloody tea then.'

She clattered on the tea tray and threw seven sugar cubes in for good measure before going back to the footstool and taking her perch. Fourteen and Ned were still locked together in their odd cup embrace, and Jenni had to clear her throat several times before Ned dragged his gaze away.

'Mhm? Everything alright, Jenni?'

'Yeah, I reckon yor tea's gone cold by now.'

Ned looked back to his hands as Fourteen took hers away. The cup was steaming, and he brought it to his lips for a sip. 'It's perfect.' He smiled at Fourteen over the rim.

'I can give youse the room if you want?' offered Jenni.

That broke Fourteen's reverie.

'No, thank you, Jenni. I am betrothed, after all. We don't want to add any more fuel to that fire.' She tore herself away from Ned and the cup and stood up. 'Try and find out what you can about the scroll, please.'

'I'll find out, don't you worry. C'mon, Boss.'

'Mhm. Yes. I'll see you…' Ned faltered and put down the cup. He did not know when he would see

Fourteen again.

She smiled sadly at him and watched the two of them leave. Her fingers trailed back to the tea tray and the red cup. It was still warm as she picked it up, sipping the tea for herself. Ned was right. It was perfect.

Chapter 25

'Did you 'ear all that?' asked Jenni as she and Ned walked over to The Slides where Jimmy Fingers could usually be found.

'Yep.' Ned decided not to say anything else.

'If Jimmy can't do anyfink about the copy, e'll know where yor bruvver is staying and then...'

Ned still didn't speak. He knew what Jenni meant; she wanted to steal the original ancient scroll from his brother. They walked on in silence, greeting the odd person here and there until Ned's stomach rumbled. He was both tired and hungry.

'Let's grab a bite before we tackle Jimmy, yeah?' he suggested. Jenni didn't take any convincing.

The Slides were the foodie part of Roshaven. A long street that had lots of different vendors dotted along a path from the top of the hill to the bottom. The more rough-and-ready establishments were found at the lower end. They had the most grease. The youngest students from the Guild Colleges would periodically challenge each other to eat something from every place on The Slides. The closest anyone had even got was three years ago when a young lad from four towns over had given it his best shot. He'd made it about half-way down and was doing great until he got to Le Chez and was offered pig knuckle stew. It's not a meal for the faint-hearted. The actual pig knuckle wasn't the problem however the stew came in a hollowed-out pig skull complete with original ears and snout carefully cured and sewn around the skull. Ned understood it was a popular tourist attraction. People came from miles around to see it.

Jenni headed towards Kronks Shack and put in an order for two lots of hot meat rolls, fried potatoes and frozen milk. Ned shook his head at her love of this quick food. Usually, she steered away from traditional human fare. Except for pizza. And cake. Fae food involved a lot more plant-based ingredients. Ned didn't even want to guess what meat went in the rolls at Kronks. Instead, he concentrated on the satisfying greasy taste and watching in amusement as Jenni dipped her fried potatoes in her rapidly defrosting milk.

'Any idea where Jimmy will be?' Ned asked once Jenni had finished eating.

'Nope.'

'Where do you want to start then?'

'Ere's good. We could 'ave a narna split and I reckon he'd be 'ere afore we done.'

Ned declined his share of the dessert, but sure enough, Jenni was right. Jimmy Fingers sauntered into Kronk's, greeting everyone like long-lost friends, and dragged a chair over to their table. Spinning the seat round, he sat on it backward and leaned on the backrest.

'You rang?'

Ned never knew how Jimmy Fingers found out people were looking for him, but like a bad penny, he just seemed to turn up.

'Ave a butchers at this, Jimmy.' And Jenni took out the copy of the ancient scroll from her pocket.

Fingers spread it out over the table and his eyebrows rose as he read.

'This legit?' he asked.

'That's what we want to find out,' replied Ned. 'I presume we can trust you not to divulge the contents?'

'E means don't tell no-one wot you just read

overwise I'll break your kneecaps.' Jenni delivered the threat whilst scraping every bit of banana split from her bowl. Strangely, it didn't detract from the menace behind her statement.

'Am I getting paid?' asked Fingers.

Ned looked at Jenni. She put her spoon down.

'Ow much?'

Fingers sucked his teeth and drummed the table.

'Tell you what, I get this scroll for you and you look the other way next time I'm fingered for a job.'

'I can do that. Provided it doesn't risk the safety of the Emperor or the city. No murders.' Ned stuck out his hand for Fingers to shake.

'Mate, I don't kill people. What do you think I am?'

'A master con-artist, forger and someone with more lives than ten cats.' Ned held Fingers hand in a firm grip and gave him the look. It was his *I'm trusting you, don't let me down* look and usually it had the desired effect.

'So where's the original of this then?' Fingers clicked for the server's attention and ordered a pancake stack.

'The Lord of Fidelia has it.'

'Exotic location work costs double.'

Jenni snorted. 'Lucky for you, e's 'ere in the city so you ain't got to go nowhere. I dunno where tho.'

'Try Madam Silk's top establishment,' suggested Ned. 'He'll either be staying there or there will be collateral damage who can tell you where he is staying.'

'Sounds like a mean piece of work,' commented Fingers, winking his thanks at the server for the food.

'Yep.' Ned clenched his fists.

'How do you know him then? Tried to arrest him before?'

Ned pushed his seat back and left enough coin on the

table to pay for the food. Jenni replied.

'It's 'is bruvver so don't cock up, cos if Theo catches you, it's night-night for you. The Boss can't save you, and Theo don't mess about. He killed Griff.'

Ned watched as Jimmy's face paled, no doubt the pancakes now sitting like lead in his stomach. Griff had been a patron to many in Roshaven.

'If I do this for you then I get the chance to upset the plans of the person who is ruining my livelihood.' Fingers picked up a second pot of syrup. 'Silver lining.'

The thief-catchers left him enjoying his pancakes with renewed vigour.

Chapter 26

Fourteen sat in the library with her head in her hands. She was running out of time to choose a name before her coronation. A name that would help stop her marrying Theo.

A gust played with wind chimes outside the window, and Fourteen allowed herself to be distracted. She watched the leaves dance in the breeze and wished she were with them. A great whoosh made her turn in alarm. What had been a small fire in the grate was now a blaze. A book or something must have fallen in, she thought as she half stood, not sure what to do for the best.

A few sparks shot out of the fireplace and singed the carpet with a satisfying sizzle. Fourteen eyed the distance to the door and was calculating whether she'd be able to make it when the flames whooshed again, doubling.

How is the fire doing that? She wondered as she backed up against the window. The wind rattled the casement and Fourteen decided to try to get out the window. The library was on the ground floor, after all. Fingers fumbling with the latch, she finally undid it, and the wind blew merrily in, whipping the fire into a greater frenzy. With the fireplace to the left of her, Fourteen felt the heat licking at her body as she scrambled out. She was in a panic and hurrying, so her exit from the window wasn't elegant. She landed with a thump in the flower bed.

Now she was outside, the wind began buffeting her hard. It was as if the wind was trying to push her in a certain direction. She staggered to her feet and tried going left, around the palace wall to a side door, but despite her best efforts she couldn't take a single step forward in the gale force winds.

Fourteen stopped trying to move, and the wind dropped. She looked at the treetops in the garden, which were suspiciously still. She began walking again only to be completely barred in her tracks by the wind once again. She glanced in the open library window and saw that the fire had gone out.

Then she realised. It was the elementals. She hadn't played with them since she was a lonely child left to her own devices in the garden. None of her siblings had ever admitted to seeing them, and none of them were inclined to play with the baby of the family. More fool them, Fourteen ended up being the surviving heir to the empire.

'Air... are you trying to tell me something?' Fourteen asked.

The wind made a nearby flower bed of tulips nod. Fourteen smiled to herself and turned around. As she did so, a tiny flame jumped out the library window and danced in front of her face.

'Fire, nice to see you again.'

The flame shined bright then danced forwards, waving at her to follow. Fourteen let the wind push her gently onwards into the gardens.

'Where are we going? And where are the others?'

In response to her question, a nearby disused fountain sprang into life, tinkling water splashing and glittering in the sunshine. A large teardrop joined the flame in front of her and continued to beckon Fourteen forwards. The ground shuddered, and suddenly Fourteen was moving faster than she expected. She almost fell, but Air caught her and helped her ride the Earth wave towards the centre of the famed rose gardens of the emperor.

Inside the gardens, narrow pebbled walkways wound complicated paths through elaborately planted rose beds. There were trailing vines decorating romantic trestle arches, bees buzzing, butterflies fluttering, and only a slight sour tang to the air from the liberal use of enchanted manure. It helped things grow faster but smelt stronger for longer than the usual stuff. Rose perfume made everything feel thick, as if you were trying to walk through a cloud. Tinkling water fell from beautiful marble fountains and statues were sprinkled throughout. The different flower colours swirled in geometric patterns. The teardrop and flame danced here and there over rose beds whilst the wind rustled leaves and the ground made the bushes dance.

'I don't understand… we removed the magics from the red roses. My father didn't enchant anything else, did he?'

The elementals stopped and the rose garden hung in complete silence for a moment.

'Okay, I'll take that as a no.'

There was a swirl of rose petals in one corner of the garden. Then the other corner and then again, another until all four corners had dancing rose petals of different colours, weaving in intricate patterns, moving closer and closer to Fourteen. She watched, entranced, as the soft petals spun and fluttered around her, gently touching her skin and bringing their heady fragrance to her. One by one the many petals fell, each one landing on Fourteen for a moment until she was standing in a pile of beautiful blooms.

Fourteen had tears in her eyes as she took in the

meaning of this gorgeous natural display.

'Rose? You want my name to be Rose?'

Air whistled, Earth rumbled, Water splooshed and Fire whooshed. Fourteen clapped her hands in delight.

'I love it, I love my new name. Thank you, elementals. I shall never forget this. I must tell the Highs immediately.' Fourteen brought her palms together in front of her heart and bowed four times to each corner of the rose garden in deference to the elements before gathering her skirts and rushing back into the palace.

*****

That went well.

Eventually.

Oh, don't be such a stick in the mud.

I'm Earth, I'm made of mud.

She has a name now, and it's beautiful.

Yes, our Rose.

And the words echoed on the wind as the elementals dispersed to do whatever it was elementals did when they weren't meddling in the world of man.

Chapter 27

Ned was about to lock up when he heard footsteps on the stairs. He groaned. He could not cope with another missing cat today. As it was, after he and Jenni had got back from seeing Jimmy Fingers, they'd found Sparks sitting proudly atop three separate reports of missing cats.

Not to cast aspersions, but each owner was a single woman in her late forties with a penchant for chintz. He'd decided to bring them all in together tomorrow so he could deliver the bad news. The missing cats were actually all the same cat who had been living the high life being looked after by three different women. The bad news was that the cat had ended up in a troll trap. It had probably been lured in by the smell of the poisoned rats the trolls left for the dwarves.

The entrance of Jimmy Fingers broke Ned's reflections. Fingers had the beginnings of a splendid black eye, tissue shoved up a bloody nose, one shoe and was soaking wet and muddy.

'Gods, Jimmy, what happened?'

Jimmy laughed weakly and sank into a chair.

'Your brother is a psycho, Spinks.'

'Yeah, tell me something I don't know,' Ned replied whilst rummaging in his drawer for the bottle of scumble he kept handy and a mostly clean glass. 'Here, drink this. You want me to get a Druid?'

Fingers shook his head and then winced.

'I'm going there next. Just came to give you this. Thanks.' He lifted the drink, tipped it towards Ned and downed the scumble in one mouthful. Wincing as the alcohol hit his throat and burned on the way down, he pulled out a tatty piece of paper.

'Is this it?' Ned was impressed. He hadn't expected Fingers to get back to them so quickly.

'Yeah, and I'll tell you this much. That ain't ancient. It's regular papyrus soaked in tea to look old, then dried and crunched up before being written in ink watered down with soot and more tea. Then passed over a candle a few times and left in a warm place to go a little brittle. Smart move using the papyrus. It's thicker than ordinary paper and is easy to treat for aging.'

Ned turned the scroll back and forth, and now that Jimmy had pointed these things out to him, he thought he could see the effects.

'How do I prove that this isn't legit?' Ned asked.

Fingers coughed and gasped in pain. It looked like he had a few cracked ribs as well.

'Couple of ways,' he said with a wince. 'You can scrape the ink off, it hasn't had time to soak in and they never covered the papyrus with any grease, resin or wax. They often preserve ancient scrolls in wax, it stops time from destroying them, mostly. If you set fire to it, it'll probably give you black ash, another sign of little aging. Old scrolls burn to give white ash. Plus, you can't snap this in half. It's not truly brittle with age.'

Ned was doubly impressed. Fingers knew his craft.

'Thanks, you've done a superb job. Now, tell me - how did you get a hold of this?' Ned waved his hand over Fingers.

'Getting in to his place wasn't a problem. Your brother is staying at the empty manor house up on Travis Point.'

'The expensive part of town. What made you check

there?' asked Ned.

'It's my job to know where all potential marks are in Roshaven. Man's got to earn a living.' Fingers grinned as Ned motioned for him to keep going.

'There weren't no-one there except young Sally working as cook and maid. We go a ways back and she was happy to ignore me having a nose around. I was digging through the study, looking for the scroll, when one of your brother's henchmen caught me off guard. He was a quiet mover despite his size. Managed to get a blow in before I shimmied lose.' Fingers pointed to his nose.

'How did you deal with him after he broke that?'

'I gave him the Jimmy Fingers Shake n' Bake.'

Ned nodded and smiled. He knew it well. Fingers would start talking at ten to the dozen, weaving side to side, placing his opponent into a sort of daze. It worked to a different degree on different people, but it always ended up putting them off their guard. The 'shake' was followed by a double uppercut to the kidneys or depending on how big the opponent, a straight finger, full hand jab to the throat. It was called a *bake* because they folded up like they were going in the oven.

'After that, I saw what I was looking for, grabbed it and scarpered. Unlucky for me, your brother had just returned. He set his dogs on me and I ended up having to jump out the window and into the creek. Hence the mud. Worked in my favour though - those mutts couldn't get my scent and follow me.'

As Fingers said that, they both heard dogs baying outside in the street. They sounded close. Fingers threw Ned a panicked look.

'Quick! Into the bathroom,' said Ned. 'There's a spare set of clothes on the back of the door and you can get out the window onto the roof. Chuck your old clothes down in the alley. Willow has a mesh of ivy up there that's easy to climb. Travel across the rooftops until you arrive at the Druid Grove. Tell High Priestess Kendra I sent you and she's to keep you safe.'

'What about you?' Fingers asked, already moving to the bathroom Ned had pointed to.

'I'll deal with Theo,' Ned replied grimly.

Chapter 28

Ned had little time to hide the scroll, so he put it on the desk and pulled a stack of reports over the top as the door banged open and a huge shape pushed through. Ned dismissed him. Despite the size, he was just a heavy to make Theo seem intimidating, and that would not work here.

Theo followed a few steps behind. He had an incredulous half-smile on his face.

'Edmund, darling. You actually live here?'

'No, Theo, this is my place of work. Can I help you with something?'

Theo smirked.

'Yes. I want to report a theft.' He said as if he couldn't believe he was uttering the words.

There was the faintest clatter from the direction of the bathroom, so Ned used that cue to push his chair back and go get a crime form from the stack by the Ficus plant.

'You need to fill this in. If you cannot write, I can complete it for you based on your verbal account,' he said.

Theo looked at the form and the pen in Ned's hand and gestured for the heavy to take the items. He left him filling in the details while he studied his brother.

'Life treating you well, Eddie? You look a little tired.'

'I'm not sleeping well, thanks to you. When are you going to get rid of this?' Ned jabbed a finger at the Nightmare whickering in the corner but Theo just feigned ignorance.

'Get rid of what, Eddie?'

Ned scowled. He needed Jenni with him to see if Theo had the contract with Barbas on him. Ned might be able to tackle Theo by himself, but he probably couldn't take the bodyguard as well. He'd have to get it next time their paths crossed, which they no doubt would. Right now he needed Fingers to get away.

'Since when did you become a Lord?' Ned asked, changing tack.

'Come, come. A little politeness goes a long way, Eddie.' Theo paced and stroked his chin. 'Why not tell you? It was, after all, your pal Griff who gave me the idea, with fingers in lots of pies he had so much revenue coming in. Chief of T.A.R.T.S was ambition enough for our father, but it really is true that money can buy you anything you want.'

'So you bought your title.'

'Appropriated is a better word. A favour here, a good deed there, and before you know it, I am entitled. In more ways than one.'

Ned's insides clenched. He forced himself to stay seated.

'How are Mum and Dad?' Ned asked, not caring either way but wanting to keep his brother talking and give Fingers plenty of time to escape.

'They are enjoying retirement and are planning a trip. Who knows, they may even come here.'

They needn't bother thought Ned.

'Where's your sidekick? She was… powerful.' Theo glanced around.

'Jenni has gone home for the day, which is what I was about to do.' Ned turned his attention to the muscle. 'Have you finished?' He took the report and pen - thief-catchers were very territorial about their pens - and had a quick look at the claim.

'Someone broke in and stole a priceless artefact? You should increase your security,' Ned commented.

'Oh believe me, it won't happen again.' Theo cocked his head to the side. 'Mind if we poke around? In case a good citizen has handed in my… priceless artefact.'

'Be my guest.' Ned hoped he'd given Fingers enough time to get away.

The muscle opened the cleaning cupboard, nosed around in the tiny kitchen and then checked the bathroom. He reappeared and gave Theo a slight shake of his head.

'You know, brother dear, consorting with criminals isn't best practice for the catcher chief.'

'I can arrest you, if you like. Sure we'll find something that sticks,' Ned retaliated.

Theo's eyes narrowed.

'I expect a full report on my case. It wouldn't do for the upstanding thief-catchers of Roshaven to be unable to solve my theft now, would it?'

Inwardly Ned grimaced, but he was careful not to show his feelings on the outside. Yes, it would be a blow to let a crime go unsolved, but these were extenuating circumstances. And he was working on direct orders of the Emperor. Besides he knew who'd done it.

'We'll keep you updated,' said Ned.

'Don't you want to know where I'm staying, little brother?'

'You're staying in the mansion up at Travis Point.'

'I see you keep well informed.' Theo pursed his lips. 'You know, Eddie, my dear, my offer still stands. If you wanted to join the family business? You could be our

Roshaven agent.'

'Thanks, but I decline.'

'Shame. It would be nice to have family here, but I have a couple of other candidates in mind. They'll be a permanent fixture soon.' Theo glanced at the mirror on the wall Willow had demanded they get and adjusted his hair. 'You heard about the engagement, of course.'

'Yes,' replied Ned tightly.

'When you brought her to Fidelia, I knew I just had to have her. She's so… imperial. And comes with a little city too. Tell me, Eddie, does she taste as good as she smells?' Theo leered.

Ned balled his hands into fists, doing his best not to react.

'Once I've taken her trading routes, I mean to plunder her thoroughly,' Theo went on.

Ned surged forwards, his anger rising, but the muscle stepped between him and his brother, an impenetrable wall.

'Aw, Eddie! Do you have feelings for her? I can tell you how she handles, you know, after the wedding night. If you like? After all, you do like to be well informed.'

'Get out,' Ned said softly.

'I look forward to hearing about my thief and having my property returned swiftly.' Theo took a few steps towards the door but turned back to face Ned again. 'I will destroy you if you stand in my way, brother dear. Utterly and completely.' He beamed and strode out, his bodyguard following.

Ned let out a shaky breath and had to mentally uncurl his fist. His fingernails had left crescent marks on the inside of his palms. Getting out the scumble again, he took a tot before recovering the ancient scroll and tucking it safely in his sock and boot. It was time to fill

Jenni in and get this document over to the Emperor. As soon as possible.

Chapter 29

Ned picked Jenni up at the bar on his way out of The Noose. She'd missed Theo and his heavy going up the stairs. Something to do with a competitive game of darts and a toad. Ned wasn't really listening as she explained. She told him she'd seen Theo leaving, and was debating whether to follow or go check on Ned, when he himself came down.

'Did Fingers get it?' asked Jenni.

'Yep. And he showed me how it's a fake. So all we have to do now is take it over to the palace and give it to Fourteen for safekeeping.'

'And Theo didn't know you 'ad it? Where did you put it? Did you ask 'im about the Nightmare?'

'I think he suspected I had something, but I hid it on my desk, beneath the filing and he denied any knowledge of the Nightmare.'

Jenni nodded sagely. Ned's filing was a thing of legend in the office. He never did any because he didn't have the time, but he also knew where every report was. It was like once he'd looked at the paper and put it down, he knew its location.

'We'll get it next time on the contract, Boss. Mebbe I can lift it. 'Ow did Fingers get away?' Jenni asked as they left The Noose.

'I sent him to the Druid Grove by way of Willow's network across the rooftops. Even with his injuries he should make it. And yeah, next time we see Theo, see if you can get hold of Barbas's contract. This Nightmare has outstayed its welcome.'

'No problem, Boss. Fingers should be awright, Willow's vines are gentle unless she barbs 'em.'

Ned reflected on the time Willow had stopped a thief in the middle of the street by wrapping him in barbed vine quicker than he could blink. It had been a terrifyingly brilliant display of power, strength and darkness.

Walking along their usual route to the Imperial Palace, Jenni tugged lightly on Ned's sleeve and finger-signed that they were being followed. Ned signed back with *two up top* and she shook her fingers slightly, indicating another three behind them.

An even five versus two, thought Ned as they passed by a broken streetlamp, which made their surroundings darker and murkier. There were a couple of loud grunts and as Ned glanced back he saw two lumps on the floor. Jenni looked pleased with herself.

'Elbow?' Ned murmured as Jenni grinned. It was a favoured move of hers and because of her short stature often proved a highly debilitating manoeuvre.

Just one more heavy behind and still the two on the rooftops. Ned hoped they didn't have arrows. He didn't feel like being shot at tonight. Besides, more fool them if they did. The gargoyles who ruled the rooftops didn't like it either. People skulking around with bows scared the birds, the gargoyles' primary food source, and gods forbid if someone shot a pigeon by mistake. Gargoyles might not be the fastest movers in Roshaven, but they were one of the sneakiest. You never saw them move. They were just sort of *there*. Ned had heard it said they moved through beats of time, so that when you blinked, they were on you.

Ned had never tested the theory but judging by the muffled scream and smack of body hitting pavement, it was sound.

'Should we check that out, do you think? Civic duty and all,' Ned asked Jenni.

She shrugged.

'Let Theo fill out a form if e's bovver'd,' she replied.

The two remaining followers made no further moves to stop Ned and Jenni, being slightly more intelligent than their counterparts.

It was late, so the Palace gates were shut and the night-guard snoring gently. It took three perfectly aimed stones thrown by Jenni to fully wake him, and then she and Ned had to wait a good ten minutes for the sleepy guard to relay their message into the Palace.

Finally, a High appeared. It could have been Left, it could have been Right. What it had was a long, stripy nightgown, fluffy slippers and a nightcap. Jenni had to turn around and stifle her giggles with a fist. Ned managed to keep a relatively straight face.

'Spinks! Do you know what time it is? You can't just turn up here at any time of night. What do you want?'

'We have important information for Fourteen, I mean, the Emperor. It's imperative she hears it immediately.' Ned tried to use his eyes and eyebrows to impress upon the High the significance of their late-night appearance.

'Yes, well, hand it over and I'll make sure she has it in the morning.' As that High was speaking, the other one appeared.

'Sorry, but we need to speak to Fourteen directly,' said Ned.

This one had on moccasins and a short kimono. There were definitely some knobbly knees on show.

Jenni was now leaning on Ned for humorous support, and Ned had to clear his throat twice in order to get rid of his bubble of laughter.

The two Highs conferred together with a great deal of ferocious whispering before nightcap High came forward and told the guard to open the gate.

Ned and Jenni passed through, and Ned felt the slightest magical tingle.

'Are you warded?' he asked.

'Physical gates are not the only night time protection for the Emperor, may they live for ever and ever!' snapped kimono High.

The two officials bustled ahead of the thief-catchers, conferring in whispers, before arriving at the bedchamber of the Emperor.

'Wait here,' and they left them in the corridor.

'This ain't where she wos last time we came,' remarked Jenni, referring to when thief-catcher Joe's sister had masqueraded as the Emperor and Fourteen had fled to the fourth floor with all her staff, triggering a protection spell. 'And it were pretty fancy in there. Wonder wot its like in 'ere.'

'Don't hold your breath, Jenni. I doubt we'll be let in there.' Although Ned held faint hope that one day he might.

They waited five minutes and then another five minutes. Ned figured he may as well take the document out of his boot, and just as he was balancing on one foot, the door to the imperial suite banged open, making him jump and lose his balance. He ended up sprawled on the floor as Fourteen glided out, an extremely thick, no-nonsense dressing gown enveloping her from neck to ankle. She did not, however, have any slippers on and Ned saw her toes bunch slightly in response to his fall.

Almost as if she were about to help him. Red-faced he stood, one boot on, one off, clutching the scroll.

Fourteen's eyes alighted on the paperwork.

'You found it?' she asked.

'Yes, and we've had it authenticated,' Ned replied passing it over, but Fourteen's face fell. He quickly explained. 'No, no, I mean it's a fake.'

'How?'

'Well, Jimmy Fingers can tell you the full details but basically it's fancy paper dipped in tea, scrunched and passed over fire. They obviously don't have very good forgers in Fidelia.'

Fourteen considered this, unsure whether she should be proud of the fact that Roshaven did.

'Ahem.' It was a High.

'Yes?' Fourteen asked.

'We were going to wait until morning but Left and I have received some disturbing news,' said the High Right.

Ned watched as Fourteen's shoulders slumped and wished he could go give her a hug.

'Out wiv it then,' said Jenni, curious to know what else could be going wrong.

'We've had reports from Molotov, Elongoo and Narborough. They've seen this scroll and have accepted its authenticity. They stand with Fidelia.'

'So. What difference does that make?' asked Ned.

'It means that we are without allies,' replied Fourteen.

'Not completely. You got the Fae,' Jenni said stoutly, puffing out her chest. 'We ain't never run from a fight afore. This is our place too. Yor city grew up round our grove and we live 'ere togever in 'armony. Ain't nuffink gonna change that. It is written.'

Written where? wondered Ned but kept that thought to himself.

'Thank you, Jenni. I appreciate the support. We may need it.' Fourteen squared her shoulders and flashed a small smile at Ned. 'Thank you for bringing me this. Goodnight.' And she went back into her suite.

The Highs shut the doors behind her and looked expectantly at the thief-catchers.

'Yeah, awright. We're going.' Jenni stomped off down the corridor with Ned following her, wishing he could stomp too.

Chapter 30

Ned tugged at his collar. It was too tight, as were the trousers and the new boots. How was he supposed to feel the mood of his city in boots that were too tight? He'd been in a foul temper ever since receiving the invitation to the Emperor's pre-coronation party. It had turned up a gilt-edged piece of card in a posh envelope so thick you couldn't see through it when you held it up to the light. No friendly word or joke or even his name written by her hand. Nothing.

They were supposed to be - well, Ned didn't know what it was they were supposed to be, but they were, and now he felt like an insignificant thief-catcher, only invited because of his rank. The impersonal invite had said plus one, so he was dragging Jenni with him. And she was late. He forced himself to put on the too stiff dress coat that accompanied the smart, barely worn Chief Thief-Catcher uniform, but he left the helmet. It had a plume. That was a feather too far.

A loud banging from downstairs broke his reverie, and he stalked down to open it. He would've hurried, but everything he wore was constricting and not comfortable to move in. Opening the door, it surprised him to see Jenni.

'What are you doing out there?' he asked.

'Waiting for youse to open the door.'

'Yes, but why didn't you just pop in? Like normal.'

'Told you earlier, me magic ain't working right.'

Ned stood to one side to let the sprite in. He checked the time. They had half an hour before guests were due to arrive at the palace.

'Let's have a cuppa, eh? You can tell me everything,' he said.

Jenni's shoulders slumped at Ned's suggestion, so he tried another tack.

'There's some beetle cheesecake left.'

'Fine. But we'll 'ave to walk there so we ain't got long if we don't wanna be late.'

Ned wasn't bothered in the slightest at being late. Truth be told, it wasn't his kind of party but he was attending in order to support Fourteen. Busying himself with the teapot, he listened while Jenni explained everything that had happened at her coming of age ceremony. When she'd finished talking and eating, there was no beetle cheesecake left and they had five minutes to get to the palace so they left in a hurry.

'Well, I'm proud of you. Going through all that and speaking up to the Source. It must have been overwhelming.' It impressed Ned, especially as Jenni hadn't had time to prepare for her ceremony. She'd handled everything superbly.

'Fanks, Boss.'

She smiled, and Ned felt less guilty at not being prepared for Jenni to go through the ceremony either. It had come as a surprise to both of them.

As they reached the palace gates, they paused.

'You ready?' Jenni asked.

'As I'll ever be,' replied Ned.

There was a set of Palace Guards on the main entrance gate. These were larger than the usual specimens and had perfected the art of looming.

'Invitation?' growled the one on the left.

'Come on lads, stop messing around. You know who I am.' Ned said, grinning at the joke. These were Mick and Rick, who had admitted him many times before.

'In. Vit. Tation,' repeated the guard.

'Alright, alright. I was just saying,' muttered Ned as he went to take the invitation out of his back pocket. It wasn't there. So he tried his front pocket. It wasn't there either. Or in his dress jacket. He patted the internal pouch. Nothing. Laughing nervously, his hand returned to the empty back pocket.

'Wot's up, Boss?'

Turning away from the smirking guards, Ned whispered to her.

'Jenni, pop back to the house. I think I've left the invite on the table.'

There was a tense moment as Jenni clenched but did not disappear.

'Jenni! Stop messing around. I don't think Mick and Rick here are going to let us in without our invitation,' said Ned.

'You got that right,' replied the guard on the left, who could hear every word.

Ned scowled at him.

'Right Boss, wait 'ere and I run back and get it. Won't take long.' Jenni turned and began trotting away before Ned had a chance to reply.

Remembering that she'd said her magics were out of sync, he mentally kicked himself for being so thoughtless. It had been an odd couple of days, what with his Nightmare problems which weren't going anywhere, his intense reaction to bean, Griff's will, and now Jenni's issues. Once they'd made it past this ceremony, Ned vowed to himself that he'd go with Jenni back to the fae realm and help her get some answers. If that's what she wanted. He wasn't about to go and stir up trouble unnecessarily.

There was a cough behind him and Ned realised he was in the way of some newly arrived guests who were clutching their gilded invitation in their hands. Ears reddening in embarrassment he apologised and moved to the side, trying to act as if he wanted to stand outside the gates and wouldn't dream of being anywhere else. The next fifteen minutes passed like treacle with far more people arriving than Ned even thought should have been invited. He was thinking he should forget the whole thing and go home to die of shame when Jenni finally came trotting around the corner.

'Got it?'

'Nah. Can't find it. Looked everywhere. You sure you 'ad one?' Jenni half-smiled to show she didn't really mean it, but Ned wasn't listening.

He was wracking his brains trying to think what he'd done with the bloody invite. He eyed Mick and Rick and took a deep breath.

'Guys. This is embarrassing. For both of us. You know who I am. I know you do. And while it's admirable that you're keeping out the undesirables, I can assure you I have a personal relationship with the Emperor and we, my companion and I, are meant to be at this ceremony. Could you look the other way, this one time?'

The guard on the right responded. He held out his hand.

'Invitation?'

'Gah!' Ned kicked the wall and then hopped around in pain. He didn't have his proper boots on.

The two guards had both lain hands on their pommels most threateningly when a familiar plume came bobbing past the gate.

'Oi! Freddie-boy!' shouted Jenni, making the poor

lad jump and his helmet clatter to the floor.

'Jenni?' He grabbed his helmet and hurried over when he saw Ned and Jenni. 'Mr Spinks, Sir. Why aren't you inside? They're nearly ready to start the ceremony.'

'We er… have mislaid our invite.'

Tutting, Fred pushed through the two guards and turned to confront them.

'Mick, Rick–what's going on? You realise who this is? It's Mr Spinks, Chief Thief-Catcher. I know he got your pocket picker last week, Mick, when you stepped out with Shirley from down Grassy End, so don't give me that just doing my job face. You're making the office of PG look bad. And you, don't you get me started Ricky. How many times has your ma lost her marbles, and it's been the thief-catchers what found them again? I've said before that a string vest does not make a good marble bag, but she's set in her ways. Old people are like that. Now smarten yourselves up fellas. You're representing the Emperor. Act sharp and let these two very important guests in.'

Neither guard would look each other in the eye, nor would they glance at Fred, Jenni or Ned, but they relaxed their stance, took their hands off their pommels and moved aside.

Ned watched as Fred nodded to himself in satisfaction and marched back inside. Ned followed swiftly before Mick and Rick could play funny buggers again.

'Thanks, Fred. We appreciate it.'

'Oh, no trouble at all, Mr Spinks, Sir. No trouble. But we'd better get you to the grand hall, they're starting any minute and I don't think they'll wait for the likes or you or me.'

'No, I don't suppose they will,' Ned said as he and

Jenni followed Fred into the palace.

Ned looked around in interest. He'd never made it to the grand hall before, and he certainly hadn't mixed with so many toffs before either. Everywhere he turned people seemed to greet each other like long lost family, yet the minute they turned their backs feverish whispering occurred between groups. The soundtrack of the room peaked with squeals of excitement and chuntered along with a charged hum. Despite recognising the odd face there was no one Ned particularly wanted to speak to, except for Fourteen of course, and he knew that was unlikely to happen.

Jenni snagged a passing tray of hors d'oeuvres and cleaned it of all the best bits, leaving the salad.

'Any good?' asked Ned with a grin.

Jenni shrugged, then muttered under her breath as Momma K floated over.

'Daughta.'

'Momma K.'

'Chil' ya left so quick. Tings were no finish. De Council axe me ta give ya dis suggestions.' She flourished her fingers, and a letter appeared in the space between Jenni and her mum.

'Fanks.'

There was an uncomfortable pause as neither fae knew what to say and Ned dithered whether to get involved.

In the end Momma K flapped her elegant wings gracefully, closing the gap between herself and Jenni and bent down to cup the sprite's face with one of her delicate hands.

'Me always 'ere for ya, chil'. Always.'

Jenni flushed and Ned could feel his own collar tightening. Neither of them were used to such public displays of affection.

Momma K turned to face him, her gaze drawn towards Ned's fourth eye, which worked whenever it was highly inconvenient and unnecessary. She licked her finger and then pressed it to his forehead with some force.

'Ya see now. When ya need to.' She glared at him. 'Protect her.' She didn't need to say the rest.

Ned bobbed his head and with a flap of her wings she had moved on, circling the room with targeted ease. There was a dull ache in the middle of his forehead now and he rubbed it gently, checking his fingers to see whether she'd left any marks. There didn't appear to be anything there.

'Ahem.' It was a familiar dry cough.

Ned pushed down his groan of recognition and tried to plaster a semi-friendly expression on his face as he turned to see the undead solicitor.

'Mr Simms. Fancy seeing you here.'

'I am here on several strands of business. Events like these make it easier to access those who prefer not to deal with civil servants. Or the undead.' Mr Simms grinned at his own joke as he unclipped the satchel he was carrying and drew out a small purple jewellery box. 'This is the next magical item. Griff wanted our beloved Emperor to be the recipient.'

'Can't you give it to her? Some other time?'

'I'm afraid tampering with the magical constraints on the will is beyond my firm's skill. Not that we'd ever change the dying request of our beloved clients.'

'Wot is it?' Jenni eyed the box suspiciously.

Ned reluctantly took the box and opened it to reveal a diamond ring. It wasn't huge or flashy. A simple cut stone in an unassuming delicate band of pale yellow.

The sort of ring that Ned might be able to afford after several months of intense saving.

'Why this?'

'I'm afraid we weren't privy to the inner thoughts of our client. Only the requested outcomes and in this case that the Ring of Truth be delivered to our Emperor.' Mr Simms was enjoying himself, as much as an undead lawyer can at an imperial function. 'Don't forget about the time limit.'

'Time limit?' Ned had a bad feeling about that, quickly followed by the name of the item. *Ring of Truth?*

'I remind you that each magical item has a window of delivery otherwise dire consequences shall unfold, according to the will that is.'

Ned decided he couldn't risk Griff's whimsy. Dire might very well be dire.

'How long do I have?' he asked.

'Oh, about twenty minutes.' There was no mistaking the grin this time. Mr Simms was loving this.

'Um, Boss? 'Ow you planning to get it over to 'er?'

Ned eyed the crowd. If he moved fast and followed the shifting patterns of nobles, he could swoop down the left-hand side of the room and cut across just in front of the main dais and catch Fourteen before the party officially began. The High Right and High Left were still mingling. He had time.

It would have worked if the lady with the crenelated dress had turned left and not right, throwing her huge needlework edifice across Ned's chosen pathway. He swerved to the best of his ability, but that put pressure on the already inadequate boots and they couldn't live up to it. They slipped on the smooth floor, failing to gain any purchase, and Ned skated with the desperation of a man who knew he was going to fall and there was nothing he could do about it.

Of course, by this time the entire room was aware of a man near the Emperor who was desperately trying not to fall head over heels, and a great deal of whispering and fan fluttering was watching Ned's almost slow motion fall into embarrassment. As he landed on the floor, his elbow cracked loudly, jarring his arm and causing him to involuntarily let go of the jewellery box he was holding.

'Gods dammit!' he yelled, causing several of the more delicate nobility to swoon and those who hadn't climbed socially that much higher than Ned to tut in distaste.

Ned took in the crowd, noting Mr Simms watching events unfold with unbecoming glee and wished Jenni would just catch the box. But he was too late as Fourteen snagged it out of the air and sent a quizzical look at the sprawled thief-catcher.

Ned rose to one knee as the soon-to-be-coronated Emperor of Roshaven opened the box. He saw her eyes widen, lips part and a small flush colour the hollow of her neck. But this was an auspicious day, and the room was packed with eagle-eyed gossip mongers and backstabbers. The whisper flashed around the room quicker than lightning.

'It's an engagement ring!'

Ned had seen Fourteen flick a glance at him and given the tiniest shake of her head, so he played the fool and attempted to sweep a bizarre half kneeling bow. This would have been the perfect occasion for a plume.

'A gift for you, my Emperor,' he called out in a mostly steady voice.

'One I cannot accept,' replied Fourteen.

'Why not?' Ned was puzzled. It was only a little ring.

'This kind of union is usually a matter of empire, not one of love,' she replied.

A collective gasp shot round the room and hundreds of ears craned that bit further forward.

'You have to accept. I'm on a bit of deadline.' Ned was doing his best to ignore the horde of nobles breathing down his neck but couldn't help but catch some muttered comments.

'It's not very romantic, is it?'
'What do you expect from a commoner? They probably think this is how it should be done.'
'Did you see it? How big is the stone?'
'Can the emperor even marry a commoner?'

That last comment jerked him to his feet and sent heat into his face as he stammered an explanation.

'No! It's not like that. I would never, I mean, not now. Not here. I mean...' Ned trailed off as he saw the hurt flash across Fourteen's face before she concealed her emotions behind her imperial mask. He tried again and stepped forwards to close the gap between them. Throwing caution to the wind, he put his hands over hers and closed the box. 'It's from Griff. He wanted you to have it.'

A combination of understanding, relief and regret flashed through Fourteen's eyes before she pulled her hands away and made a slight gesture to one of her ladies-in-waiting, handing them the jewellery box.

'Thank you for delivering the item. The empire thanks you for your service and would respectfully request such deliveries be made during work hours and not during state functions.' Fourteen swept away without a backwards glance at Ned.

'But…' Ned watched the crowd of nobles close around Fourteen. His unresisting body was slowly pushed further and further away. He looked for a glance, a gesture, anything that showed she was aware of his presence, but all signs of his Fourteen had disappeared and only the Emperor of Roshaven remained.

It filled him with remorse. Of course she'd thought it was an engagement ring, who wouldn't? And now he'd made her, and him, appear like a fool in front of the assembled lords and ladies. That had not been his intent, and he was sure Griff wouldn't have wanted it either. Ned should have thought of a better way of delivering the ring. Maybe if he'd just walked up to her, it would've looked like her thief-catcher wanted a quick word. After all, the Emperor cannot break protocols at a state occasion.

Ned's heart ached as he recalled the flash of hurt across Fourteen's face. That was the last thing he'd wanted to do. Recognising the familiar scent of Jenni, Ned turned away from the pomp and ceremony.

'C'mon, Jenni. I think we've outstayed our welcome.'

For once, the sprite had no witty comeback and instead swiped a large slice of chocolate gateau off the desserts table as they left the Grand Hall. No one stopped them on the way out, and the two walked silently out of the palace gates.

Chapter 31

'Well, that was embarrassing.'

Ned's shoulders tensed as he recognised that voice. He didn't want to turn around.

'Why are you 'ere?' Jenni challenged the man behind them, whilst licking her chocolately fingers.

'I was invited.' Theo pushed off the palace wall where he had been waiting for them. 'Nice try with the proposal, brother dearest, but she's already taken. And your little trinket is hardly a match for what I'm offering.'

'It wasn't a proposal. It was a gift, from Griff,' retorted Ned.

Theo waved one hand dismissively in the air.

'How are your dreams?' he asked.

'Wonderful, thank you.' Ned looked his brother in the eye. 'You?'

'Eddie, darling, don't be gauche. I just wanted to say hi, see if you've caught any thieves lately. You know, do the brother thing.'

'Fine. You've done it so now you can leave.' Ned half turned, then glared back over his shoulder. 'And you can take your damn Nightmare with you.'

'No can do, amigo.' Theo leaned conspiratorially closer to his brother. 'Really, Eddie, did you think you could get rid of me that easily? Tell me about this ring, is it valuable? What about the other items you have to deliver?'

Ned pushed away the hurt face of Fourteen from his mind's eye and tried not to let his brother's words get under his skin.

'It was from Griff and I have delivered it to its rightful owner.' Ned jerked his head at the bejewelled fingers of Theo. 'What do you want with a trinket like that, anyway? You've got more than enough on your left hand alone to make up for that little thing.'

'Looks can be deceiving, Eddie dear. Take me. Whoever would've thought that the most feared criminal mastermind in Fidelia would have a lowly lawkeeper as a brother? It's ridiculous.' Theo pulled a piece of paper out of his pocket. 'This is your contract with Barbas and I would be happy to annul the agreement, in a heartbeat. Just get me the ring and the rest of the magical items.'

Ned wondered how Theo knew about the things in Griff's will. He was probably only after them because he thought they would give him power or wealth or both.

'They're not for you,' he replied.

'Eddie! Griff is dead. He doesn't care who gets them. And don't worry about stiff old Mr Simms. I'll get my people to have a word with his boss. You'll still make your delivery boy fee. Whaddya say?'

Ned stayed quiet for a moment, as if considering the offer.

'You know what, *Teddy*? I'm glad you've found a place you can use your unique talents and carve out a piece of happiness for yourself. But if you think you can show up here, in my city, and take whatever you want, you'd better think again. As for Griff's will, he may be dead, but he was a close personal friend of the Emperor and if he wants her to have these things, that's what will happen. If I were you, I'd leave Roshaven. Now.'

For the briefest moment, fear flashed across Theo's face.

'You don't scare me!' he hissed at Ned before

stalking away.

'Did you get it?' Ned hoped that Jenni hadn't lost her quick fingers as well as her magic.

'Corse I did, Boss.' Jenni flourished Barbas's contract in her hands and then secreted it away again. 'Do you wanna go see him now?'

'Might as well. It's not like I'm going to get a decent night's sleep, is it?'

'Nope but… we need to 'itch a lift so if you could mebbe pretend to go to sleep or summink that would be grand. I need to see the Nightmare to catch it.'

'C'mon then. Let's go home via Bucket Street. I want to fill up.'

The pair strolled right rather than left to take this detour. There were power wells dotted across Roshaven, constructed by the fae wherever ley lines crossed paths. Some were on walls and some were on lampposts. They all looked like miniature taps. Ned began refilling his personal well by tapping into the one on a lamppost. He caught Jenni watching with interest.

'What's up with you?'

'Jus' looking.'

'It's just a refill, Jenni. I do it fairly regularly.'

'Yeah, I know… 'ow do you do it though?'

'You see this spigot? You give it a wiggle to loosen it and then put your power well underneath and you've got to, sort of will the power up and out.'

'Will it?' Jenni craned her neck to look even closer. She could see the raw magic flowing out into Ned's power well. It sputtered and disappeared.

'Wot 'appened?'

Ned cleared his throat.

'It's not exactly easy to perform with an audience. A man and his spigot need a little room.'

Jenni took the hint and moved back a couple of paces while Ned tried to reconnect with the power line that connected to this hub. It was like reaching for something through treacle, but he finally grabbed hold and finished recharging.

'Ow do you knows if you've got enuff?' Jenni was checking out Ned's well again.

He pulled his overcoat closed and did up the buttons, hiding the power well and his utility belt.

'The well knows. It stops and you're full. Refuelling is a very intuitive process. Jenni… why are you so interested? You've got a direct line, don't you?'

'I dunno wot I got now.'

'You ought to find out. It could end up being crucial in a life or death situation.'

Jenni began to object that they were never in those situations and then stopped, agreeing with him. They had been in several in the last year alone. Not to mention the incident with the Yeti. They both shivered at the memory.

Back at the house, Jenni tried to warm some milk for Ned in an effort to help him fall asleep, but after she'd burnt the third saucepan full Ned shoed her out of his kitchen and grabbed a bottle of scumble.

'This'll be as good as anything else,' he said, taking a swig.

In the end, it took about twenty swigs and some bad singing before Ned finally crashed out. The Nightmare appeared a few moments after Ned's eyes closed. It was very wispy at first, but soon became more corporeal. Jenni shook Ned awake and grabbed a handful of mane before the horse could disappear.

'Get on!' she yelled.

Ned tried to marshal his limbs effectively but

couldn't swing his leg up.

'Stand on the sofa,' ordered Jenni as the apparition began frisking under her grip.

Ned stood to a wobble and launched himself at the beast.

'I made it!' he exclaimed in triumph, landing backwards on the horse.

'Yeah, if you say so,' muttered Jenni as she vaulted onto the Nightmare to sit behind its head, her back pressed against Neds.

'Where's the head?' Ned asked, peering blearily at the tail in front of him.

'Take us to yor master,' coaxed Jenni as the Nightmare skittered beneath them before gathering itself into a powerful leap and galloping out of the room.

Ned felt Jenni flinch as they passed through the brick wall.

'What happened?' he asked.

'I weren't sure if we could go through the wall or not.'

Ned watched the building recede away from them.

'I'm guessing we can.'

'Yep.'

Chapter 32

The fresh night air soon brought Ned back to his senses. He decided to ignore the fact that he was astride a phantom horse backwards and instead took in the scene. His fear of heights kept tapping his shoulder, but the view of his city, his Roshaven spiralling out below him with all its foibles and idiosyncrasies brought a tear to his eye. Taking a deep breath, his gaze lifted, and the sky demanded his rapt attention.

'Stars…'

'Wot about 'em, Boss?'

'They're so… so…' Ned couldn't explain how small he felt and how vast the sky seemed.

'Yeah, shame ain't it.'

'What is?' Ned tried to turn his head, but that wobbled his seat upon the Nightmare and the incessant shoulder tapping got a little harder as his stomach swooped, his breath caught and his skin went clammy.

'Them stars, right, they're all gone and they're so far away only the echo of their light shines at us.'

'Really?' Ned was surprised, both at the fact and at Jenni knowing something like that.

'I'm impressed.' A dry voice near his ear made Ned flinch and suddenly the Nightmare had disappeared and he was tumbling to the ground.

'Argh!!!' The wind flew cold past his face and the streets of Roshaven rushed towards him. Ned shut his eyes and clenched. Nothing happened. He risked an eye-open, and the ground was still accelerating to meet him, so he squeezed it shut again. Still nothing. He opened both eyes and dragged their gaze sideways.

Jenni stood on a cloud, hands on her hips as if she were about to give the tall fellow next to her a rather large piece of her mind.

'Jenni,' Ned wheezed.

'Just stand up, Boss. It's an illusion. Piss poor one if you ask me.'

Ned's thundering heart didn't agree, but he gingerly pressed down with one knee and when it touched a solid surface, he pushed himself to standing, refusing to check what exactly his feet were standing on.

'Your fear,' the tall man inhaled. 'It's so…primal.'

'Barbas?' Ned asked Jenni, she confirmed with a brief nod, so he directed his attention at the man. 'Barbas, we're here to return your contract.'

'Return?' Barbas cocked an eyebrow and regarded Ned with the same stern, disapproving stare he had received from many a teacher, senior work colleague and of late, Fourteen.

'Whilst I appreciate the efforts you've gone to - very good craftmanship by the way - the Nightmare is no longer required. I spoke with my brother and have returned the contract to you for official… finishing.'

A bead of cold sweat trickled down Ned's back and the palms of his hands were clammy. He swallowed and tried to gauge what Barbas was thinking. The stony face gave nothing away. It was like being on trial for his life, only a thousand times worse. Ned fought the urge to look down to see if he was naked and ignored the sudden desire to find out who those thousand pairs of eyes that were boring into his back belonged to.

'Oi, lay off 'im. You've made yor point.' Jenni stomped on Barbas's foot and thrust the contract under his nose. She didn't appear to quail in the slightest as the fear demon shifted his calculating gaze from Ned to her, but her tail twitched nervously.

As soon as he was released from Barbas's power, Ned took a deep shuddering gasp, patted his clothes against his body and risked a quick glance over his shoulder. There was no-one there. The movement of his eyes reminded his body he was standing on nothing and he clenched his teeth once more, dragging his attention to Jenni and Barbas.

Barbas had taken the document and was peering at it.

'Usually I require both parties present for the cancellation of such a contract, but seeing as you brought such wonderfully fragrant fear with you, I'll just collect the rest of the essence I'm owed and we can negate the deal.'

'No-one said anyfink about collecting nuffink...' Jenni tried to intervene but Barbas had already crossed the space between himself and Ned and had both hands pressed to the side of his head.

Ned's eyes rolled back. He turned deathly pale and arched back, arms splayed, toes barely touching the invisible floor. His mouth opened in a silent scream, the cords on his neck standing out and his fingers curled into open fists. A huge grey miasma lifted out of his body and Barbas collected it with a large glass vial he'd conjured out of nowhere. As the last of the fear was captured, Ned's body collapsed into itself and Jenni rushed forward as he hit the ground with a slap.

*****

'Wot did you do to 'im?'

Barbas regarded the sprite with a sneer, the vial of Ned's fear disappearing with a wave of his hand.

'You might think you have your fears under control

but you can't hide them from me, they smell delicious.'

She glared back at him. Barbas snapped his fingers, dissolving the contract.

'Consider the contract paid in full.' As Barbas and his Nightmare faded into the night sky, his disembodied voice rang in Jenni's ears. 'Be seeing you.'

Jenni had no time to consider the threat as, much like last time she'd visited Barbas, she was now falling through the air. She'd had the presence of mind to grab hold of Ned's body and was riding him like a quick lead balloon. She clicked her fingers. Nothing. She squeezed her eyes shut and muttered a prayer to all the Gods above and below before willing her spell forth. Still nothing. The ground was now scarily close, and Jenni gripped Ned with both hands as tightly as possible and braced herself for impact.

A rush of power ran down her arms and silver sparks flew as she barely cushioned their landing onto the street cobbles. Her heart was pounding in her chest as she let out a shaky breath and turned her hands over. Already the power was receding. She could feel its warmth travelling back up her arms to the core of her being.

They were safely back on firm ground, in the middle of a blast circle of dead weeds, lichen, moss and other small city foliage.

*****

'Jenni? Are you sat on top of me?'

'Yes, Boss.'

'Thought so.'

There was a brief pause.

'Do you think you could, you know, move?'

'Corse, Boss.' Jenni scrambled off and offered Ned a hand to help him to his feet.

'Why are we on Chuffing Street?'

'S'where we landed, after Barbas.'

The pair started walking, heading for HQ as it was closer than Ned's place.

'That's the end of that then, eh?'

'Hope so, Boss. I ain't too keen to chat wiv Barbas again anytime soon.' A faint gallop in the distance caused them both to turn and look up at the night sky. A shadow flitted across the moon, making them both shiver. 'Yeah, we're well out of that, Boss.'

Chapter 33

It was the morning after Fourteen's party and Ned's visit with Barbas. Ned's mouth felt thick, and he had a crick in his neck. He tried to focus on where he was. It looked like a floor. Was that a pile of filing? He squeezed his eyes shut tight, then checked again. Yes, it was, so that meant this was the Thief-Catcher's office.

There was the sound of glass clinking as Ned pushed himself up to a seat. Peering around blearily, he saw two empty bottles of scumble. Two! He touched his head; it wasn't a particularly terrible hangover so there was no way he'd drunk both.

'Morning, Boss!'

Ned winced at the loud, cheerful greeting. Jenni must have been his drinking partner. She always said that swigging scumble was like giving her entire body an apple-flavoured buff. Claimed it cleared out all the vital organs.

'Water?' he croaked, but Jenni thrust a bacon sandwich and a mug of hot tea in his hands instead. Ned's stomach roiled, and he put the plate of food down.

He sipped the tea, in case it turned out to be a druid tonic and not tea at all. Ned tried to remember what had happened last night. He'd embarrassed himself at Fourteen's coronation party with that damn ring from Griff. Then Theo had mocked him, Jenni had stolen the Nightmare contract, and they'd been to visit Barbas. He shuddered. And then… then there was scumble, he guessed. An eventful night. He ought to go see Fourteen, make sure she was alright and not upset about the ring.

He took another sip as the office door opened.

Inwardly groaning, Ned pulled himself to his feet, but when he saw who it was, he dropped into his chair, splashing a little tea on his trousers.

'Good morning, Mr Spinks. I have the next item,' said Mr Simms.

'Yor kiddin', right? Couldn't you 'ave given us that yesterday or woteva?' asked Jenni.

Mr Simms's lip curled and one eyebrow rose. 'I don't make the magic rules. Perhaps you should have a word with your mother.'

'Yeah, right.'

'What is it this time, Simms?' asked Ned.

The undead lawyer reached into his briefcase and pulled out half a brick.

'Woah, easy!' Both Ned and Jenni reacted combatively. Ned had half crouched and was wielding a broken bottle of scumble he'd smashed on the side of his desk. He watched as Jenni sparked her fingers, muttering under her breath as she looked around for somewhere to pull power from. A half-brick was a deadly weapon this close to the Black Narrows, and many young lives had been affected in one way or another by this kind of missile. Best results came from it being dropped at height, but anyone handling a half-brick could cause at the very least a ruckus, but more usually a fracas, and at times even a brouhaha.

Mr Simms blinked in surprise and placed the half-brick on the corner of Ned's desk. Then seeing that action had little effect, took two measured paces backwards.

'This is the Half-Brick of Courage. It's the next magical item from the will of...' He was about to launch into the long list of titles but caught the tone of the room and changed tack. 'From the will of Griff, the er… entrepreneur.'

Ned tossed the broken bottle into the waste bin and Jenni stopped sparking.

'Wot's a trepenor?' she asked.

Ned shrugged. He wasn't sure.

'Something to do with losing money, I think.'

Mr Simms tutted and took a further step backwards whilst Jenni and Ned approached the brick.

'You said it's called the Half-Brick of Courage?' asked Ned.

Mr Simms nodded.

'You put that inna sock and you'll 'ave all the courage you want,' remarked Jenni.

'Who is it for?' asked Ned.

At this question, Mr Simms barked a cough of embarrassment. He smoothed his pinstripe suit with his zombie hands.

'It's for the Emperor, may *she* live for ever and ever. Must get used to saying that.'

Ned shook his head, igniting his hangover, and swore under his breath.

'Yes, quite. It's a little embarrassing for us as well. If I ever see Griff on the undead circuit, I shall be having words.'

'Are you likely to?' Ned asked.

'Given the sizeable amount of money awaiting you, losing ownership of his trading routes, and these magical items… I should think not. What would he possibly have to come back to?'

For half a second Ned had the slightest glimmer of hope that his friend might not be dead after all. Or if he was dead, maybe he was only mostly dead and they could find a cure. Even after having seen him get killed, attending his funeral and making that burning arrow shot. A tiny spark.

'Ow do we know this is genuine?' Jenni poked the half-brick, and it wobbled.

'Jenni, don't play with the magical items. If there's nothing else, Mr Simms?'

Mr Simms inclined his head and turned for the door. Just as he was passing through, he stopped.

'We have two more magical boxes at our offices. Waiting for their seals to open and the instructions to be read. I think, perhaps, I may be back here again.' He tipped his finger towards the thief-catcher and left them to their half-brick.

'Wot you finking then, Boss?' asked Jenni.

'Well, last time you couldn't hear the humming of the cup, so it could be something that's just tuned into humans.'

'Into you and Fourteen you mean.'

'Yeah,' said Ned, distractedly as he bent down to inspect the half-brick. 'We've got to go take this to the Emperor, so let's go via the kitchens and see what Ma Bowl's got put away. I'm sure she will have saved something from the party last night.'

Jenni brightened up at that prospect, although Ned was wishing he didn't have to go back to the palace so soon. At least his brother wasn't staying there yet.

'I fink she's waiting.'

'What?'

'Youse look like yor cogiwotsitting–I fink Fourteen will call off the wedding once she's been proper coronated and all them trade routes 'ave been sorted. I 'eard it ain't going well.'

'Who did you hear that from?'

'Sparks.'

Ned splashed some water in his face and grabbed a handful of mint to chew. He didn't have a razor at the office–it was too much of a dangerous weapon to keep on the premises given their usual suspects, the pub downstairs, and the proximity to the Black Narrows.

'How did he find out?'

'He's in with the afids at the palace. They're terrible gossips.'

Ned rubbed some water through his hair and tried to style it so it lay that way on purpose.

'Aren't aphids the little green bugs that eat roses? Does the palace even have any of those?'

'Oh yeah, infested. Little blighters they is. We good?'

'Yep, let's go.'

They walked out of the office. Ned reappeared two minutes later, panting from running back up the stairs. He'd forgotten the half-brick. Not wanting to walk down the street holding half a brick, he put it in a discarded sock and shoved it in his capacious overcoat pocket. That action alone filled him with such purpose and direction that he felt he could conquer the world with half a cabbage and a paperclip. Shaking his head to break the spell, he realised he could still smell cabbage. The housewives of the Black Narrows, the most dangerous occupants in there, must have been preparing the daily gruel. The stomachs of many desperate men ran on the thought of cabbage soup.

Chapter 34

The gates of the palace were still closed. Ned wondered if its residents were also suffering the effects of the morning after. He hoped they wouldn't have the same problem getting in that they did last night.

Ned pushed the gate, just on the off chance, and it swung open. He peered sideways to see if there were any guards around. There weren't, so he and Jenni let themselves in and closed the gate behind them with a soft click. If no-one else had noticed, he wasn't about to tell anyone. Provided no crime had been committed. Then, of course, he would be obliged to tell someone.

'Stop it,' ordered Jenni.

'What?'

'Yor nervous finking. It makes me ears twitch. I fink most everyone is gonna be asleep. Are we going to the kitchens first or wot?'

Ned grimaced at how well Jenni knew him and then nodded, letting her lead the way. A nice friendly mug of something from Ma Bowl would be lovely. And a couple of honey cakes, if she had them going spare. It would help with the hangover which had just decided it was hungry now.

The kitchens had the same comforting bustle as always. There was Ma Bowl sat on her high stool watching the scullery girls closely to ensure eggs were being poached to perfection. The lads were doing the toasting. They had egg duty yesterday. Ma Bowl was firm but fair.

'Cake on your left, trifle on your right. Everything

else is being mopped up to make various,' said Ma Bowl by way of greeting.

Not for the first time Ned was struck by how Ma Bowl might not be looking in your direction yet knew where you were. The woman had fantastic peripheral vision.

Jenni claimed the bowl of trifle, leaving Ned to choose from cherry and almond cake, lemon cake and chocolate cake. Feeling a little less hungover, he went for the balanced option - a little of each. Two hot mugs of tea were delivered to a corner table for them and stools were slid across the floor. Ned and Jenni slotted into the kitchen whilst brunch flowed around them.

'What was all that about then? With the ring?' Ma Bowl asked after Ned had eaten his cake. She had a soft spot for him, said he reminded her of late husband Derek, which was probably why she'd given him the option to finish his meal before grilling him.

'It wasn't my ring, it was from Griff. The Ring of Truth, apparently. No idea why it looked like a diamond ring.' Ned took a slurp of tea. 'You've heard about the magical items Griff left in his will?'

Ma Bowl nodded. Ned wasn't surprised. The imperial kitchen was another nexus for gossip.

'Well, I'm the official deliverer of these items and each one comes with a time limit or something. The ring turned up last night. It wasn't my fault I tripped over that woman's foot.' Ned felt his ears redden.

He'd basically been on one knee in front of the woman he loved with what looked very much like a typical engagement ring. He cringed inwardly.

'It's not right to lead a lady on,' said Ma Bowl.

It was a statement but delivered with such gravitas that Ned felt contrite and squirmed a little on his stool.

'E'll marry 'er when this is all over wiv. Won't you, Boss?'

Ned just puffed out his cheeks. He wasn't even sure Fourteen would still have him.

'Ma? I gotta question—why ain't the coronation today? Seems silly not to 'ave it when all these posh 'uns are 'ere.'

Ma Bowl glowed at being asked such an important question.

'The tradition of having a coronation party and the actual coronation two days later stems from the former Emperors. They were rum ones, always partying and carrying on and such like. That's where the recipe for thrice-candied duck comes from. Been passed down through the generations.'

Ned's mouth watered and Jenni was almost drooling. Thrice-candied duck was a glorious Roshaven delicacy.

'Too many dignitaries ended up missing out on the coronation on account of bad heads or dicky tummies. So the ruling council decided to include an extra day of celebration or, as you and I call it, a day of recovery.' Ma shifted on her seat a little. 'Coronations are lengthy, and it's important to at least appear like you're paying attention. That's why the big feast is the day before the coronation. It gives people something to do and fills them up for the ceremony. Not that our Emperor's coronation won't be wonderful. I hear she is wearing a beautiful dress.'

Ned watched as Ma's eyes glazed over. She'd been head of the imperial kitchens ever since Fourteen was born. He felt a twinge of despair. He still had the feast and the coronation to live through before they could get rid of his brother and this ridiculous engagement. And his social standing as Chief Thief-Catcher meant he definitely wouldn't be at a high table. He would be too far away to hear anything.

Jenni was happily slurping jelly, so Ned had to wait a moment for her to finish.

'I think the feast might be somewhere Theo will try something, only I don't know what,' he said to her.

Ned caught Ma Bowl watching the two of them with interest.

'I can't say anything, Ma. Official catcher business. You understand.'

'Oh yes. I understand. I also understand that your brother is a miserable toe-rag and I will hold you personally responsible should he get his grubby little mitts into my Emperor.'

Ned nodded in agreement and privately thought that miserable toe-rag was an extremely nice way of describing his brother.

Cake demolished, he popped his plate in the sink, giving the dish girl a wink for her trouble. Going over to Ma Bowl, he stopped to give her a kiss on the cheek for which she reciprocated with a cheeky bum pinch. Ned and Jenni left the kitchen with full bellies and smiles. The mood didn't last long.

'Where should we go to announce ourselves?' Ned asked Jenni. 'We can't just roam around the palace.'

'I fink we just 'ead for her study. If she ain't there yet she will be soon, I reckon.'

So that was where they went and were sitting comfortably by the fire, Ned half dozing when the door banged open and Fourteen stalked in.

'I hope you've come to apologise after your shenanigans last night.'

Ned relaxed. If she'd used words like diabolic

behaviour, then he was in big trouble. As it was, he wasn't out of hot water just yet.

He was about to explain when he caught Jenni glaring at him in much the same way as Fourteen, so he hastily stood.

'The ring was the second item from Griff. Simms sprang it on me at the party and said there was a very short time limit to get it to you,' explained Ned.

'What was it going to do, explode?'

Ned shrugged helplessly. 'I have no idea what the side effects would have been, but with that many people in the grand ballroom, I wasn't going to take a chance. Besides, I would have made it to you discreetly if that damned woman hadn't got in my way. I never intended to embarrass you. I wouldn't do that.'

'I know.' Fourteen dropped the semi-furious act and slumped into a chair, her head in her hands.

'What's wrong? Hangover?' asked Ned.

'Gods, I wish.' She sighed. 'I thought we had him on the ropes. I found a name.'

'And?' Ned asked eagerly.

'Rose, my new name will be Rose.'

'Beautiful, really beautiful. It suits you.' Ned grinned. It was the perfect name for her.

'Yeah, that's lovely. Fab choice.' Jenni gave the newly named Rose a thumbs up.

'It's being formally recognised and signed into the imperial register tomorrow at my coronation, where it will also be announced. I'm glad you like it,' said Rose, beaming.

'I do.'

'On top of my name, you found the ancient scroll and we have the evidence that it's a fake. Gods, I'm even going to be crowned tomorrow but... the trade agreements are a mess.'

'Why? What has Theo done now?' Ned was wary.

'I thought it was all going too easy. He's been in touch with everyone previously, that much we guessed, but what he's done is slur Fat Norris. Told them tall tales about his inefficiency and fed them rumours of his corruptness,'

''E is corrupt. 'E runs the docks,' commented Jenni.

'Yes, but Theo has informed our trade allies that Fat Norris sanctioned the traffic of slave children. And apparently he showed them *significant proof.*'

Ned's face paled.

'The only way he could show them *proof* like that would be if he were trading in slave children himself,' he said.

'But I can't prove that,' said Rose. 'I've got my hands full trying to convince trade partners who have dealt with men their entire lives that they can trust me. A single woman with no heir to the throne and no man by her side to step in and take over. And now I have to do something in the face of this *proof* otherwise I'll be seen as a weak ruler.'

'Surely that's not stopping things from moving forward?' asked Ned. 'Everyone knows Roshaven is a strategic place on all established trade routes. Perfect for supply stops, for making a quick sale and changing cargo.'

'I know, I know, but…'

'But what?' Ned leaned into Rose and put his hands around hers.

'Fidelia,' she said.

'What about it?'

'Theo has been improving their bay. He's had a harbour carved out, and a shipyard is being built, plus he's got enough room for twenty ships to anchor. He's started to build infrastructure, and it's not that much further along the coast from us. If I can't get these men to listen to me and see that Roshaven is still the powerful trading partner we've always been, then I'm going to lose the trade agreements. And…'

'Go on,' said Ned gently.

'If I do marry him, then he'll take over Roshaven and I'll be relegated to breeding stock. Oh, don't look so shocked, Ned. You know it as well as I do.'

Ned tried to school his face to comforting instead of concerned.

'So don't marry him,' he said. 'Easy.'

'If I don't marry him, then he's going to steal all our trade. This one meeting today is the only opportunity I have to convince these trading partners we are a solid bet, a safe harbour and a dependable source of wealth. I can't rely on Fat Norris. They believe the rumours about him. In fact, if I don't remove him from his position as Lower Circle, they will more than likely consider me as in cahoots in the whole thing.'

Jenni had been listening.

'Well, to be fair, 'e is getting old. And since Two-Face Bob lost 'is 'ead 'e ain't got the 'art wot 'e used to. Fingers'd be better for you.'

'Fingers?' Rose was confused.

Ned grinned.

'Of course. Jimmy Fingers. He'd be a great person to promote to the role of Lower Circle. He's got that nickname because he's metaphorically got fingers in lots of pies and studies the trading flow. There is a little illegal activity on the side but give him that responsibility and I think we'll see a fair bit of legalisation happening. I can send him over, if you like.'

'Do you think he'd take the job?' asked Rose with a touch of hope back in her voice.

Ned and Jenni looked at each other, smiling.

'I think I can guarantee it,' said Ned.

'That's great. At least I can announce that news at today's trading meeting. I'll talk to Norris first, so he's prepped. I think it will relieve him.'

'Yeah, 'e will. E's got a 'oliday home all set for 'im and the missus once 'e retires,' said Jenni.

'Where did you hear that?' asked Ned in surprise.

Jenni shrugged.

'Around,' she replied.

'Well, as nice as this brief conversation has been, I have to get ready. Wish me luck,' said Rose, rising reluctantly from the chair.

Ned got up with her and his coat knocked against his leg.

'Oh! I have something for you.'

'Not another ring, I hope?'

'No, it's er… well, it's a half-brick.' Ned pulled the sock out of his pocket and retrieved the brick.

'You're giving me building material?' Rose was confused.

'It's the next magical item from Griff. It's the Half-Brick of Courage,' explained Ned.

'You're kidding, right?' Rose looked at Jenni for confirmation. She just smirked.

'Hold it. Trust me.' Ned held the half-brick out to her.

She looked at his face, as if trying to decide if he was pulling her leg. She must have concluded he wasn't as she took the half-brick from him. Suddenly she was standing straighter and looking confident and feeling powerful, like she'd just run a race and won.

'Woah!' she breathed.

'I know, right? Take this with you to the meeting and it will give you all the courage you need to convince those traders that sticking with Roshaven is in their best interest.'

'Ow is she gonna walk inta meeting wiv that, Boss?'

'Oh, Jenni. You'd be amazed what you can hide under ceremonial robes,' teased Rose. She hefted the half-brick in her hand and then touched Ned's arm in thanks, unspoken emotion in her eyes. 'I'll see you at the coronation.'

'See you then,' Ned whispered back as she left the room.

'Do you fink she'll do it?' asked Jenni, scratching an armpit.

'Yes. Yes, I do. Come on, Jenni. Let's get back to the office. We've got a criminal to employ for the Emperor.'

'Wot if 'e says no, Boss?'

'Fingers won't miss out on an opportunity like this. He's been building support for a coup for a while. It was Two-Faced Bob's murder that started everything. He was the one person Fingers couldn't get around,' explained Ned as the two of them walked out of the palace.

'Cos of the two faces. Gotcha.'

'Something like that.' Ned smiled. Theo could sow all the lies and deceptions he wanted, but Rose was going to win everybody over. He could just feel it.

Chapter 35

When Ned and Jenni returned to The Noose, there was a queue spilling out on the street. It took a good deal of excuse-me-sorry and squeezing through on Ned's part before they even got half-way through the inn. In the end Jenni had to whistle loudly, which she was able to do on a sub-sonic frequency, causing everyone to clutch their ears in shock, turning to see the source. After that, a path was made.

Inside the office, Willow, Sparks and Joe were trying to field enquiries as best as they could.

'What's going on?' asked Ned.

'They're all here because an ad in the paper said we'd pay a silver bit for information,' explained Willow, holding up the offending advert for Ned to look at.

'Information about what?' he wondered.

'Anything. Everything. It's mad, Boss. What do we do?' Willow's leaves were all fluttering in agitation and buds, thorns and creepers were rapidly appearing and disappearing. It was most discombobulating.

'OI! Listen up.' Ned banged his desk. 'This is the deal. Write your information down on a piece of paper with your name and address. If it's useful, we'll pay you. If it isn't, we'll pass it on to *The Daily Blag* to print. You can all be famous.' There was an undercurrent of muttering at this statement, so Jenni added a bit.

'If you don't like it, I can pass yor details onto Momma K.'

That shut everyone up. No one wanted to come to Momma K's attention on purpose. Jenni might turn you into a toad, but Momma K would turn you inside yourself and force you to come to face to face with your inner demons. Most people weren't built to deal with things like that, and the odd idiot who sought Momma K out probably wished he was a toad. If he had any coherent thought patterns left.

There was a bit of queue shuffling as some decided their information wasn't worth sharing after all, and for twenty minutes there was some intense pen scratching on paper from those who still felt it was. Ned went to brew some tea and wondered whether Mariah Neeps, owner and reporter at *The Daily Blag,* would tell him who submitted the ad. They were on semi-shaky ground after the business with the rose thief.

Jenni squeezed into the kitchenette and double-checked for biscuits. She looked disappointed, but then there were only fig rolls left in the biscuit tin as Ned had already discovered and she clearly wasn't that desperate, yet.

'I fink it were Theo that put in that ad.'

'Yeah, you're probably right,' replied Ned. 'One of his little games designed to throw a spanner in the works.'

Bringing his tea back to his desk, he saw the last person in the queue was leaving the office.

'Okay then, what have we got? Anything worth having?' he asked.

There was a period of intense paper shuffling.

'Not really, Boss.' Willow waved a tendril over her pile. 'Some of the same old complaints. Mr Briggs says his neighbour keeps stealing bricks out of his wall and putting them on the other side, but you know Mr Briggs. He has that syndrome.'

It was a polite way of saying Mr Briggs was as mad

as a box of frogs and his neighbours were actually the kindest, most generous people you've ever met. They'd enclosed Mr Briggs's little cottage within their gardens to keep him safe.

'Mr Briggs made it to the thief-catchers office? By himself?'

'No. Mrs Moffet was with him.'

Mrs Moffet was one of the kindly neighbours.

'Right, well send all that paperwork over to Neeps at *The Daily Blag*. Say thank you very much for the publicity. Here are the replies and explain that the person who placed the original ad will cover the cost of printing these,' instructed Ned.

'Why do you fink Theo bovver'd, Boss? S'not exactly a major fing.'

'Theo likes to be petty. He finds all kinds of ways of getting into your head, Jenni. Sometimes by doing lots of small, silly things like this so you spend all your time looking out for the next little thing and then bam! He drops the giant hammer.'

'Whose giant hammer?'

'It's a metaphor, Jenni.'

'Oh,' replied Jenni darkly. She didn't like metaphors. 'So he's just doing this for a laff?'

'More or less.'

Sparks was flashing a complicated pattern.

'Yor not wrong there, mate,' replied Jenni.

Ned declined to find out what was flashed. He already knew Theo was a lowlife.

'Apart from these informative snippets, do we have any fresh cases?' he asked.

Joe picked up the clipboard to check. He was very attached to the clipboard. Ned wondered if it made him feel important and useful. Joe took his time, checking the list and lifting the page just in case any recent information had been added since he last looked.

'Nothing new to report, Boss,' he said.

Ned sighed. He could do with a simple crime.

'We could always go catch Jimmy Fingers again, offer 'im that job wot the Emperor said about,' suggested Jenni.

'Can do. Only I don't think he will need catching. He's probably still at the Druid Grove. Theo's muscle did a bit of a number on him.'

Ned left instructions for Willow, Sparks and Joe to firmly shut all doors and windows if they were to leave the office. He hoped Theo wouldn't stoop to it, but he had dabbled in pyrotechnics in the past. It would be a real shame if an attack on Ned resulted in the burning down of The Noose.

As ever, Jenni accompanied Ned, and they headed to the Druid Grove. Despite druidic power not being claimed felt calming and she always enjoyed visiting.

There was a new druid at the welcome desk that Ned didn't recognise.

'We've come to visit Jimmy Fingers.'

The new druid, a young man with far too much long luxurious hair, ran a manicured finger down the ledger.

'Sorry, there's no one of that name here.'

Ned cast about in his memory to find Fingers' actual name.

'Er… what about James Laforny?'

'Ward two, bed eleven,' replied the druid with a smile containing multiple bright white teeth.

Ned nodded his thanks and strode off to the inner sanctum, Jenni scampering alongside.

'He were a bit too good looking, weren't he?' she said.

'Dunno, didn't notice.'

'Them teef, and that 'air. It were well nice.'

'Probably just some young model hiding out for a while, letting the heat die down on the illicit affair he had with Judge Michaels' wife.'

'That's ever so spific, Boss.'

'It was in one of the reports.'

'You gonna shop 'im?' Jenni wondered.

Ned shook his head as he pushed the door open to ward two. It was only a third full, and they found Fingers easily enough. He had three female druids laughing at something he'd just said.

'Spinks.'

'Fingers. Mind if we have a brief chat?'

'Ladies, duty calls. We'll talk later?'

The druids glided away after each one had touched Fingers lightly on the arm or leg.

'How do you always do that?' wondered Ned aloud.

'What can I say? I'm great with people,' said Fingers.

'Well that's good because the Empress, may she live forever and ever, wants you to become Lower Circle.'

Fingers held himself very still. Ned could almost see the cogs whirring as the con artist weighed up the pros.

'What's the catch?' Fingers asked finally.

'No catch. Legalise some of your business and help the Empress rebuild our trading relationships. It's win-win.'

Fingers was silent for a long time, nodding to himself before he spoke.

'Long live the Empress.'

Chapter 36

Ned was about to congratulate himself on a job well done when he recognised an undead figure in the groveyard.

'Mr Simms? What are you doing here?'

'Ah, Mr Spinks. I have the next item for you.'

'You're kidding, right? We only just delivered that last one.' Ned wanted to shout but didn't want to make a scene. That would be unprofessional. He leaned in menacingly to the solicitor and poked him in the chest. 'It better not be for the same person.'

'Yeah, we ain't the runners,' complained Jenni, who had been listening.

Mr Simms smoothed what was left of his hair across his pate.

'I'm afraid this item is in fact for our Empress. And it needs to be delivered today between seven and nine pm.'

'That's specific. Wait… that's when the coronation banquet is happening. How am I supposed to do that?' Ned asked in disbelief. Despite thinking he would, he hadn't received an invitation.

'You don't have an invitation?' Mr Simms sounded surprised. As surprised as a dead man can sound.

'No. Do you?'

Mr Simms shook his head and reached into his briefcase.

'Nevertheless, you must deliver the Fork of Plenty to the Empress, may she live for ever and ever, between seven and nine pm, or else.' He passed the utensil over to Ned who took it reluctantly. 'Look on the bright side, Mr Spinks, there is only one magical item left after this delivery and then you will have fulfilled the requirements of your inheritance.'

Ned was turning the fork over and over in his hand. He could smell the most amazing roast chicken dinner with sage and onion stuffing and golden, crispy roasted potatoes, buttery and peppery carrot and swede mash with real gravy and more crispy roasted parsnips, broccoli and peas so green they glowed and a huge Yorkshire pudding with delicate crunch on the outside, yet soft on the inside, the perfect bowl for that gravy.

'Boss? You awright?'

'Mhm?' Ned swallowed and tried to clear his mind. His stomach rumbled appreciatively. Mr Simms had gone.

'You've stood there for like five minutes or summink. I fink yor acktually drooling. Lemme see this fing.' Jenni took the fork out of Ned's hand, but for her, it was only a way of getting food from plate to mouth. She tucked it into Ned's shirt pocket. 'You okay, Boss?'

'Yes, I... Jenni? When did we last eat? That fork just tempted me with an incredible roast dinner. Like something Ma Bowl would make for you. I could taste everything. It was so good. I'm famished.'

'You got all that from the fork? Weird, I got nuffink. Yor probably 'ungry cos of the 'angover. You wanna sausage sarnie or summink, Boss?'

'That sounds perfect. Then we can figure out how to get me into this dinner tonight.'

'Can't you just turn up? They let you in last time.'

'Yeah, but I was supposed to be at the ball and that was only because Fred passed by. I am not risking him being on duty to bail us out. And tonight is an enormous deal. It's a state dinner.'

'Steak? Why's that a big deal?'

'State, not steak. It means there will be dignitaries from neighbouring countries and top religious officials. Important people. At least, people who have enough power to be important, anyway.'

'So Theo will be there?'

'Yes. And if I can get in to the dinner, up near the top table to watch him, I can make sure there are no unexpected surprises.' Ned tapped a finger to his lips. 'Come on. We must know someone who is being invited? What about Kendra here?'

'Nah, the druids don't get invited to fings.'

'Why not?'

'Cos…' The answer dawned on Jenni and she swore.

'Jenni? Because what?'

'Cos Momma K represents all the fae and associated wotsits like the Druid Grove at state functions. Most nominations can't be bovvered to go to the 'uman fingys. No offence. So Momma K does it all for 'em.'

Ned smiled in relief.

'Well, that's that sorted. I'll ask Momma K if I can be her guest. Come on. Let's grab something to eat before we travel through to the fae realm. It's close to here.' Ned set off to find the nearest sausage sarnie vendor whilst Jenni traipsed behind him.

After demolishing his food and half of Jenni's, Ned finally realised his sprite wasn't very spritely.

'Jenni? Is everything alright?'

She sighed.

'I ain't 'zactly told you everyfink.'

Ned waited.

'I said no to me wings, and you knows Momma K has a lovely pair so she's probably seeing that as a right kick in the teef cos me being her daughter and everyfink and then… there's the ovver fing.'

'Go on,' coaxed Ned.

'I gave up the frone and I ain't 'ad chance to talk to 'er 'bout it.'

It took Ned a moment to translate *frone*. He'd always known Jenni was Momma K's daughter, but he thought it was more an all-fae-are-my-children scenario rather than a direct descendant in line for the throne scenario. His trusty sidekick was royalty.

'Um…' Ned wasn't really sure what to say. He was bowled over that Jenni had chosen this life she had here with him and the thief-catchers over a position of power in the fae realm. He tried to rally. 'Look, are you alright going to see Momma K? I can manage without you if you've got some… er… paperwork or something to catch up on.'

'I appreciate the fawt, Boss, but I gotta go wiv you. She'll probably take your first born in a deal if I'm not there.'

Ned nodded, then the details of what Jenni actually said percolated through.

'My first what?' He wasn't sure if she was joking or not.

'C'mon, we ain't got long and she might need some convincing.'

Chapter 37

Ned always felt some trepidation when dealing with Momma K, but this time it was tenfold. If she didn't say yes to him being her plus one, then short of breaking the doors down, he was out of ideas on how to get to the dinner.

'Just be polite and give 'er yor gift. You got a gift, right?' asked Jenni.

Ned panicked, then remembered the sugar snails in his inside left pocket. Kendra had given them to him as he was leaving the druid infirmary. She'd said they were good for crunching but they had looked way too life like for Ned to try them. He was also pretty dismissive of replacing bean with sugar. It was an insane idea. Pulling the bag out, he was glad to see the snails were intact, their little shells still shiny and pearlescent.

'Wossat?'

'My gift.'

'Fair enuff. C'mon, she's in the lemon grove.'

Ned didn't ask how Jenni knew or why there was lemon grove. He supposed everyone had to make lemonade.

Momma K was inspecting a harvest of lemons and the poor pixie holding the basket was shaking so hard that the fruits were at risk of falling out.

'Wat ya want?' Momma K didn't even bother to turn around.

'Momma K, I brought you a gift,' said Ned.

The petite fairy spun gracefully, her dreadlocks chiming as the tiny charms in them danced. She gazed at

Ned for a long moment, saying nothing and then regally extended one hand. He placed the bag of sugar snails into her palm. It looked huge.

'Wat ya bring me, catcher-man?' she asked in a delighted voice, moving the bag in her hand and hearing it chink slightly.

'Sugar snails. They're very… whimsical.'

Momma K opened the bag and peered inside. She took one of the sugar snails and placed it in her mouth, crunching with glee. Merriment pranced in her eyes as she regarded Ned, ignoring her daughter completely.

'Wat ya want?' she repeated the question, softer this time.

'I er… I want, I mean, I'd like to be your um… plus one, please. At the coronation dinner, I mean. If you'll have me, that is.'

Momma K's brow creased in confusion, then she laid a small hand on Ned's arm.

'Ya no invited? Ya poor ting. Sure ya want ta see? 'E be dere and 'e no good fo' da city. 'E no good fo' she.'

'I know. I need to be there because I have to deliver this.' Ned reached into a different pocket this time and brought out the fork. 'It's the Fork of Plenty. I have to give it to Rose. Griff said.'

Momma K had been listening to Ned with a quizzical expression on her face, but when he mentioned Griff's name, her eyes slanted and she smiled slyly.

'Ya want ta take me to da feast ya gat to change. Ya no wear dat.' She clicked her fingers at his clothes in distaste.

'Of course, anything. I can wear my dress uniform if you like. It's clean.' Ned was sixty percent sure it was clean, but he couldn't remember when it was last laundered.

'No chil', dat na good fo' me. Me tink me send ya sometink. Sometink long.'

Ned blinked. Long didn't sound too bad.

'Okay, great. Where shall I meet you?'

Momma K glanced at the still trembling pixie and the lemon basket.

'Me lemon coach will pick ya up at seven. Doh be late. Me no wait fo' ya.'

'No, of course. I mean, yes I will,' stammered Ned, amazed that sugared snails had secured him the invitation he needed.

Momma K glided away, leaving the lemon pixie to gratefully put down her basket and release a deep breath.

'Did you not want to talk to her?' Ned asked Jenni, surprised that she'd been ignored by her mum.

'Don't matta. Come on, let's see wot she sends. Bet it has a codpiece.'

'What?' Ned groaned and scrambled after Jenni, his mind racing. He hadn't considered the implications of a codpiece.

They exited the fae realm without incident, but one step into the real world and had a strong yearning for Rose. All his worries and fears for her crashed over him.

'Yeah, sorry about that,' said Jenni.

'What?'

'When you go in the realm, anyfink wot yor worried about goes away, but when you come out again, it all comes back double wallop. S'not fair. I shoulda said. Sorry, Boss.'

'It's alright. I'll get through.' Ned tried not to dwell on his dark thoughts and instead began prepping his pipe. After a few puffs, he could talk again. 'You think the outfit will already be there?'

'Momma K don't mess about wiv fashion. She loves it. There might be ruffs.'

Ned wasn't convinced if Jenni was joking or not. He was only vaguely sure he knew what ruffs were, so it was with some trepidation that he headed upstairs to his room once they got home.

There was something laid out on his bed, so he took a deep breath and went to investigate. It was a pair of black trousers and a red shirt with a sheen to it. No codpiece. Exhaling, Ned held up the shirt to the mirror and figured it was better than yellow or green. The shade made him look sharper somehow. Like it pulled out hidden hues in his eyes and hair. Stepping back a step, he tripped over something. Looking down, he saw a pair of boots.

Dropping the shirt back on the bed, he reverentially picked up one of the new boots. They were Gunningtons. The leather was so soft and that hand-finished turning - it was exquisite. Gunningtons had to be built around the individual foot for that perfect fit. They were the boots Ned dreamed of.

Hardly daring to breathe he shook off his old boots and carefully put a foot into the new one. It was like wearing thousand gold bit gloves for your feet. Shaking his head to himself, he walked a few steps and luxuriated in the comfort and support they gave his feet.

There was a loud whistle of appreciation from the doorway. Jenni was checking out the Gunningtons.

'They fit!' said Ned in amazement.

'O corse they fit.'

'But how? Gunningtons have to be built around your foot. Everyone knows that.' Ned looked down. 'Wait. Does this mean there is someone out there who has the same feet as me?'

Jenni sniggered.

'Nah. It just means Momma K got the measure of you is all. She's good at that. Wot else did you get?'

'Oh, a shirt and some trousers. But the boots, Jenni, the boots.' Ned let out a radiant smile and didn't notice Jenni leaving him to it.

In the end, Ned got ready too early and spent forty-five minutes picking his fingernails, wondering whether he ought to have something to eat before he left, but fighting with the nerves in his stomach that voted firmly against the idea. Jenni had gone out, wishing him the best of luck. She had said something about having plans with Willow and Joe that may or may not have involved a game of skittles. Ned hadn't been listening. He was window-watching, wondering what on earth a lemon coach looked like.

When a giant lemon rolled down the street on huge golden wheels, he had his answer. He was about to hurry out the door when he remembered the fork, so he dashed back inside and the lemon was about to roll away as he grabbed the door handle sticking out the pith.

'Ya late.'

'I forgot the fork.' Ned looked around in interest as he got in. The inside of the lemon gave the impression of being juicy with almost bouncy seats and an intense citrus aroma, but everything was held in place by Momma K's magic. There was no way anyone would be juicing this fruit. 'This is amazing.'

Momma K chuckled and there was a cascade of twinkly noises. Ned gaped as he regarded the fae queen. She had dressed to impress, wearing a glowing white lacy dress that looked like a spider had spun it. Knowing Momma K, it probably had. Her wings had been tinted red to match Ned's shirt, and her usual dreadlocks were now gorgeous curls that hung in bouncy ringlets.

'Wow! You look incredible.'

Momma K smiled and inclined her head at recognition of his compliment. They spent the rest of the brief journey in silence. Ned casting about for something to say but dismissing each topic. But at least it kept his mind occupied until the lemon coach passed through the palace gates and the butterflies took over.

It was Rose's coronation dinner. She would be busy impressing visiting dignitaries and would have no time for him, but he hoped that, as Momma K's plus one, he would be sat nearby. If not, he'd have to think of an ingenious way to get the fork to her without drawing everyone's attention. Then, of course, there was his brother to cope with.

Ned clambered out of the lemon and remembered to offer his arm to Momma K. She tinkled with laughter and graciously touched his arm with her hand whilst she fluttered beside him. She was smaller than Jenni and would have looked tiny next to him if she had stood. As it was, her wings moved the fabric of his shirt, setting off the shimmer so it seemed to transform under the lights.

Feeling some confidence ooze back into him with each step in his perfect Gunningtons, Ned held his head up high as they were announced into the ballroom. As was customary there was a lull in conversation at the announcement of each new guest, but this time the silence stretched as guests desperately tried to place the dashing man beside Momma K.

There was a rapid rustle of whispers as someone finally twigged it was Ned and passed it along. Ned watched in amusement as recognition dawned and facial expressions either turned impressed or sneering. He followed the whisper as it reached the newly named empress, who stood on the other side of the ballroom wearing a shimmering golden dress and simple circlet in her hair.

Rose's beautiful brown eyes sought him out and the tiniest of smiles lifted the corners of her pink lips. Ned's heart thudded so loud he was sure the rest of the room could hear it, and it was only the stiff pinch from Momma K's fingers that drew him back to where he was and who he was with.

'Come chil', let's go find our seats.' She steered Ned closer and closer to the top end of the table, and he was both thrilled and terrified to see they were seated at the immediate right of the Emperor with Momma K next to Rose.

He could easily get Rose the Fork of Plenty at this rate. Glancing across, his jaw clenched as he saw Theo wearing some ridiculous purple ensemble and sporting an oiled goatee. That had to be a stick on. He didn't have it last time Ned had seen him.

Theo saw Ned and did a double-take. For the first time in a long time, he looked worried, so Ned took some small comfort. Hopefully being across from the table to his brother, he could avoid any direct conversation. And being Momma K's plus one would mean that Momma K would protect him from any deadly missiles or poisons his brother might attempt.

The last of the guests arrived, and a gong announced the imminent service of dinner. Everyone took their seats, looking forward to the culinary delights of Ma Bowl and her bevy of kitchen staff.

Ned thought even Theo wouldn't be able to ruin dinner for him. All he had to do was ignore the man, concentrate on being a great guest for Momma K and get the fork to Rose.

The Empress was the last to sit and as she took her place, the servants danced. At least it looked like a dance to Ned. Some darted in with wine and water whilst others whisked in various delicacies based on each guest's likes and dislikes. He was impressed to find mini Yorkshire puddings with medium-rare slivers of roast beef on his plate. He glanced sideways at Momma K's dish, then quickly averted his eyes. There had been a lot of legs. He didn't want to know what those legs were attached to.

Nobody started eating until Rose picked up her fork, then everyone tucked in with gusto. Watching her pick at the food in front of her, Ned could feel sadness emanating from her. *She's hating all this*, he thought. Without thinking about it, he stood up and walked past Momma K's chair until he was beside Rose. Crouching down, he pulled the Fork of Plenty out of his pocket.

'Another present from Griff,' he whispered.

'Ned! Go back to your seat,' hissed Rose, trying to see if anyone was looking. The entire room was riveted.

'You look so sad. You're not alone, you know. I'm here for you.'

'Ned, please.'

The pleading note in Rose's voice took Ned aback as he pushed the fork close to her hand and for the briefest moment their fingers touched. An instant warmth bloomed inside him and his stomach skipped. She moved her hand away but didn't take the fork from him. Breathing in her heady cinnamon perfume, he returned to his seat with the cutlery and tried to stop the shake in his hands that threatened to spill his water.

'Ya a fool, catcher-man. A love-drunk fool.'

Ned looked at Momma K, expecting a frown, but

she was smiling at him. She patted him on the shoulder and went back to her delicacy. Ned tried to do the same but his stomach was skittering all over the place and his eavesdropping talents kept bringing him snatches of conversation peppered with his name. In the end, he only managed half a Yorkshire pudding and made a mental note to thank Ma Bowl next time he popped in the kitchen.

He refused to look across the table at his brother, despite feeling his eyes boring into him.

Chapter 38

Ned had hoped Rose would talk to him, but she seemed to be studiously ignoring him. He thought he would be able to reach past Momma K and pass her the fork but was then worried it might get cleared away between courses, so he waited for the main to be served.

It was roasted everything. A vast range of meats, some fish, every vegetable that could conceivably be roasted and a few that probably shouldn't have been attempted. Ma Bowl had gone all out.

Ned saw Momma K glancing at him from time to time and he knew he needed to get this cutlery delivered, so he cleared his throat, trying to think of something to say to Rose.

'Darling, you ought to try this.' Theo had a piece of roasted meat on his fork and was holding it out to Rose.

Ned watched while she looked at him coolly before taking it and resting it on the side of her plate. She wasn't eating and her wineglass was untouched.

Momma K tutted. She put down her utensils and flew up out and over her chair until she was hovering behind Ned.

'Change place catcher-man. Me want ta talk to dis lovely person.' Momma K gazed adoringly at the man they had sat Ned next to. It was some dignitary or other, he'd told Ned his name, which Ned had promptly forgotten.

In his haste to get up, Ned knocked the table with his knee hard and caused all the tableware to dance a little. A couple of glasses toppled over, and some cutlery fell to the floor, including some of Rose's.

Ned scrambled over to the side of Rose, trying to be quicker than the servants.

'Here, take this one. It's from Griff,' he whispered as he pressed in into her hand before he was shushed back to his seat by servants who deftly cleared up the mess.

He glanced at Rose and saw that she was holding the Fork of Plenty tight, a look of wonder in her eyes. Ned wondered what meal she was imagining, and some of his appetite returned. He helped himself to a couple of nearby dishes and tucked in with a sense of achievement. Another magical item delivered.

It seemed that visiting dignitaries didn't really eat because, before Ned even had a chance to go back for thirds, the servants were clearing the plates and bringing out delicate sugar bowls and spoons.

Theo had given up trying to entice Rose with titbits and was instead showing off to the women next to him. Ned felt a little guilty. He did not recognise her either. He looked up and down the table and realised that he barely recognised anyone except Madame Silk and Jimmy Fingers who were seated at the other end.

Fingers looked at ease, which was more than could be said for Ned. He had been stopped at the last minute by Momma K from wiping his greasy fingers on his trousers twice now, and apparently he'd used the wrong knife to butter his roll. Contemplating the sugar bowl in front of him, he wondered whether the guests knew they were edible. They tasted like nothing and weren't worth the effort, but he remembered Ma Bowl teasing him once with one and him being convinced for days that she could eat glass. He'd been younger then.

They placed a tiny slice of chocolate cake and a

delicate curl of ice cream inside his bowl. Ned waited, but nothing else was forthcoming, so he grabbed a spoon.

'Not that one,' whispered Rose and she took up another spoon that looked exactly the same to Ned, but he switched, pleased that she was finally talking to him.

He scooped up the entire desert in one go, caught Rose's eye, and scoffed the lot. She tried to smother her giggle but couldn't hide her shaking shoulders.

'My love, are you okay?' Theo clicked his fingers importantly to summon a servant, but no one paid him any attention, and Rose just waved his faux concern away.

Feeling like he'd won a point, Ned allowed himself to relax a little until the gong rang again and conversation seemed to buzz along the table.

'What's happening now?' Ned whispered to Momma K.

'It time fo' dancing,' she replied delightedly, but Ned's heart sank. He wasn't a great dancer, and he doubted the toffs at this so-called party knew the dippy duck or the firefly hoop-la.

At some hidden signal, everyone stood, and Rose led the guests into the third best meeting room. Another bevy of servants swirled around offering brandy or port.

Ned looked for the musicians but there weren't any.

'You sure we're dancing?' he asked Momma K, and she just tinkled with laughter.

Sipping his brandy, the back of his ears burning, Ned felt a little hard done by. It wasn't his fault he didn't know how these things worked. This was his first formal palace dinner.

The gong sounded again and Rose led the way back into the dining room. Only this time there was no sign of the tables and chairs.

Ned let out an impressed whistle. That had been fast. And now he could see the band at the top end of the room. He was semi-relieved to see there was a fiddle. He should be able to move to fiddle music. Hopefully Momma K wasn't much of a dancer.

'Dis me favourite bit. Me love dancin.'

So much for that, thought Ned gloomily. But he didn't have to worry. Momma K was an important person in her own right and there were plenty of toadies desperate to dance with her. Ned was jostled out of the way. He spied Jimmy Fingers and went over to speak with him.

'Jimmy, how's it going?' said Ned.

'Not bad, Spinks. Can't beat a slap-up meal for your first official job, eh?'

Ned lowered his voice. 'Has Theo recognised you?'

'Nah. The druids did good work and I heal fast,' replied Jimmy.

'Good, good. Did you make it to the meetings?' Ned was keen to find out how Fat Norris had taken the replacement and whether things had gone Rose's way.

'Yeah. It was alright. Your girl did good. Got 'em all in line. And Norris blustered a bit. But between you and me, he was happy to be well out of it. You should've seen…' Jimmy was interrupted by a buxom blonde who wanted to dance with him, so Ned watched as the former con artist shrugged helplessly and allowed himself to be led away.

Ned wondered what it was he should've seen. Time was running out for his brother to add too many more spanners. They'd sorted out the fake scroll, replaced the incompetent trade official, and Fourteen had been renamed Rose. All she had to do was get through tomorrow's coronation and be approved by the gods.

There. That was it. Ned's stomach plunged, and he broke out in a cold sweat. What if Theo had made a deal with one of the gods? He'd taken out a contract with a fear demon for the hell of it. A deal with a god was nothing. There were plenty of innocents in Theo's path he could sacrifice.

Ned had to talk to Rose, warn her of what was coming next. He craned his neck to look for her in the crowd, not realising he was stepping further and further out into the ballroom. Turning in frustration, he bumped right into her as the band began playing a slow waltz.

'Dance with me?' Rose asked as Ned instinctively took her hand and cupped his other around her waist.

The two of them moved in time with the music, their awareness of other people in the room having faded away.

'You look beautiful,' Ned said.

'As you are handsome. This colour suits you.'

'That was all down to Momma K.'

'I'm glad you're here. I'm sorry I couldn't invite you but…'

'It's okay. I'm no one.'

Rose's face wrinkled in disagreement.

'No one to these people here, I mean. Not to you,' he explained.

'No, not to me.'

The two moved closer, Ned holding Rose's hand against his chest and their hips pressed together, swaying in time to the music.

'I need to warn you.'

Rose looked up at him, her huge brown eyes like liquid bowls of chocolate Ned wanted to dive into. He shook his head slightly to clear his thoughts.

'Watch out tomorrow. I have this horrible feeling Theo has done something.'

Rose took a deep breath, pressing her body even closer to him, and Ned thought his knees might give way.

'He can't stop the coronation. It is written.'

'But the fake scroll. Have you confronted him about it yet?'

'No, I… I got all the trade agreements, Ned. I did it.' Pride shone in her eyes. Ned grinned at her.

'I knew you'd do it. You're amazing.'

Before Rose could reply, there was a tap on Ned's shoulder.

'Mind if I cut in, Eddie. After all, she is my fiancée.'

It was Theo. Ned looked past him at the dance floor. Nobody else was dancing, they were all watching him and Rose. They hadn't even noticed they'd become the centre of everyone's attention. Ned let go at once and he saw Rose's mask return. The Empress stood in front of him so he made a weak leg and moved back, letting his brother whisk the love of his life away from him.

'I need a drink.'

'Me taught so.' Momma K held out a glass of something which Ned knocked back in one. 'No worry, catcher-man. Tis in de stars. Ya victory be worth de great sacrifice ya make.' She smiled encouragingly at him, but it did little to lift Ned's spirits.

Chapter 39

Theo sat in a high-backed chair before the fireplace, fingers steepled, an invoice on his knee. *The Daily Blag* had sent him a bill for the printing of all the waste of time answers the citizens of Roshaven had given the Thief-Catchers. He'd pay it, eventually. But for now, he was annoyed at his brother for shifting this expensive annoyance back his way. Things were not going exactly as he had planned and the empress had ignored him for most of the evening. His brother had kept trying to give her a fork. A fork, for gods sake. It must be one of Griff's pathetic gifts. Either that or his brother had some strange notions on gift-giving which might well be the case, considering the company he kept. Theo smirked as he remembered cutting in on Ned's dance. He'd put him in his place then.

The corners of the room darkened and Theo felt fear tickle the back of his head.

'What do you want?' he asked, trying to keep the quake out of his voice.

There was no reply but the tension in the room lifted and when Theo looked behind him there was only a piece of parchment on the floor. He went to pick it up.

'Gods sake!' He balled the parchment up and chucked it into fireplace.

'Everything alright, Sir?' One of Theo's men poked his head round the door, alerted by the angry shout.

'No, everything is not alright. Barbas just informed me the contract has been paid, in full. That bloody sprite did something, she must have.'

'Anything I can do, Sir?' asked the lackey.

'Yes, order the job. Make sure it's finished by tonight and everyone is well aware what will happen if they don't do what they're told. You can chop bits off for all I care, just get it done.' Theo breathed heavily through his nose. 'And get me my scholar, now!'

He spent the next five minutes pacing, his thoughts whirling. The fake scroll wasn't going to work for much longer and someone had stolen the fabricated original from Theo's paperwork. It was that slippery eel they'd almost caught the other night. Theo was sure he'd been at Ned's place of work, hiding somewhere. He'd been so close to catching him.

And then today, that woman had sailed into their meeting with the trade partners. All that careful planning, arm twisting and blackmailing had been for naught as she'd somehow won them all over. She'd fired that slob of an overseer and put an ambitious young man in place who would do the work. Shame the slave children story hadn't worked. At least he was getting paid for the cargo.

There was a nervous knocking at the door and a skinny bespectacled man let himself in.

'You wanted to see me, Sir?' His voice quavered.

'Have you found something I can use?' Theo barked.

'Well, actually, there is reference to an ancient rite. Seems to have gone out of fashion but it was never changed so if they adhere to the law, they'll have to agree.' The scholar beamed short-sightedly at Theo.

'Agree to what?'

'Ah yes, well that's the interesting bit you see. Take a look at this.' The man passed an old book to Theo, holding it open at the relevant place and pointed with a finger. 'See here? This could be useful.'

Theo peered down and after reading a little, he took the book from the scholar and smiled, continuing to read.

'Yes, yes. This could work for us. This could be just the thing.'

Chapter 40

Ned had spent the morning trying to explain to Jenni what he thought Theo was planning to do next.

'So you reckon 'e ain't gonna do nuffink today, at the actual coronation?'

'No, because he wants Rose to be officially the Emperor. He knows we had a hand in stealing the fake scroll and that we'll have told her how to disprove it. So now he's got to come up with something else.'

'But a priest? Ain't they meant to be 'oly and stuff?'

'Meant to be,' muttered Ned. He and Jenni were chatting over tea and toast at his place as they waited to go to the coronation. This time there was no invitation, and as officials of the city, the thief-catchers had a designated spot in the grand hall.

The grand hall was also the ballroom, which was also the best meeting room so adaptations had to be made. It was achieved successfully with several sets of different coloured curtains, seasonal ceramics and an impressive array of rugs.

'Which one?' asked Jenni.

'Which one, what?'

'Which priest do you fink it will be?'

Ned puffed out his cheeks as he considered the options, although it was tough to keep track of all the religious symbols that appeared and disappeared in Roshaven. There were many religions to choose from, not including the druids and the fae. Fae gods were numerous and ever changing. He was pretty sure even Jenni didn't know all of them. There was some confusion about whether Momma K was one or just a conduit to them. When you have magical powers, Gods aren't quite so impressive.

Sister Eustacia represented the dominant religion of a higher power. It was unclear what exactly this power ran, but all its believers agreed it was something on high. It required no sacrifices and had specific cakes for certain religious days, making it very popular. Sister Eustacia preached togetherness and forgiveness. After a religious exchange program, she'd taken on an honorary position within the druid grove and enjoyed herself so much she'd never left.

There were the monks of Schway who attended regular chanting sermons at regular times. So regular in fact that many residents of Roshaven ran their clocks by them. It was said if a clock ran to Schway time then you'd never be late. Ned dismissed them as being harmless hummers.

It was the old-fashioned fire and brimstone priests that he worried about. Human sacrifice had gone out of fashion a few decades ago, but that didn't mean that the odd missing person hadn't ended up speaking to the gods. These gods were more or less nameless. Except for the Great God Unami they were old, vengeful, blood thirsty and powerful, speaking to rage and righteousness. These were the ones who would appreciate an acolyte like Theo. If his actions were done in their name, well, there would be a little extra power behind those acts.

The only other priest was Father John. He looked after the sick animals and was scoffed at by most citizens in Roshaven for looking after the pigeons and rats, but he was also one of the most well-known religious figures as he healed pets. Father John appeared to talk to the animals and Ned had on more than one occasion requested his presence at a crime scene which included a rabid animal.

'Fire and brimstoners I reckon,' Ned said, having completed his inner survey of all the candidates.

Jenni just nodded. But then she'd often told him she thought religion was a waste of time. Her opinion was that if you didn't honour nature, then it was going to slap you, end of. That was all the faith you needed as far as she was concerned.

'It'll be tomorrow,' Ned went on. 'The day after the coronation, when Theo can try to enforce that fake scroll.'

'But Rose's already nixed it all, ain't she?'

'That's what I mean. She'll try to discredit the scroll to get out of the engagement, and that's when Theo will pull his trump card.'

'Ow do we get round that one then?'

'Without knowing who it's going to be, there's not a lot we can do. Get our eyes on as many fire and brimstoners as we can, see if any of them are acting more suspiciously than usual. And we need to try and make sure we're in the room when Theo shows his hand, if possible.'

'And when we know who it is?'

'Undo whatever promise Theo made.' Ned tried to sound as confident as possible so that Jenni wouldn't have any doubts, but privately he was far from certain they would be able to overturn anything Theo had used to blackmail a priest. 'And we're going to have to come up with a way to delay the wedding.'

'Already sorted that.'

Ned blinked at Jenni in surprise.

'How?'

'Me 'n Willow were finking 'bout that and we

reckon we use the dress excuse.' Jenni puffed her chest out with pride, but Ned had no idea what she was talking about.

'The dress excuse?'

'Yeah, you know.' She affected a high pitch voice and tiptoed around the kitchen. 'Oh lordy, lordy, I ain't got nuffink to wear. Oh lordy, lordy, I gotta go shopping. Oh lordy, lordy I ain't got no shoes wot match.' She had to stop because she was laughing so much.

Ned couldn't help but join in. It took a few moments before he regained his composure.

'You really think that will work?'

'Way I 'eard it, the wedding dress is the most important cloves you'll ever wear, so it's a fact that you 'ave to 'ave the exact right one. It's fing. The law.'

Ned was almost certain it wasn't a law of the land, but if it were a socially accepted rule, he would definitely support Rose's right to take as long as she wanted to find the right dress.

'Maybe we could get you and Willow assigned as security for this top-secret mission. You know, to drag things out a bit more and keep things hush hush so Theo doesn't know that you're not even getting a dress.'

'I fink she'll wanna look at least.'

'Why? It's not like she's going to end up marrying Theo. That is not happening.'

'Granted, but…'

'But what?'

Jenni shuffled her feet but was saved from answering as the other thief-catchers arrived. They were all getting ready at Ned's house so he could make sure Joe didn't forget to shine his boots, Willow didn't forget to wear clothes, and Sparks didn't forget that he couldn't invite all his friends and relations.

Ned made a mental note to ask Jenni exactly what she was talking about later. Right now, he had coronation to attend.

It had been with some pride that Ned had arrived with his thief-catchers at the palace. Everyone's boots were shiny and whilst the thief-catchers didn't have set livery, everyone had their thief-catcher badge prominently displayed.

It was with dismay that when they had been shown their seats, Ned found himself stuck behind a pillar, so couldn't get a good look at anything without craning his neck uncomfortably and impeding someone else. And it had been with a great deal of boredom that they had been waiting the past two hours. Apparently, it was a requirement to gather all the guests well before the coronation was due to begin. For no legitimate reason at all, as far as Ned could tell.

Although now that Ned thought about it, it was probably so that people got excited when the ceremony started, although it too was probably long and boring.

A gong sounded, and the crowd hushed. Gongs were very popular in Roshaven. They'd tried ringing bells but found that most Roshaven citizens dismissed bells as being harbingers of angels. And no-one wanted an angel on their shoulder. They were heavy, and the feathers made you sneeze.

A procession began. Several of the high priests from the different religious orders, the two Highs looking as proud as punch, Upper Circle, Lower Circle and Stalls. Then, after a small gap, came Rose.

There was a collective ooh from the masses. Their Empress wore a simple white gown with a square neckline and a fine net train attached to the shoulders. The train had tiny roses in all different colours embroidered upon it.

Ned craned his neck as much as possible in order to watch Rose walk past him. She looked so young, and yet there was an air of determination about her. For a moment, Ned imagined the half-brick of courage hidden in her dress somewhere, and it made him chuckle. Then a sharp elbow in his ribs reminded him he was encroaching on someone else's viewing, so he reluctantly drew back.

Stupid pillar.

Ned could still hear the coronation speeches and investments. First, each priest gave a speech about their gods and how they looked down upon, protected, and valued the Imperial City of Roshaven. Then the members of the Imperial Cabinet each gave a small speech on their dedication to their own role and how it uniquely supported the Empress and the City. Jimmy Fingers did well considering he hadn't been in his official role for long. Then there were the prayers. All seventeen of them, each one long and sonorous, repeating the same declarations in overly fulsome language, but phrased to meet the requirements of each different deity.

Ned was just nodding off when he heard Rose's voice. She was accepting the duties of empress and pledging her life to her empire. As her words rang out clear and strong, Ned felt a huge sense of relief and pride. That was his empress. And Theo hadn't stopped her coronation. Her words seemed to infect the rest of the crowd as everyone sat a little straighter and prouder in their chairs.

'Wot 'appens now, Boss?' whispered Jenni. 'Are we 'aving a party?'

'No, that was the other night.'

'So wot about the wedding and stuff?'

Ned couldn't answer. He didn't know.

'Citizens of Roshaven. I give you your empress, Rose Mahcitsea, first of her name. Long may she rule,' declared the High Right.

Ned glowed. A beautiful name for a beautiful woman and roses were, of course, the symbol of the city of Roshaven, famed for its rose garden. Some people might think it a little cliched, but Ned thought it suited her perfectly.

The crowd seemed to hesitate. The old saying had been *may he live for ever and ever,* but this was new. One of the Highs was less impressed with the hesitation and banged his staff on the floor.

'LONG MAY SHE RULE!' came the triumphant reply.

Unseen by Ned and his catchers, a priest had placed the imperial crown on Rose's head so now as she walked past, the jewels caught the light and twinkled. Her eyes flitted sideways at Ned so briefly he wasn't sure he'd even seen it, but it tugged at his heart. He wanted nothing more than to leap over and protect her fiercely from anyone and everything.

'You alright, Boss?'

Ned looked down at Jenni and realised he was clenching his fists.

One of the Highs' spoke.

'Our empress, long may she rule, will now proceed throughout her city and greet her citizens. Go forth and cheer, for today is a day of celebration.'

But Ned and his catchers couldn't go anywhere because they were wedged in behind the pillar and had to wait for the slow caterpillar of people to wend their way out of the room, the palace and into the courtyard.

'Do you fink we can watch 'er? If we find a place somewhere?' Jenni asked as they finally got out into the street.

'You can try.' Ned looked up at the flags and banners. 'I'm going to head home. It's been a full on few days and we still don't know for sure what Theo will do next.'

There was a brief whispered discussion among the catchers.

'Awright, Boss. Me and the ovvers are gonna go see wot we can see. Catch you laters.'

Ned watched his team for a moment, then turned and walked away from the crowds and the excitement. He was glad the coronation had gone without a hitch for Rose and adored her new name, but he was also sad, sad that she seemed further from him than ever before.

Chapter 41

Rose was humming. She'd eaten her breakfast with the Fork of Plenty, drank her morning tea from the Cup of Good Luck, and was wearing the Ring of Truth on a chain around her neck. It was tucked away from curious eyes. Each item had bolstered her confidence and increased her positivity about solving the issues ahead. The Half-Brick of Courage also nestled in a hidden pocket within her dress. Thank goodness for voluminous skirts.

Today she would face Theo and debunk his ancient scroll. Then, with her new trading routes in place and Jimmy Fingers fulfilling the role of Lower Circle, she could concentrate on Roshaven and her imperial rule.

Rose went over in her head the things Ned had told her were wrong with the scroll and was certain she had memorised them. She was looking forward to the expression on Theo's face when he realised he'd lost. She only wished Ned could be there to see it too.

With a jaunty step and the urge to whistle pushed down, Rose walked to the second-best meeting room, where today's talks would be held. Ma Bowl had said there would be honey cakes, and she wanted to get there before the Highs ate them all.

Schooling her face to an emotionless mask, Empress Rose nodded at the palace guards to announce her.

She entered into a room of men. The Stalls and the Upper Circle were nowhere to be seen, and Rose's heart sank as she realised she was the only woman. Granted, she was also the Empress but... *never mind,* she told herself, lifting her chin a little higher. Rose glided to her chair and was delighted to see a small plate of honey cakes had been set to one side for her.

She took her seat and waited for a cup of tea to be poured for her before helping herself to a honey cake and watching the priests in the room. There had been a few respectful nods in her direction, but no-one took her cue and sat down. Or indeed stopped their terribly important conversations with each other.

Rose coughed, but it had little effect. The High Right stood close to her chair, so she leant over and banged his staff on the floor. To his credit, the High Right was only slightly taken aback and recovered quickly, ushering everyone to their seats before calling the meeting to order.

'We are gathered here today to discuss the Empress's upcoming nuptials to Theodore Michel de Silverthorpe, Lord of Fidelia. My empress, would you like to begin?'

Rose nodded her thanks to the High and took a moment to look around the table at the faces before her. The half-brick was a reassuring bulk on her lap.

'It has come to my attention that there are some discrepancies with the ancient scroll from Fidelia...'

Before she could get any further, one of the older priests interrupted.

'The scroll has been ratified and sanctified by the Great God Unami.'

'And by the gods of war, plenty and good weather.'

'And by the gods of home, hearth and hops.'

One by one, each of the priests chipped in with their religious approval for Theo's fake scroll until they came to Father John. There was a long pause. The priest looked at Rose with a great sadness in his eyes and in a broken voice added his support to the fake document.

Rose caught the faintest smile flit across Theo's face and despite the Half-Brick of Courage, her insides squirmed with fear, anger and worry all at once.

The High Right leaned in and whispered urgently in her ear.

'My Empress, we cannot ignore the might of every religious order in Roshaven. We'll be excommunicated from everyone. If you choose to stand against religion and ignore their sanctity, the balance of religious power will shift. They will no longer recognise the Imperial Crown as having any authority.'

The High Left added his own hiss.

'One person cannot stand up to that much religion, not even an empress. You must please the majority to maintain the balance. Your reign needs religious acceptance.'

Rose muttered out of the corner of her mouth.

'Someone is blackmailing the priests, surely? I will not let that continue.'

Both Highs nodded, trying to show how considerably they agreed with the wisdom of their empress without acknowledging the enormous elephant in the room.

'With this much support, I think we can be confident that the Gods are smiling down upon this union and we should set a date as quickly as possible.' Theo oozed intense satisfaction. 'How about Thursday?'

It was Tuesday.

There was instant uproar from the Highs, each one trying to out-shout the other at how an imperial wedding couldn't possibly be put together in two days. Rose let them get it all out before she spoke.

'Whilst I am, of course, excited to be wed, I'm

afraid there are several purification rituals that must be observed. Isn't that right, Father John?'

The priest looked like she had caught him between a rock and a very hard place.

'Yes, extremely important,' he wheezed.

'And then there are the prayers, meditations, fasting and tributes to be paid to each house of worship. How many was it at last count, Father John?'

The priest warmed a little to his role.

'Several dozen, my empress - several dozen at least.'

'And we cannot rush these things. You understand, Lord Theo. It's a matter of *religion*.'

Every religious eyeball turned towards Theo and he conceded with a sharp nod of his head.

'Finally, there is the most important decision of all. The dress.' Rose allowed herself to gush. 'I simply must have the most perfect wedding gown.'

Several of the more fatherly priests got a little misty eyed and there were a few *hear, hears* from the collective.

'Father John, you will still be my spiritual advisor, won't you? As we prepare for this auspicious event?'

The priest looked like a dwarf realising he'd walked into a troll bar by mistake. He couldn't speak but managed a weak nod.

'Wonderful,' said Rose. 'Once we have worked everything out, then I shall gladly let you know the timeframe, Lord Theo. It may be that you even have time to return to Fidelia for a spell.'

Rose gave Theo her most beguiling smile and could see from the look in his eye that he almost believed her.

'If there is nothing else?' The Empress looked to her Highs for their guidance and the High Left banged his staff.

'Meeting adjourned.'

'Oh, Father John. A moment, please?' Rose called as the priests gathered themselves to leave.

Father John sank back into his chair and avoided looking at anyone, especially Theo as the room slowly emptied. Eventually it was just Rose, the Highs and the priest.

'Honey cake?' Rose offered innocently.

Chapter 42

Ned hurried after Fred, heart pounding in his chest. It was most unlike the affable young palace guard not to indulge in random conversation. To remain on point and keep a sense of urgency meant something was very, very wrong.

He almost wanted to run, but he didn't want to start a panic on the streets. There had been an incident a few years ago that had involved a rolling cheese and a running scullery maid that turned into the biggest, ugliest, most competitive foot race Roshaven had ever seen. No-one won that cheese though. A story for another time. Ned tried to think what new drama his brother might have cooked up, but when his brain wouldn't stop going off on tangents that ended up with Rose missing a limb, he told it to shut up.

Gritting his teeth and attempting to look authoritative Ned marched through the palace gates and leaving Fred in the courtyard, headed for the second-best meeting room. His heart stopped thudding at a thousand miles an hour when he saw Rose was safe and sound. He clocked the Highs and Father John. That was odd. Why was Father John there?

'I came as soon as Fred found me. How can I help?' Ned asked.

'Tea?' asked Rose in a pleasant voice but not waiting for the answer. She poured one anyway. 'I requested your presence, Mr Spinks, because I'd like a lawkeeper present when I talk to Father John. For clarity.'

Ned looked more closely at Father John and noted the beads of sweat on his brow, his ashen complexion and a look of quiet desperation in his eyes. Not knowing what was expected of him, Ned took out his notebook and pencil. There was one vacant chair on Rose's side of the table, so he risked it and sat. A High placed the tea the empress had made in front of him and Ned wanted to pinch himself to make sure all this was real, but suppressed the urge. Mostly. He ground his heel onto the top of his other foot. Just to be sure. Definitely real.

'Now that everyone is here, Father John, can you tell me why the different religious factions of Roshaven are in complete agreement?'

Ned blinked. He'd obviously missed something huge. The numerous religious orders in Roshaven never agreed on anything.

'Well, I... I'm not sure I'm the best qualified priest to answer...' Father John reached a finger to his collar and tried to loosen it.

'Maybe not. There are priests of a higher standing than you, but you at least, feel some remorse for what you're being made to do, don't you?' asked Rose.

'Yes, I mean... I shouldn't...' Father John looked to Ned for some support but seeing as Ned didn't know what was going on, he couldn't help. Nevertheless, he tried.

'Can I ask a question?' Ned half raised a hand. 'What exactly is it Father John is meant to have done?'

The High Left answered.

'This morning the entire religious body representing the great and many gods worshipped in Roshaven, categorically supported, endorsed and approved the veracity of the Lord of Fidelia's ancient scroll.'

Ned's inner dictionary took a moment to catch up.

He felt slightly sick and a little panicked.

'They think the scroll is real? Why?' asked Ned.

'That is what Father John is going to explain, aren't you Father?' Rose smiled sweetly at the priest.

The Father said nothing for a while, and Ned was just wondering whether he ought to start questioning the suspect when the man finally spoke in a very soft voice.

'He killed my goldfish. Not something that might bother many people, but me and Goldy had been together nigh on twenty years. He was long-lived for a goldfish. Always happy to see me return from prayer and a constant companion. Brutally murdered, you understand?'

Rose's face was a picture of compassion.

'Of course, a tragedy and one that brings you great pain, but why support him after such an act?' she asked.

Ned didn't want to hear any more. Killing pets was not a new trick for his brother. It was usually the first in a long line of much worse atrocities. Especially for women who spurned his advances. Theo wasn't used to being told no.

'He killed Goldy because I wouldn't agree to ratify the false document,' Father John continued. 'Then he dognapped Bertie, my golden retriever, and he... he...' The priest swallowed the lump in his throat. 'He sent me his ear and told me he would return Bertie to me in pieces if I didn't stand with him.'

Rose looked at Ned with horror in her eyes. He knew what she was thinking. *What kind of man mutilates a dog?* Ned was ashamed to know that if Father John had had a rabbit, it would have been a full pelt returned to him and very possibly a rabbit pie.

'Father John? My condolences for your goldfish and we will, of course, do everything in our power to get the rest of Bertie back to you safe and sound. But I have a few questions, if that's alright?' Ned asked gently, and the priest nodded. 'Meaning no offence to you, your animals or your holy order, why you? Why choose you to torture in this way? You are not the most powerful religious leader in our city.'

Ned saw his question had sparked in everyone's mind as both Rose and the Highs leaned forward to better hear the priest's reply.

'I am, predominantly, a spiritual leader for those who love animals and it's true, I also spend a lot of time looking after the spiritual health of pets.' Father John focused on Ned. 'People, as a rule, love their pets. Consider them to be part of the family and want the best for them. Especially during times of sickness. I give what comfort I can, you understand?'

Ned had no idea, having never owned a pet in his life, but he nodded sympathetically.

'The other priests, they are all animal lovers in one way or another. Whether it's a learned raven or a sacred serpent, their daughter's gerbil or wife's turtle. There's a lot of love for animals.' Father John wasn't looking at Ned anymore. His gaze had turned inward. 'The Lord of Fidelia hasn't just pet nabbed Bertie. He's taken one or more animal from all our spiritual leaders. He found the thing that connected us all—not a deity or a prayer, but a pet. He took the pets.' This time Father John turned to Rose and leaned towards her. 'If I don't ratify that fakery, he will kill them all. I cannot bear to have that bloodshed on my hands. I cannot.'

The priest was now chalky white and shaky. Rose murmured to the High Right, who hurried over to the far corner of the room where a decanter of brandy stood. He returned with a large tumbler for the priest and encouraged the holy man to drink.

Rose gestured for Ned to walk a few paces away with her.

'Does that sound like your brother?' she asked.

'I wish it didn't but, yeah, it does.'

'What do I do? I can't have the lives of every priest's beloved pet on my conscience. I won't.'

'Are you… do you have any, er… pets?' asked Ned.

'No. I don't like the smell. But the fact remains that I don't want innocent bloodshed on my reign, whether it be human or animal. Your brother has crossed a line here, Ned. What should we do?'

Despite the severity of the situation, Ned's heart skipped a beat as Rose asked him what they should do. He knew he shouldn't dwell on his faint hope they could somehow have a relationship once they had dealt with Theo, but he couldn't help it. She was his silver lining. He thought quickly.

'If I could borrow Lower Circle, Fingers I mean, then his network together with mine should be able to locate and liberate the animals. We'll have to be quick though, act tonight. Theo might just kill them all, anyway. Was he in the meeting when you singled the Father out?'

'Yes. Yes, he was.'

'Then we've got to move fast. Really fast. Can you send Fingers to me? As soon as possible?'

'Of course, do you need anything else?'

Ned wished he could ask for a good luck kiss, but instead he grabbed Rose's hand and gave it a quick squeeze before hurrying back to HQ. He had a menagerie to save.

Chapter 43

Ned sprang into action as soon as he got to the Thief Catcher's office.

'Sparks, go chase Fingers, tell him to hurry. Willow, can you reach out to your plantwork? Tell them we're looking for a large collection of animals that shouldn't be together. Joe, I want you to take a message to Queen Ann, we're going to need her help too. Jenni, will you start a chain letter?'

Sparks had already left by the time Ned had finished speaking and Willow was leaning out of the window in deep discussion with the lichen on the roof tiles. Ned grabbed a piece of paper from his desk, double checked it wasn't anything important, then wrote his note.

My liege. We humbly request your help in finding a hidden collection of animals. Father John has been blackmailed and many lives are at risk. Send word in the usual way. Payment will be doubled. Yours in city, Spinks.

'I don't understand,' said Joe after having read the words over Ned's shoulder.

'My brother has stolen an eclectic bunch of pets that belong to the priests of Roshaven. If we don't save the animals, he is going to force the priests to ratify the fake scroll that dictates Empress Rose must marry him and hand over her empire and power. He's already tried to take all our trade away from us and killed a goldfish. We don't have a lot of time because he was at the meeting with the priests when Rose saw Father John was the weak link and pushed. If we don't hurry, they will murder multiple innocent pet lives. Got it?'

Joe's mouth gaped, and he nodded, one hand out for the note.

'Good lad. Now take that to Queen Ann as fast as possible, then get back here.' Ned ordered Joe out of the office and for once the lad scarpered off at speed.

'Wot do you want in the chain?' asked Jenni.

'Ask if anyone has seen a dozen or so animals together. Best keep it simple.'

Jenni nodded. They had both experienced a bad chain letter when the sacred mushrooms had been stolen. It hadn't been pleasant.

A magical chain letter worked on the premise that all words have power, some more than others, but every combination is essentially a magic spell waiting to be cast. With the right focus, direction and buckets of intent, it was possible to pass a brief message across an extensive network of fae in seconds. There was a general agreement that they only used a chain letter in matters of extreme emergency like stolen children and substantiated death threats. Ned had a feeling Momma K might demand payment for this request, but you could never tell. Most people had a soft spot for one animal or another.

'Give us a boost?' Jenni nodded towards Ned's power well.

He took a deep breath and focused on opening his well. Once he could sense the energy brimming on the edge, he touched Jenni's shoulder and willed the magic to flow into her. There was some resistance - there always was. Magic had a certain wilful wildness to it and fought being told what to do, especially in large quantities. Jenni would have to direct the power carefully.

Ned watched Jenni steady herself as through the connection she felt the power within her grasp and concentrated.

Any groups of animals in one place wot shouldn't be, report in. LOD.

There was no need to say who had sent the chain letter. Each magical wielder had their own signature and fae were a lot more sensitive to that sort of thing than human magic users. Every fae would realise the message came from Jenni and therefore know who to reply to.

Ned had felt the surge, so he let go of Jenni and tottered backwards a few steps. She'd drained his power well, and judging by the hollowness he was experiencing, she'd taken most of his own stored magic too.

'What does LOD mean?' Ned asked before bending to put his hands on his knees and catch himself. He was exhausted, like he'd just run to Fidelia and back.

'Life or Death. 'Ere Boss, you awright? Did I take everyfink?'

Ned wheezed a little, still fighting the aftereffects.

'Yeah, pretty much. It's not a problem. Remind me to refill the well when we next go out.' Ned cast an eye over the sprite. 'What about yourself? Still got juice?'

Jenni concentrated.

'I got summink, but it's slipping and sliding, I ain't got the hang of it all yet. You know, cos of the strictions and stuff.'

Ned nodded. He thought Jenni was effectively now a level one magic student. All non-fae started with knowing they had access to magic but were unable to use it without training. So far in his life, Ned had only ever drawn on his innate magical powers when Rose had been in danger. But he could use the magic he took and stored from power wells for small, everyday things with a lot of practice and luck. It didn't always work. Judging by how empty he felt, it would take a few replenishes to get the well and the quick draw spells back up to full strength.

'We'd better make a stop once we know where the animals are being kept.'

'Ow long do you reckon we'll have to wait?'

'Hard to say…' Ned was cut off by the return of Sparks, who was flashing so rapidly it was difficult to tell whether he was trying to communicate or he was just really, really excited. 'Jenni, a little help?'

Jenni focused on the bug for a few moments.

'Ohhh, well yeah that is pretty impressive.'

Ned waited a moment.

'What? What's impressive?'

'Oh yeah, right. Sparky-boy says Fingers can speak lightbug, ain't that good? I never 'eard of an 'uman who could do that afore.'

'And? Is Fingers mobilising?'

Jenni focused again. She had to ask Sparks to slow down three times before she got the entire message.

'Yeah, Fingers is gonna have a word. See wots wot on 'is end. And 'e told Sparks e'd send bug word if 'e 'eard owt.'

Ned had to give it to Jimmy Fingers. He was a man of hidden depths. Being able to speak firefly though, how did that help with his forgery business? Ned filed that question for another time.

Next to report in was Joe. He was breathing hard, like he'd just been running.

'Everything alright, lad?' Ned didn't think he'd offended Queen Ann, but you never could tell with beggars.

Joe nodded and gulped in some air.

'I didn't want to miss anything.' A few more gasps. 'It's exciting.'

'That's one word for it,' muttered Ned.

Willow pulled herself back into the room.

'Sorry, Boss. There's not much clear plant chat about a large group of animals. I mean, obviously, they are enemies, so I've got multiple options. I can try to narrow it down a bit more, but it will take time.'

'Thanks, Willow. See what you can do.'

There was a patter of footsteps from the corridor and a small grubby child appeared. It darted to Ned and pressed a piece of paper into his hand, then bolted back the way it had come.

'Score one for the beggars,' murmured Ned as he read the note. 'Let's go. We're headed for the docks.'

Ned mused on the note. It meant that the animals were more than likely in a warehouse. The rose thief had proven you could hide anything down at the rent-a-warehouse section.

'There's a lot of buildings down there, Boss. It'll take us ages to search 'em all.' Jenni sounded doubtful.

'According to the note, we need to check the large one at the end of Hangar Lane. There's been some recent activity there involving many new animal deliveries.'

Ned led the thief-catchers and strode confidently from The Noose toward the docks. He made a slight detour to the nearest well and refilled, setting up a couple of stun spells. It took him three goes before he could get the magic to behave because his mind was all over the place. Thinking about what was at stake for Rose helped him to focus, and once magically armed, Ned felt more confident.

'Eyes open, Catchers. We don't know what we're

walking into, but my brother is no fool. Those animals will be guarded in some way or other. Look after your buddy.'

The thief-catchers operated on a buddy system when going into a potentially dangerous situation. Joe and Willow kept an eye out for each other whilst Ned and Jenni did the same. Sparks was the alarm system who called for back-up. There was some uncertainty about what exactly that back-up would be, but it was available.

Suddenly a swarm of bees surrounded Sparks, buzzing excitedly. Jenni translated for the others.

'Fingers says end warehouse, Hangar Lane, a lot of four-legged recent activity.'

Ned was impressed. Fingers could talk to bees too? Absolutely the right person for Rose to have looking after her trade and busy docks. Or soon-to-be-busy docks.

At the top of Hangar Lane, Ned attempted a plan of action. Or he would have if a lookout on the road hadn't noticed them and signalled for attack. There was an explosion of whizzing spells and harmful missiles through the air. The thief-catchers huddled behind some handily stacked crates.

Chapter 44

Ned considered their options. A suicide run to the warehouse. Stay where they were and hope Theo's men got bored. Jenni popping. Each option felt equally flawed, and Jenni's magic was ropey at best at the moment.

'Jenni, how do you feel about popping?' Ned had to ask.

'I ain't sure, Boss. But you could do it, if you tried 'ard.'

Ned let out a bark of laughter. There was no way he could disappear himself and reappear in a warehouse a good five hundred metres away.

'Nah, you're right. You ain't the stones for this kinda fing. You're just a washed-up catcher wot got the chiefdom frew dumb luck more'an anyfink else. Wot a waste.'

Ned felt his ears turning red and his skin prickling. He knew what Jenni was trying to do. Extremes of emotion usually punched through his spellcasting block. Jenni leaned in a little closer.

'You sit there and you fink that it's all gonna get sorted. But 'ow? Yor bruvver is gonna take yor kingdom and yor girl and there's nuffink you can do about it. 'E wins. Again. Just like 'e always does. And you? You lose. Loser.'

The other catchers were dumbstruck. They'd never heard Jenni talk to Ned like that before, and they hadn't cottoned on to what she was trying to do.

'You didn't protect Griff. You didn't protect yor old

girl back in Fidelia. Now yor failing Rose. And wot you got to show for? Nuffink. Can't even do a simple spell. Why you even 'ere? Ain't a bottle of scumble got yor name on it?'

The Griff comment had lit a fire in Ned. He clenched his fists and glared at Jenni. But she wasn't done.

'You are gonna end up alone like some old, fat, washed up nobody. No friends, no family, nuffink. And yor bruvver is gonna be Emperor, have loads of babies and ruin that woman wot luvs you. E'll break 'er in half, like that!' Jenni clicked her fingers and there was a blinding explosion of light that no-one was prepared for.

The stench was layered and Ned was sure he'd stepped in something squishy. He tried to focus his light-blinded eyes on his surroundings and flinched as a cold nose pressed itself into his palm. It belonged to a dog wearing a bandage where one of its ears should have been. They were inside the warehouse, surrounded by the stolen animals.

For a moment there was stillness. The dogs recovered first, barking loudly–half excited, half in intruder mode. The cats hissed and arched their backs. Birds chirruped in alarm, flitting away out of danger, as did the multiple smaller squeaking rodents.

Fending off wagging tails and wet noses, Ned processed what he'd done. He'd popped, taking all the catchers with him. Willow looked greener than usual, and Joe had added to the distinct aroma with that morning's breakfast. Jenni blinked twice and looked about.

'Good work, Boss. Very impressive.' She cast a sideways glance at Ned as if to say, *we awright?*

Ned gave her a quick nod. He was still smarting

from her truths, but she'd done what needed to be done and now they were inside. Getting the animals out would hopefully be easier.

'Anyone got any ideas?' he asked the others whilst trying to shush the dogs before a guard investigated.

'It stinks in here, Boss,' said Joe.

'Yeah, thanks for that, kid.'

'No, I mean, beneath the animals and that. I think there's a sewer grate in here.'

Ned perked up. They used some warehouses for livestock, and if this was one of those, it would have sewer access.

'Spread out, see if you can find the hatch. But quietly. We don't want Theo's goons realising we're in here.'

The thief-catchers searched across the warehouse floor, trying to avoid squishy parts and animal tails, but the animals got excited too and the dogs started barking joyfully again.

'What's all that racket?' A voice could be heard from outside the building. Everyone froze.

'Probably just fighting over a rabbit or something,' replied another person.

'Do you think we should check it out?

'Nah, it's fine.'

Ned breathed out and held his finger to his lips whilst looking at the other catchers. Joe responded by waving madly.

'Over here, I've found it,' whispered Joe, pointing down. There were a pair of double doors set into the floor and the sewer stink was stronger.

Joe and Ned heaved them open, and the stench made their eyes water, so much so that Joe lost hold of his door and it clanged shut. Everyone hunched and held their breath. Easy to do in the environment.

'I definitely heard something this time,' said the first voice. The other person sighed loudly.

'If you want to check it out, be my guest, but if any of those animals run out the door, it's your neck on the line.'

'Then it's yours if they're escaping somehow,' retorted the more conscientious lackey, but he made no move open the warehouse and check within.

'Here, use some of this,' offered Willow as she handed out something sticky and yellow. 'It's tree sap, it will stop the smell if you rub some under your nose. Don't worry, this one doesn't harden.'

The catchers all applied and things got instantly better.

'Okay, new problem. How are we going to get all these animals down there without too much fuss?' asked Ned.

'You could just ask 'em,' suggested Jenni.

Nobody offered any other ideas, so Ned cleared his throat and addressed the menagerie.

'Attention animals. We have a way out of here to take you back to your homes, but it involves climbing down this hole into the sewers. We need to be quiet. We don't want to alert the guards. So I want you to form an orderly queue and follow us.'

He did not expect his words to have any effect, but incredibly the animals lined up. In twos, which was handy. Two snakes wound themselves around Willow, who didn't seem the slightest bit concerned, whilst the smaller rodents like the hamsters and gerbils found pockets to ride in. Ned himself had a mouse, gerbil and guinea pig.

'Is that everyone?' Ned looked around the

warehouse and noticed several cats who'd kept themselves apart. Whilst the dogs had pushed to the front and were eager to get going, the cats looked like they had paid no attention and had no plans to move.

'Don't worry about 'em, Boss,' said Jenni. 'Cats is cats. They'll leave when they wanna. So bloody minded.'

Ned dithered for a moment. He needed all the animals to return to their priests. Otherwise Rose wouldn't be able to make all the religious orders to denounce the ancient scroll.

'Alright, let's go people. And animals.' He waved his arms in a herding motion and watched the menagerie move. There was a great deal of yipping, yapping, meowing, barking, grunting, squeaking and chirping.

It was too much noise. The curious guard risked opening the door.

'Oi! Stop!' he yelled.

The dogs, pig and snakes had gone with Willow and Joe. Sparks was guiding the birds, ducks and terrapins. Ned and Jenni had the pockets of rodents and a few rabbits who were hopping alongside.

'Come on, move!' shouted Ned and the animals on legs ran.

As Ned clambered down the built-in ladder from the warehouse down to the sewer tunnel, a couple of shapes flitted over the head. He flinched and nearly yelled when one of the shapes used his shoulder as leverage for a better leap.

It was the cats. Not the guard trying to stop him. He did yelp, however, when a blasting spell ricochet off the sewer door and singed one of his eyebrows.

'Run!' he yelled, mis-stepping on the ladder and half falling the rest of the way down. He was battered and bruised, smelly and covered in poop of many kinds. He spied a broken broom handle in the sewer tunnel. Taking a tremendous risk, he clambered back up the short ladder and grabbed the first door. He swore loudly as a crossbow bolt thudded into the second door, mere millimetres from his fingers. The small animals in his pockets were chittering in panic and little claws had started scrabbling. With an almighty heave, Ned pulled the second door shut and threaded the broom handle through the sewer door handles. It would hold long enough for the catchers and animals to get out of there.

Ned breathed a sigh of relief and began jogging down the tunnel to catch up with the others. It was time to take these animals back home and get the signatures Rose needed to reject Theo's scroll.

Chapter 45

Ned decided that trying to deliver the individual animals to each owner would take too long, and he wanted to report back to Rose before Theo tried anything else.

It was well known that the priests from the different religious orders liked to gather of an afternoon to talk theology. Quite a few residents in Roshaven hedged their bets by visiting different churches, sermons, services and masses, but because the priests communicated regularly the religious messages were usually similar. It also meant the floating devout had more religious holidays.

Ned, his catchers and the animals headed for the Lower Barn. Despite its name, it was a very grand building, funded by the religions of Roshaven. As they arrived, they could hear the shouting from the outside. It had timbre.

'IT IS OUR WILL THAT YOU SOLVE THIS ISSUE WITH FATHER JOHN,' boomed a voice.

'We shall not tolerate you standing against Father John,' sang out another.

Ned pushed open the door cautiously. Gods could be tricky.

There were several nebulous shapes hovering above the ground, pulsing in different colours. Below them were arrayed the discretion of priests, and priestesses, of Roshaven. Every single eye and nebula swivelled to glare at the newcomers. Then they registered all the animals.

'Fluffy!'

'Oh, look at the state of your fur!'

'Mittens, here, girl.'

All the rodents from various thief-catcher pockets scurried to their masters, and the snakes unwound themselves from Willow's trunk. The cats allowed their servants to stroke them whilst the dogs were so happy to see their owners there were more than a few puddles.

A luminous cloud coalesced into the Great God Unami and strode towards Ned. Its translucent nostrils wrinkled as it registered the stench of the sewers. A brief flash of light and all the thief-catchers had freshly laundered clothes that smelled of roses.

'THANK YOU FOR RESCUING THE ANIMALS. LARGE SEGMENT OF FAITH YOU KNOW. BOTH CREATURE AND OWNER. FATHER JOHN FUNNELS MANY PRAYERS OUR WAY.'

Ned was a touch overwhelmed at being in such proximity to the Great God Unami. He was by no means a devout follower, but he knew the gods were, well, gods. He never expected to ever stand so close to one.

The Great God Unami's priest came over with a snake draped across his shoulders.

'Spinks, isn't it?'

Ned nodded.

'Thank you. For this.' The priest gestured at the animals. 'Your brother threatened to kill everything. We couldn't take the chance, you understand.'

Ned didn't. Not really.

'Why not just ask yor god to whack Theo for you?' Jenni had no problem asking.

The priest took on an indulgent tone.

'We don't pray to our Gods for our own fulfilment. We are the messengers of their almighty grace.'

'Sounds a bit flim flammy to me,' muttered Jenni,

eyeing up the celestial being standing next to her.

'Will you condemn the fake scroll now?' asked Ned.

'Of course,' replied the priest.

'Sign this then.' Jenni flourished her own paperwork. It was a document from the Empress citing all the evidence why the Lord of Fidelia's alleged ancient scroll was a phoney and had the names of all the religious leaders with space for signatures.

It took a good ten minutes to line up all the priests and priestesses to sign the document with the Great God Unami encouraging the illiterate to add their own marks.

'I still don't see why they didn't just flame 'im,' muttered Jenni. 'Supposed to be all-powerful wotsits or summink.'

The Great God Unami overheard and with a twinkle in his eye bent down to whisper something in Jenni's ear. Ned watched as Jenni reacted with a frown and then a grin. He was going to have to find out what the God said, but first they needed to get this signed declaration back to Rose.

'Where is Father John?' asked one religious leader.

'He's at the palace, with the Empress. She thought it would be wise for him to stay there while we looked for the animals, in case Theo tried anything else,' replied Ned.

'How did you find them?' piped up someone.

'I know people,' Ned replied with a grin as he and the thief-catchers left the pets to their owners and gods.

As soon as they were out of earshot, he leaned over to Jenni.

'So, what did the Great God Unami say?'

Jenni smirked.

'No, seriously Jenni, what did he say?'

'Oh, some flannel 'bout 'ow we is all drivers of our

own fate and it affects the cosmic balance or summink if they interfere too much.'

'Why did that make you smile?' asked Ned.

'Cos it means the Gods ain't all that more powerful than the fae. Momma K's gonna love that.'

Ned couldn't help smiling. She really would.

Chapter 46

It was a very different meeting this time. Rose blazed
with authority and self-confidence. She knew the ancient
scroll was a fake, and she had the expert advice to prove
it. The priests would no longer stand in her way. In fact,
many of them had approached her to shake her hand,
give thanks and in some cases, even praise Ned. A sure
sign that the theft of their pets had emotionally affected
them.

Ned couldn't be here at this meeting, despite Rose
arguing for it. The Highs had advised it would be too
flammable to have the two brothers in the same room,
plus with Ned came Jenni, and the priests, no matter how
thankful they were for their rescued pets, might be tetchy
around fae.

Theo was running late. No doubt trying to figure out
how he could pretend he knew nothing about the pet
thefts, thought Rose sourly. Finally, the door opened as
the Lord of Fidelia was announced.

Theo looked rumpled. As if he'd slept in his clothes,
or perhaps hadn't slept at all. Rose smiled on the inside.
They were going to win this one, she could feel it.

The priests had been swirling around the room,
coming together and drifting apart. Their current pattern
left Father John momentarily alone. Rose watched Theo
swoop towards him.

'I hear you have a few more animals to minster to
than normal, Father John,' Theo commented with a
sneer.

'Every creature is beloved by God. Even those that

live under rocks,' replied the priest.

Rose mentally congratulated the Father. That was fighting talk for a man of the cloth. She noted with interest as the back of Theo's ears reddened like his brother's did when angry or embarrassed.

It looked as if Theo was trying to come up with a rebuttal, but he failed and stalked away to the other side of the room where the tea was laid out.

Rose decided at that moment to take her place and call the meeting to order. The others filed to their seats, Theo trailing in last.

'I would like to open this meeting with the matter of the erroneous scroll discovered in Fidelia archives.' Rose focused on Theo and spoke unemotionally. 'The scroll has been tested and regrettably, my lord, I must inform you it is a fake. It holds no weight in this imperial court, has no legal standing, and its authenticity has been refuted by the religions of Roshaven. A report has been written. You each have a copy.' Rose gestured to the paper reports in front of each of them.

Only Theo was checking the report, and he was muttering under his breath as he read the evidence supplied by Jimmy Fingers. He gave little away if you didn't know what to look for, but the reddening ears were a clear sign to Rose that the Lord of Fidelia was fighting a strong emotional reaction. He cleared his throat.

'My deepest apologies for the unintended error. My archivists will be thoroughly punished for this lapse in judgement.' Theo inclined a stiff head in Rose's direction. 'My intentions towards you remain the same. Ancient scroll or no scroll. My hand is still extended in matrimony.' He leaned further forwards. 'With Fidelia and Roshaven linked, we'd be a mighty force to reckon with.'

'As much as we are flattered by your offer, my lord, we regretfully decline.' Rose was trying her best to fight her rising relief and happiness that she had escaped the clutches of this odious man.

But an evil glint had appeared in Theo's eyes, and he steepled his fingers for a moment, as if gathering his thoughts.

'Then I invoke the Right of Champion for your hand,' Theo declared, looking very much like the cat who got the cream.

There was an instant low hubbub as the priests and council members at the table reacted.

The High Left leaned into Rose.

'It's a fight to the death, my empress. Theo against your champion.'

'Do I have a champion?' whispered Rose, hoping fervently it was not one of the scrawny Highs holding a mostly ceremonial position.

The two Highs exchanged a glance, as if willing the other to be the one to tell her.

'Spit it out!' hissed Rose.

'The Emperor's traditional champion is the Chief Thief-Catcher, my empress.'

Rose went still. Ned was her champion. Ned had to fight his brother to the death, and she couldn't refuse the challenge if she didn't want to get married. She had to speak to him first, she couldn't make this decision by herself. Not when it affected them both.

'Do we have any time?' Rose asked in a low voice.

'Traditionally twelve hours to show up and fight, otherwise it's a forfeit.'

Rose addressed Theo coolly.

'By law, the Empress of Roshaven has twelve hours

to answer your ultimatum and either accept or stand with their champion. We shall reconvene in the Great Courtyard at sunset. Well within the twelve-hour window. Is this acceptable?' Rose hoped her voice wasn't shaking as much as she was.

'Sounds good to me.' Theo rose, ready to leave the meeting. 'Give Eddie my love, won't you?' He said with a smirk before leaving.

Rose's face was pale as she slumped in her chair. Would Ned risk fighting his own brother when he might lose and die? Did she even have the right to ask him to kill his brother for her? What frightened her the most was that she didn't know if she could ask in the first place.

'Get me my Chief Thief-Catcher now,' ordered Rose. 'I'll be in my study.' She swept out of the room, leaving her Highs, members of her council, and the discretion of priests to gossip and condemn the man she loved.

Chapter 47

Ned knocked on the door to the Empress's study. He wasn't sure what to expect, but he figured that if it had been good news, she would have met him somewhere more public. Unless she wanted to discuss... other things. That made his knees wobble. They'd been avoiding their relationship status ever since they got back from the quest that killed Griff.

'Come in.'

Rose was sitting by the fireplace and a blue-green flame danced in the grate until Ned drew closer, then it returned to the usual orangey red glow.

'Was that...?' Ned wasn't even sure what he was asking.

'An elemental? Yes. They named me.'

Ned didn't even know how to respond to that, so he just waited.

'Do you want some tea?'

He shook his head, aware that he wasn't making things easy for her, but he just wanted to know what the problem was - what new nightmare had Theo dreamt up?

Rose gestured to the empty chair across from her, and Ned was about to refuse when his fourth eye caught the utter misery emanating from her. His eye was wonky at best and usually only operated with a magical assist or in the presence of intense emotion. He quickly sat and reached out to take her hands in his.

She reluctantly drew them away from him and smoothed her skirts over her knees.

'The priests supported the illegality of the ancient

scroll, so we have squashed that power play,' she said.

'That's great news.' Ned could feel the but.

'But… there's been a development. The Lord of Fidelia has requested my hand in marriage by right of ancient duel. To the death.'

'Not yours? You're not going to fight him, are you?' Ned caught her slight head shake and exhaled in relief. 'Not that you can't hold your own. I've seen you fight.' His voice softened. 'You're amazing.'

'The Lord of Fidelia, Theo, will fight my champion.' Rose looked sadly at Ned. 'My Chief Thief-Catcher.'

Ned sat stunned for a moment.

'But… that's me.' He whispered, his mind racing. 'Hang on. Did you say to the death?'

Rose nodded.

'So I've got to kill him or you've got to marry him. And if I don't fight, you have to marry him anyway. And if I lose…'

'We both do.' Rose's bottom lip trembled, and a small sob escaped before she launched herself into his arms. She began sob-talking, but he could barely make out what she was saying, so he just held her and let the tears flow. His own mind was racing.

He and Theo had never seen eye to eye, drifting further and further apart as they got older and their career paths branched in opposite directions. That was the main reason Ned had moved to Roshaven. So he could start again without being under the criminal shadow of his family.

Ned was numb. He had to kill his brother to save his love. And to save Roshaven from being ruled by a megalomaniac.

Rose eventually stopped sobbing and pushed herself out of his embrace, back into her chair, grabbing a handful of tissues as she did so.

'I think I made your shoulder soggy,' she said in a small voice.

'It doesn't matter, it will dry.' Ned held her gaze for a moment before Rose cast her eyes downwards. He reached out and tipped her chin up so she was looking at him again. 'I take it you want me to fight or… or do you want to marry him?'

This was the chance for Rose to save Ned from having to kill his brother. She tried to speak, but her body failed her. She could not accept marriage to such a monster. Not even at the cost of destroying the man she loved.

Rose took a sip of her tea, now cold, but it helped her find her voice.

'I don't want to marry him. More than anything, I don't want to marry that man, but I can't ask it of you. I can't.'

Ned knelt in front of Rose and retook her hands in his again, bringing them to his lips and pressing a kiss to them.

'I would do anything for you. Anything. If this is the only way to be rid of him, to save you and our city, then I fight.'

Rose pressed her forehead against Neds, and he could feel her trembling. He breathed in her cinnamon perfume and became oddly calm and reassured. Despite murder being on the table, it seemed like the right thing to do. Slowly the two of them moved apart and Ned gave her hands a squeeze before he stood. He needed to pace.

'How long do I have?' he asked.

'Sunset in the Great Courtyard.'

Ned nodded. He had a little time to put matters in order.

'There are a few things I need to do. Messages to send and so forth. Will you be alright?'

Rose huffed a small laugh but said nothing. Ned understood. She had placed him in an impossible position. It was natural that she felt awful.

'I'll see you later.' He cupped his hand on the side of her face and gazed into her eyes, hoping that she saw the immense love he had for her. She pressed her cheek into his hand in response.

Ned had to pull himself away and walk out of the room. He needed to tell Jenni before she heard about it from someone else.

Chapter 48

Ned soon found out Jenni was looking for him at the same time he was looking for her. They spent a couple of hours going round in circles, checking in with people only to be told *they was just here,* which wasn't very helpful.

In the end Ned decided to wait for Jenni to turn up at HQ. She would eventually, hopefully before the fight. The other catchers were out on patrol, so it left Ned alone with his thoughts. He began pacing, trying to untangle how he felt.

He knew he loved Rose. He knew he didn't like his brother, was embarrassed and ashamed by his criminal dealings, and wished more than anything that he would change the direction of his life. But deep down, Ned didn't think he hated his brother. Why hadn't Theo just threatened Rose's safety in front of Ned? A reaction arrow through the heart could be explained and justified. Probably not to his parents, but to his own conscience at least.

Now he had to fight Theo. In public Ned was guessing. All it would take would be the slightest hint that this duel was happening and the entire city would come out to watch. Nothing like a fight to the death to bring people together.

Ned's pacing had adopted a complicated infinity pattern on the floor.

It had been a long time since he'd last fought Theo. Really, they'd been kids. Fingering the small scar above his left eyebrow, Ned remembered how his brother had retaliated at being beaten. No-one knew where he'd got the blade from, and it was only thanks to Ned's own quick reflexes and a thick sleeve that the cut above his eye hadn't been any deeper. He would have been blinded otherwise.

Ned had to assume that Theo would cheat if he could and resort to name calling. Well, that was fine. Ned had been putting up with his odious brother for his entire life. He wasn't about to lose his temper over some snide comments. He couldn't say the same for Jenni. There was a good chance she'd loose a fireball or two. He really needed to talk to her.

There was a clatter on the staircase. Ned's mood leapt, then fell. Jenni would never clatter on the staircase. The appearance of a plume confirmed it. It was just Fred.

'Hello, Fred. What can I do for you?' Ned's voice sounded calmer than he felt.

'Oh, Mr Spinks, Sir. I just heard the news, from our Brian, and I wanted to say that I'd be honoured to be your second.' Fred's earnest look was almost too much to bear.

'That's very kind of you, Fred, but I think I'm sorted.' He smiled at the young lad, trying to ease his mind. 'Was there anything else? A message?' His heart flopped at the thought of Rose sending him something. He was disappointed.

'No, Mr Spinks, Sir. Just me wanting to tell you that I'll be rooting for you as will all the lads from the Palace Guard and the gardeners and the handy-men and the carriage drivers and the kitchen staff and the groundsmen and those that do things but no-one really knows what it is. We're all for you, sir. Every one of us. And Ma Bowl said if you didn't win, she'd eat her own bowl and we all know that would never happen, so it's obvious.'

Ned thought he'd followed along pretty well, but the ending he was less sure about.

'Obvious?'

'Well, she's never going to eat her bowl, is she? So that means you're going to win, Mr Spinks, Sir. No doubt about it.'

'I appreciate the confidence, Fred. If there's nothing else, I need to prepare.'

Fred nodded solemnly but couldn't help himself.

'How are you going to prepare, Mr Spinks, Sir? Only our Brian said he'd never be able to kill me on purpose. although accidentally in the night would just be a tragedy like those plays that come to the city sometime. Brothers fighting is like something out of a saga, isn't it? Our Brian said it'll be the biggest event Roshaven has ever seen. Even bigger than that time the elephant escaped and trunkpaged down the High Street. Never forget that. An elephant!'

Once more Ned caught up with Fred's words whilst nodding in what he hoped was an appropriate fashion.

Fred bounced on his toes for a moment, as if he were double checking to make sure Ned wasn't about to say anything to him. The silence lengthened.

Ned cleared his throat, trying to figure out how he could get the young guard out of his office, but was spared as Fred began again.

'I'd better go back. I'm meant to be on duty, only our Brian said that at times of great need it was alright to take five minutes, nip off and nip back, so long as no-one notices you're gone and you shout *Alls Well* when you return whether it is or it isn't. It's comforting, you see,' Fred beamed.

'Very good. I'll see you later. In the courtyard.'

Fred nodded his head so vigorously his plumed helmet was in danger of flying off.

'Right you are, Mr Spinks, Sir. See you later.'

With a half wave, Fred bowed himself out of the room and began his clattering way back down the stairs.

Butterflies that had been thinking about going for it were now swirling round Ned's stomach in a violent storm. Where was Jenni? He needed to talk to her.

But next to arrive at the office were Willow and Joe.

'We just heard, on the grapevine. Everyone's rustling. Is it true? Are you really going to fight him?' Willow's foliage was fluttering.

'Fight who?' asked Jenni.

Ned groaned inwardly. Trust her to turn up at that exact moment.

'Ned's fighting his brother. To the death!' Joe explained.

'Wot?'

Sparks flashed in and whirled around everyone's head before flashing like crazy at Jenni.

'Yeah, in a min, Sparko.' Jenni fixed her gaze on Ned, but the firefly was distracting her. 'Sparky, mate, chill out for a minute, yeah? Boss, wot's going on?'

But Sparks was too agitated and flew back in front of Jenni's face, his light pulsing wildly. Jenni reacted instinctively and swatted him away. Sparks flew across the room and landed with a smack against the opposite wall.

Instantly Willow, Joe, and Ned rushed to their fallen comrade with Jenni half a step behind.

'Easy, give him some air. Are you alright, Sparks?' Ned asked the dazed bug.

Sparks' tail light flashed erratically twice before

slowly building to a continuous glow. Then it started beating out a rhythm.

'E'd 'eard yor fighting to the death and didn't believe it.' Jenni knelt down by the firefly. 'Sparks, mate, I'm sorry. I didn't know eiver. I didn't mean it.'

Sparks darkened for a moment, then his light buzzed so brightly it made the others cover their eyes.

'E says I'm forgiven,' Jenni explained in a small voice. Without looking up at Ned, she asked again. 'Wot's going on, Boss?'

Ned went to his drawer, pulled out the scumble and asked Joe to get four mugs. He waited until he'd poured out a dram for everyone, including a splash in the bottle top for Sparks.

'It's Theo's final plan. He lost the trading rights. Fingers saw to that. His ancient scroll got disproven, and we foiled his blackmail on the priests. He's lost, so in typical Theo style, he's gone for the jugular. In this case, mine. He's invoked something called Right of Champion to fight for Rose's hand. The High's confirmed its imperial law, old but still law. And the Chief Thief-Catcher is traditionally the Emperor's champion. Or in this case, the Empress's champion. So now we fight, to the death, this evening in the main courtyard. By now, it will be all over the city and I guess we'll have a few spectators. Everyone likes a fight, right?' He tried to laugh it off, but he could tell it fell weakly on the distraught ears of his team. 'I love her. I love this city.'

He held up his mug.

'To the best thief-catchers Roshaven has ever seen.'

The others echoed 'To the best!' and downed their scumble. Willow pushed out the toxins immediately through a fungal growth whilst Joe coughed and spluttered as the fiery alcohol travelled down his gullet.

Wheezing, he managed a weak smile. Jenni was licking her lips and double checking there wasn't any left in her mug as Sparks fizzed slightly. Ned watched him anxiously. A concussion plus scumble was not the best idea.

'Wot weapon you gonna choose?' asked Jenni.

Ned half shook his head. He hadn't fought his brother in years, but when they were growing up, they'd both had some sword training, done a bit of wrestling and archery. But that was all a long time ago.

'In a fight this big, the Highs will probably say we get to choose a weapon. It's been a long time since the Emperor - sorry Empress - has been challenged. I'll go with knives. That rules out any other blade.'

'Bit risky, though. 'E might pick pistols or summink.' Jenni said it with disdain. She didn't approve of killing sticks.

'He won't. He's a crap shot. It would be a waste of bullets and I'm good. At least I was.'

'Well, at least you know 'e won't choose magic, eh?'

Ned nodded his agreement, but Jenni's words had sent a chill down his spine. Of the two of them, Ned had manifested ability but had struggled his entire life with a magical block. It was rare indeed that he ever did magic on spec. A power well and pre-made spells were the best he could hope for. And he didn't think he'd be allowed to bring that into the duel. What if Theo had somehow gained some magical ability?

'Boss, what are you going to wear?' Willow asked tentatively.

Ned glanced down at his clothes. At least they were good boots.

'Could I suggest wearing this? Underneath I mean?'

Willow was holding out a woven tunic that had a greenish sheen to it.

Ned took the clothing and marvelled at how supple it felt.

'What is it?' he asked.

'It's a combination of hemp and jute. The two strongest plant materials. Woven together, they will provide some protection against a blade. From a glancing blow at least.'

'Right. Don't let him skewer me. Got it.' Ned had meant to lighten the mood, but his comment made the sap run from Willow's eyes.

As Ned put Willow's plant armour under his shirt, Joe stepped forward with a blade.

'I'd like you to have this, sir. It's a... a family heirloom.'

Ned looked at Joe sharply. His father had been an evil sorcerer, and his twin sister had tried to usurp Rose's throne.

'Don't worry, nothing but good mojo. What I mean is, it won't let you down. You aim and it will make it,' explained Joe.

'I can't use a spelled blade, lad. Where did you even get this from?' Ned wondered if Joe had been walking around Roshaven all this time, armed like this.

Jenni sniffed the blade.

'It ain't spelled. Like 'e said, mojo. Can't beat a good bit of mojo.' Jenni gave Joe a wink that had him grinning widely.

'I've been storing in the weapons cupboard, in case we ever needed it,' said Joe with a hint of pride in his voice.

'Fair enough.' Ned picked up the knife and noted the perfect balance. He felt a connection. This blade would always strike true, he just knew it.

'I fink we ought to walk down to the square. I'll get the gargoyles moving. We don't want any blighters trying to stick an arrow in you while yor fighting Theo. It's the sort of fing he'd do.'

'Yes, it is. Sparks? Are you up to sending a message?' asked Ned.

The firefly shook his fiery bum and threw a sharp salute. Shame no-one else could see it.

'I need you to ask Queen Ann if she'll keep an eye on things at ground level. We don't want any assassin blades ruining things.' Ned double checked with Jenni. 'They've got a bug translator over there, haven't they?

'Yep.'

'Go on then, Sparks. See you back at the square.' Ned looked fondly at his catchers. 'It's been an honour.'

'Yeah, well, it ain't over yet. Come on, let's go if we're going,' said Jenni.

'You go, I'll catch you up. I just need to grab something,' replied Ned, heading towards the weapons cupboard.

Jenni saw what he was doing and nodded in approval then stomped off, the other catchers falling in behind. Ned caught them up outside the Noose and all the way to the courtyard, Jenni peppered Ned with fighting advice.

'If 'e stands low, it means 'e's got a low centre of gravity and will swipe or try an' get you off balance.'

'Watch out if 'e leans, that means e's gonna kick yer, and that's not allowed neiver.'

'Look at 'is eyes, they'll tell yer where e's going. Don't pay no attention to 'is fists.'

'If 'e starts leaping round like a chicken, just watch 'im. E's trying to tire you out and you ain't falling for that.'

By the time she repeated the advice for the third time, Ned had to stop her.

'Jenni. I know how to fight. I know my brother. I got this.' He knew that when it came down to it, in a fight, thinking flew out the window and it was all down to how you reacted.

He must have sounded much more confident than he felt because Jenni stopped giving advice. They were almost there.

Ned heard a dull thrumming noise, but before he could work out what it was, they turned the corner, and a roar rang out throughout the courtyard. It looked like the entire population of Roshaven had come to bear witness. Troll stood next to dwarf. Fae mixed with human. There were mobile snack carts doing a roaring trade. Even Ma Bowl had come out of the kitchen, but she had bought her tall stool. The commoners were crammed in so tightly that the nobles–not that there were that many in Roshaven–had standing room only. The only person with a little space was the Empress, and she had both Highs, Fingers, and Madame Silk bunched up with her on a small platform. Ned's nerves ran the full gauntlet twice, heart thumping in his ears, stomach churning, and a strong desire to turn and run had to be quashed. Looking at Rose calmed his jitters a bit, and he took strength from his love for her.

Someone had been efficient. There was bunting and flags. Lights had been strung all around the courtyard and Spark's many friends and relations added to the glow. There was cheering from the crowd for Ned and boos for Theo, who was stood on the other side of the courtyard, surrounded by his minions.

A path was being made towards Ned. It was

Momma K.

'Momma K. I'm honoured to see you here,' he said.

'Is no honour in dis. Ya bruder fight ya and if he win, we all lose. No mercy, no quarta.' Momma K's voice was low and forceful.

'No pressure,' muttered Ned, as if he wasn't already feeling the pressure. He knew he'd be dead if Theo won.

Momma K exchanged a meaningful glance with Jenni, who returned a small nod.

'Oi, none of that.' Ned quailed under the fierce glare from the queen of the fae. 'No magical assistance. I have to do this. Just me.' Ned's honour was burning. He was a law-man, and if a life had to be taken, he would take it the right way. This fight would be between him and his brother with their weapons and skills. Nothing else. 'I love them.' He didn't need to explain to Momma K he meant Rose and Roshaven.

Momma K sagged into herself, some light going out of her aura.

'Me know ya do, boy. Me know.' She lightly touched his shoulder. 'But me root for ya. We all do.' Casting an arm over the gathered crowd it acted as a signal and the people began roaring, cheering, clapping and shouting Ned's name.

Ned could feel the backs of his ears reddening. As much as he was dreading what was about to happen, the fact the entire city was behind him made it slightly better. His half-smile slipped from his face when he saw the druids. They only had one medical station set up. Only the winner would need to be treated for his wounds.

A solemn drumbeat thrummed out into the crowd.

The Empress rose from her throne and walked to the front of her platform. Both High's followed and stood either side.

'The Challenger will approach,' announced a High, and amidst booing, Theo sauntered over.

'The Champion will approach,' announced the other High. Ned tried to ignore every fibre in his body that wanted to run far, far away and began walking towards them.

The crowd cheered and whistled and clapped. Jenni grabbed his hand, stopping Ned in his tracks.

'Don't die, Boss,' she said with a crooked smile. But Ned could only half-nod in response.

His legs felt like lead as they walked across the courtyard, and it seemed to him to take forever to reach the others.

'Lord Theodore Michel de Silverthorpe of Fidelia, you have challenged the Imperial throne to a duel for the hand of the Empress Rose. You may now withdraw if you so wish.'

Everyone held their breath.

'I do… not.'

There was a collective hiss from the crowd.

'Edmund Spinks, Chief Thief-Catcher of Roshaven, you are the Empress's champion. You may choose the weapon.'

Ned had to swallow twice before he could speak.

'I choose knives.'

There was a swell in crowd chatter as the pros and cons of knife fighting were discussed.

Theo looked put out.

'Knives? Really Eddie, I thought you would've chosen something a bit more flashy, like swords. Knives are so… provincial.'

Ned said nothing. His gaze had locked with Rose and he was trying to say goodbye with his eyes, hoping she got the message that he loved her.

'Do you both have knives? Or do you need one provided for you?' asked the High Left.

At least Ned assumed it was the Left, because he stood on the left of the Empress. He should've taken the time to learn which was which. Too late now. Ned pulled Joe's knife out of his belt and held it up for inspection.

There were some nods of appreciation at the blade. Theo produced his knife. It was two inches longer than Ned's and straddled more the sword side of weaponry than knife, but it was within the measurement allowance. If at the extreme end.

With both weapons approved, the fighters were asked to face each other.

'You have chosen to fight with knives,' intoned the High on the right.

Ned noticed he said knives plural. He had obviously had the same thoughts as Ned. Theo would cheat. By saying knives, Ned wouldn't be disqualified if he produced another blade to counteract Theo doing the same.

'Upon entering the arena, a magical force field will keep spectators out. The field will be lifted on completion of the fight. If you, Ned Spinks, Champion of the Empress, choose not to fight or surrender, then the challenger will win. If you, Theodore Michel de Silverthorpe, Challenger to the throne, choose not to fight or surrender, then the champion will win. The fight will last until one of you surrenders or dies. Do you understand?'

Both men nodded.

'Fight with honour.' The High held his hands palm out to Ned and Theo, a gesture for them to shake hands.

Neither one moved.

Ned looked his brother in the eye. How did they come to this? He didn't want to duel his brother to the death.

'Theo, I...' but Theo never gave him the chance to finish and instead strode confidently to the middle of the courtyard. It had been marked with a blue circle by Fred earlier that day.

Ned glanced around the crowd and clocked Fred standing with the other thief-catchers. Remembering what Jenni said about the gargoyles, he looked up at the sky-line and saw every rooftop seemed to have some kind of winged, demonic stone masonry upon it. The gargoyles would make sure no-one intervened.

The drumbeat changed tempo and sped up as Ned walked to the blue circle. Momma K was in his periphery. She had flown higher than the crowd and was extending her arms wide. The entire radius of the crowd glowed as Momma K completed an incantation. The magical barrier was up. There would be no interference from any of Theo's goons who were no doubt dotted about in the crowd.

Abruptly the drumming stopped. It was time to fight. The two brothers circled each other warily, Theo feinted a few times, trying to see how skittish Ned was.

'Feeling nervous, brother dear?' asked Theo.

'I don't want to kill you.'

'Then put down the knife and I'll make it quick.'

Ned tightened his grip on his blade and said nothing. They continue to circle, feinting here and there, but making no serious attacks. Ned recalled what Jenni had said about Theo trying to wear him out, so the next time his brother took a step forward, Ned took two steps forward and slashed at Theo's face.

The knife met arm and sliced through Theo's leather jerkin.

Theo danced back, malice glinting in his eyes, and changed hands with his blade, leant down and pulled another out of his boot. It wasn't as long but looked wickedly sharp.

'You never said how many blades, Eddie boy.'

'No. I didn't.' Ned shook his thief-catcher coat off his shoulders and kicked it to one side. Now he had access to a leather harness, criss-crossed around his front and back, which held two slightly curved fighting knives at the back and one shorter blade in the front. 'I know you, brother.'

The crowd went mental; feet stomping, hands clapping, voices shouting and screaming, all in approval of Ned's weaponry.

But the two men were so focused on each other that they had tuned out the noise. Ned pulled the short blade out. Now both brothers were doubly armed and the true dancing began.

Ned found he and Theo dropped back into their natural rhythm of old. Neither brother wanting to commit to defence or attack, preferring instead to exchange blow for blow. It wasn't getting either of them very far.

Ned decided to chance it and dropped back to a more defensive position. Theo reacted immediately, but instead of pushing forwards, he also dropped back. So now both brothers were crouched further apart than before.

'What are you playing at, Theo?'

'Just want to give the rabble something to talk about. It wouldn't do to kill you in the first five minutes.'

The crowd began muttering, they'd come to enjoy a

fight and so far, they'd seen nothing much. They couldn't even hear the fighters. Momma K took matters into her own hands and cast an incantation. Now the crowd could hear every word.

Chapter 49

The Empress sent a summons through the crowd, and the thief-catchers pushed through to where Rose was standing. There was no space on the platform itself, so the catchers thronged themselves in front. It was a prime viewing spot and several citizens had to be evicted.

Willow was watching the fight through her fingers, half-planted behind Joe, so she had someone to screen her should things get too tense. Sparks was flitting around, mirroring Ned's movements. Jenni clambered up on the edge of the platform so she sat at the feet of the Empress.

'Jenni?'

'Your Emperoressness?'

'Do you think Ned will win?'

'Depends.'

'On?'

'Ow much 'is bruvver cheats and whever Ned loses 'is temper or not.'

'He doesn't seem to be that hot-headed. Not normally, I mean.'

'No, 'e ain't usually, but this ain't usual.' Jenni stopped talking to join in the collective cheer as Ned drew the first blood. 'Watch 'im now, Boss. E'll be lookin' to taliate!' she yelled.

And sure enough, Theo rushed Ned furiously. Double blades flashing. But Ned saw the attack coming. He dodged the thrust. Theo unbalanced, overextended and sprawled to the floor.

'Finish him!' screamed the crowd.

'E won't,' commented Jenni to Rose. 'Gotta get 'is 'ead in the right place. S'not there yet.'

Rose watched as Ned gave his brother time to get up off the floor and collect his wits.

'He can't win this fight by being the better man, can he?' asked Rose.

'Nope. Let's 'ope 'e realises afore it's too late.'

Rose was filled with mounting fear as the two men continued to test each other. Whilst Ned had drawn first blood, it hadn't taken Theo long to retaliate, and the brothers were soon sporting a variety of defensive cuts on their arms and one on the ribs for Theo.

A particularly ferocious clash of blades had Rose wincing as Theo seemed to get in a lucky swipe at Ned's stomach, but Ned came away none the worse for wear.

'Jenni? Why didn't that attack effect Ned? You didn't cast a spell, did you?'

'Nah, it ain't me. Willow made 'im some special armour. 'Ere Willow, wot's that stuff you gave the boss?'

Willow rustled closer to them. 'It's a combination of hemp and jute. It won't stop a direct hit, but it will help to deflect blows. Why? Have I done something wrong? He won't be disqualified, will he?'

Rose hoped not and turned slightly to the High Right who had been listening to every word.

'My liege, there is nothing in the ancient rules that precludes prior preparation,' he said.

'Eh?' Jenni looked quizzically at Rose.

'It means you did nothing wrong, Willow. And thank you.'

The wood nymph blushed blossom and returned to clinging on Joe's arm as the fight continued.

Rose could see both men were tiring and the gaps

between attacks were getting longer. She didn't want Ned to have to kill his brother, but if the act had to happen, why did it have to drag out?

Ned and Theo had been quiet, but the taunts from Theo began anew. Rose and the entire crowd hushed to listen as he launched into a derisive monologue.

'Why don't you just give in, Eddie? Like you always do. You can't win because even if you beat me, you've lost. A good man like you–you'll lose your respectable name. Everything you've worked for. You'll have to quit your job. Can't have a murderer as a thief-catcher now, can we? You'll have to crawl back to Mum and Dad and beg them to forgive you for killing their favourite son. Beg them for a ground level grunt job, working in the muck and the grime with the other murderers. You'll never be able to look any of your friends in the eye again. You'll be an outcast. A loner. A nobody.'

Rose could see it was having an effect. The backs of Ned's ears were bright red, and the knuckles wrapped round his knife were white with what she assumed was clenched rage. Theo carried on.

'You can kiss goodbye to all your fae friends. When I am Emperor, that'll be my first decree. All the oddballs and freaks with their funny names and weird customs. I'll round them all up and put them to work in the mines. That or they can return to their namby pamby realm with me kicking the doors behind them. What good has magic ever been? What good did it ever do you apart from those gut-wrenching stomach aches and skull splitting migraines? You never mastered it. You, a freak like the rest of them, can't even perform a basic spell. Wrong it the head, Father called it. I say, they didn't drop you hard enough when they found out you had *the gift.*'

Rose listened to Theo sneer that last comment with

rising hatred. The man was an odious toad and absolutely full of it if he expected to get out of that courtyard alive. Nearly half the audience had magic, herself included. She glanced around and saw open anger and disgust on the faces of the surrounding people.

'Jenni? Momma K won't… weigh in, will she?' Rose risked a glance at the High Right. 'If anyone interferes, the fight is forfeit and as Challenger, Theo will win by default.'

Jenni grumbled a bit to herself before answering.

'Nah, she won't interfere. She abides by the laws of Roshaven, when she's 'ere. She knows she can't kill 'im for Ned. Believe me, we would've done that already.'

More baiting from Theo interrupted them.

'That little imp that follows you around, how much does she go for, eh?'

That was as far as he got before a roar escaped Ned. He slammed Joe's knife back in its sheath and threw the other with all his might at Theo. The knife cartwheeled through the air before the hilt slapped Theo's fingers with a loud smack, causing him to drop one of his knives. Caught off guard, Theo barely had time to react before Ned barrelled into him and the two of them grappled to the floor. Still armed, Theo tried to stab his brother in the neck. Somehow Ned kept blocking him and pushing the blade away. He grabbed Theo's wrist and twisted, forcing him to drop the second knife. They descended into fisticuffs and rage. Each man raining solid blows into opposition ribs, kidneys and jaws.

Rose saw the abandoned weapons fly across the courtyard and embed themselves in the side of the Emperor's platform. She looked for Momma K who wasn't that far away from her, a self-satisfied look on her face. Glancing at the Highs, Rose breathed out a sigh of relief. They hadn't appeared to have noticed. Just then, Theo reached round and drew one of Ned's fighting knives.

'He has your blade!' shouted Rose, unable to stop herself, but she needn't have panicked. Ned had clearly felt the knife leave the sheath and had instantly rolled away from his brother, rearming himself with Joe's blade at the same time. He crouched up to a cat stance, ready to fight, with the crowd completely behind him.

Chapter 50

Ned could sense his power skittering under his skin. Every taunt and jibe from Theo had hit its mark. His blood boiled. His magic often surfaced during times of great need and high emotion, but he knew he couldn't actively use it here, so he twirled the knife in his grip. When they'd been younger, Ned had always tried to fight fair, but Theo had always cheated somehow. It was time to force his hand.

'You'll never win,' said Ned in what he hoped was a confident tone. The crowd cheered.

'Not only am I going to win, Eddie, but I will take your woman and break her. I will take your city and reduce it to rubble. I will destroy every good thing you've ever touched,' said Theo.

'My name is Ned,' replied Ned through clenched teeth, his voice loud in the hushed courtyard. A persistent buzzing filled his ears.

'You're such a fool,' sneered Theo before launching an attack.

Ned reacted with quick feet, all down to his boots. He parried the dangerous blows whilst dancing to the side. He risked a rib-grazer and was impressed when Joe's blade connected with Theo's clothes, slicing through the material and drawing a thin red line.

The two men broke apart and Theo touched the slight scratch, then checked his fingers.

'Not quite, Eddie. You need to try harder, but then that was always the case, wasn't it?'

Ned breathed out hard, trying to keep his temper in

check, but his skin was throbbing and his hands were tingling. A faint shimmering had appeared on the edge of his vision. He shook his head, but it made no difference. They continued to circle.

'Come on, Eddie. Make a move, already. I've got things to do,' taunted Theo.

But Ned was waiting. Their constant motion had moved them from the centre of the courtyard over to the north side, closer to the Empress and closer to some looser cobbles. Only Theo didn't know about them. Ned did. It was his city. These were his streets and his cobbles, and if he could manoeuvre his brother into the right place, he'd lose his balance. Just… there. Theo wobbled. It was enough for him to momentarily lose focus. Ned struck like a cobra.

But Theo was faster than Ned had remembered and blocked the stab to his chest. The knife cut deeper this time and blood dripped down Theo's arm.

The crowd roared its approval and Ned's magic pulsed, desperate for release. Both men were breathing more heavily now. Ned's power was growing, surging, trying to break free.

'Nice try, brother dear.' Theo wasn't finished with the taunting. 'With you and your band of do-gooders out of the way, I'll take your pretty little Empress and show her what a real man is capable of. How far have you got, eh? A bit of tongue? A quick fumble under the skirts? Or is she a goer? Seems like she'd be an easy lay to me. Her mother is probably just a common street walker–it's not exactly imperial blood that runs through her veins, is it? Her father was a known philanderer. No wonder Roshaven is such a slutty dump…'

A gate within Ned suddenly opened. Magic flooded out of him and slammed into Theo. Raw, wild, protective. There was an enormous clap of thunder and a blinding flash of light. An energy shock wave blew Ned and Theo to opposite ends of the courtyard whilst knocking most of the crowd off their feet. There was a great deal of muttering as people got back up. Then silence fell.

Neither Theo nor Ned moved.

Momma K lifted her magical barrier and Jenni darted over to Ned.

'E's gotta pulse!' she yelled.

One of Theo's lackeys had rushed to his side, but before he made it, the body rapidly sank into itself and disappeared with a puff. There was nothing left except a pile of black sand. The lackey picked up a handful and let it run through his fingers.

'Did he win?' Rose grabbed the High Right's arm. 'I can't bear it.'

The High patted her hand.

'I've seen magic explode like that before. It's completely involuntary. Unpredictable. Only huge emotional strain can set it off,' he explained, a small smile on his face.

'You knew? You knew it might happen?' Rose was stunned.

'One thing I have learnt, my liege, is there are no certainties in life but yes, we hoped. Just as we hoped Ned would win the fight by whatever means necessary. You are safe, my Empress. Long may you rule.'

The High Right's voice rang out over the courtyard.

'I declare Ned Spinks, Chief Thief Catcher and Champion of Empress Rose, the winner.'

The crowd was slow to react.

Some of them were still dazed from the fight and magical blowback. Gradually the noise built. Cheering, whistling, clapping, foot stamping and a great deal of hugging was going on.

Ned groaned and tried to sit up. He winced as his body protested.

'Jenni? What happened? Where's Theo?' He looked blearily around the courtyard. 'Is it over? Am I dead?'

'Boss… you s'ploded. Your magics I mean. E was all up in yor face and saying all those fings. I reckon it musta needled you right deep down cos, Boss, you blew.'

'I blew? That's… bad?'

'I dunno. Old 'igh and mighty declared you was the winner.'

'What happened to Theo, Jenni?'

'When you blew, both of youse flew cross the courtyard. You this way, 'im that way, and neither of youse was moving or nuffink. Momma K let the barrier down and I ran over 'ere. Checked you for a pulse–good work, Boss. One of 'is lackeys went over there but afore 'e got there, Theo sorta dissolved.'

'Dissolved?'

'Yeah, e's a load of black sand now.' Jenni rocked back on her heels and looked into Ned's face.

He wasn't sure what she was looking for, so he didn't make eye contact. He was still trying to figure out how he felt. Pushing himself up onto wobbly legs, Ned began walking over to the other side of the courtyard. He wanted to see for himself.

Sure enough, there was a pile of black sand on the floor. Theo's lackey had stood in some of it.

'Huh,' said Ned.

'You wanna go see Rose?' asked Jenni.

'Yeah, let's do that.' Feeling like an old man, Ned made his way over to the imperial platform, the cheers of the onlookers drowned out for him by the look of gratitude and love tinged with sorrow from Rose.

'I believe your throne is now safe, my liege,' he said.

'Thank you, my champion.'

Ned nodded.

'I think I'm going to go home. Have a bit of a lie down.' He cast an apologetic smile towards Rose. 'I'll see you later.' And he turned with a wobble, ignoring the people who wanted to talk to him. Instead, he instructed his boots to carry their numb inhabitants home. And they did.

Chapter 51

Ned sat motionless in his armchair. He hadn't taken his boots off. To be fair, he usually didn't, and sometimes even slept with them on. It always paid to be prepared. His blood-stained clothing added to the suspect stains on the faded, floral pattern of the armchair. An untouched glass of scumble sat on the side table next to him, it's ice chunk melting. Ned's pipe lay beside the glass, primed and ready to light, but Ned hadn't got that far. In his mind, he was back in the courtyard.

It was quiet, though Ned was sure the crowd had been noisy. He could sense his power swirling deep down in his gut as he got madder and madder. He was upset about the things Theo had said, but he was also cross that he, Ned Spinks, had abandoned his brother to become this monster. He should have convinced Theo to go with him when he left, but he thought he was doing the right thing by leaving him behind. A life on an uncertain road with no money, no future was no life for a bright lad. Or so he'd thought. If he'd just taken Theo with him, he might have been a doctor or a lawyer or something else grand. Instead, he'd grown into a villain.

Ned relived every blow, both physical and verbal, wincing at his own that fell on Theo. The power was growing, surging, begging to be released, and Ned could feel his fingertips getting tingly. Theo taunted him again, and suddenly a gate opened. Magic flooded out of Ned and slammed into Theo. Raw, wild, protective. It was a wonder that he hadn't taken out anyone else. Then Ned remembered Jenni saying Momma K lowered her boundary to let people into the courtyard.

Hadn't she also touched him several days before the fight? Ned finally moved, wincing as he touched his forehead where Momma K had opened his fourth eye for him. Or so she said. The fourth eye was a magical extra that only some people possessed. It allowed the bearer to sense things, sometimes danger, sometimes opportunity and often another person's magic, but Ned had never been able to get his fourth eye working properly. Just like he'd never unblocked his magic. The only time he'd reliably been able to cast any kind of spell was during huge emotional stress concerning Rose. And even then, those were more accidental than purposeful.

Did Momma K give him a release spell of some kind that had been triggered by thought? Was Jenni part of it? Could he trust either of them?

Ned's thoughts strayed to Rose and his breath caught in his ribs, reminding him they had been badly bruised, much like the rest of his body. Would the Empress of Roshaven make it so that her champion would win, no matter the stakes? Ned thought an empress might do that, but Rose was… well, Rose. She would never force someone to kill someone else. Unless it was for the betterment of the realm. And getting rid of Theo was certainly for the betterment of Roshaven. Ned winced as his body shouted a little louder about its various hurts.

Thinking like this, he was going to keep running round and round in circles, which wouldn't do anyone any favours. He needed to have a bath, physically wash his own and his brother's blood off his body and make sure there were no serious injuries. Ned could feel the residue of his power skittering under his skin. He tried to grab hold of it, but it wouldn't be caught. Looked like his magic may have been unlocked but was still no closer to being tamed.

'As long as you're there when I need you, I guess that'll do,' Ned said to himself before hauling his body up out of the armchair and through to the kitchen where his bathtub sat. Indoor plumbing had caught on fast in Roshaven. Heated water, not so much. Ned lit the charcoal pit beneath his tub and began filling the bath with water. Once more his mind strayed back to the courtyard. It was quiet, though Ned was sure the crowd had been noisy.

Chapter 52

BANG! BANG! BANG!

The noise dimly registered with Ned. Someone was banging. Loudly. And very possibly at his door.

'Gngh.'

BANG! BANG! BANG!

'Alright! Alright, I'm coming.' Ned flung the covers off and gingerly levered himself up, out of bed. His body hurt. He limped down the stairs to the soundtrack of more banging on his door. He swung it open before they could knock again, and bright sunlight hit his eyes, making him squint and scowl. 'What?'

'Ah, Mr Spinks. Congratulations on the duel.'

It was Mr Simms. He was holding a large, pink, frilly pillow with extra tassels.

'What do you want?' Ned wasn't feeling very polite.

'This is the last item from Griff's will. The Pillow of Peace.'

'Let me guess, it has to be delivered to the Empress.'

Mr Simms allowed himself a small smile.

'Indeed, it does. But there is also the subject of attire.'

'Attire?' Ned was suddenly wary. 'What does it matter what I'm wearing?'

'Apparently the magical stipulations for this item are that you deliver it at one pm, dressed in your finest apparel.'

'Fine.' Ned grabbed the pillow and chucked it behind him where it landed on his armchair, wobbled then gave in to gravity and hit the floor.

Mr Simms flinched and then cleared his throat, a leftover affectation from when he was alive. As a zombie, he had no need for throat clearing.

'Do stop by the offices of Barnaby and Simms upon successful completion of this delivery. It will delight us to present you with your inheritance. Good day.'

He had barely tipped his hat before Ned slammed the door in his face.

Ned cursed Griff under his breath as he bent to pick the pillow up. With both hands on the soft furnishing, the tense knots in his shoulders eased, his furrowed brow relaxed, and he took a deep, calming breath. Placing the pillow on his armchair, all his stresses returned, but at a more manageable level.

'Jenni!' Ned yelled on the off chance that she was here, although he knew she was far too nosey to not answer the door herself. Where was she? Sighing, Ned considered going back to bed, but he wasn't sure he'd be able to sleep now. Less than twenty-four hours ago, he'd killed his brother. He supposed he ought to let his parents know.

Ned tried to plan a message in his head whilst rummaging for clothing that wasn't too rumpled. Once he was dressed, he forgot the time delivery instructions Mr Simms had given him and tucked the Pillow of Peace under his arm as he headed for the Imperial Palace hoping to see Rose.

As he strode through the city, it seemed that everyone he passed either smiled and waved or said a few words to him. Congratulations and well wishes at every turn. Ned was embarrassed and walked faster. When the palace guards saw him and raised three cheers, he near ran into the palace and he was slightly out of breath when he knocked on Rose's study door.

'Ned! Are you alright?' Rose gave him a hug which was unexpected but wonderful. He held on to her for as long as he could.

'I'm fine. I think. I've brought you this. It's the last item from Griff's will. The Pillow of Peace, apparently,' replied Ned.

'Oh, how… unique.' Rose raised an eyebrow at the ruffles and tassels. There was a lot going on for one pillow. 'Just pop it over there and I'll look at it later.' She pointed to a chair and Ned obliged. 'Can I get you anything? Tea? Honey cake?'

'Oh no, I can't stay. I've got to send a message. To my parents.'

As he spoke, Rose stopped smiling.

'Ned, I… if you need me to… what I mean is…'

'No, it's alright. Better if it comes from me.' He let out a short laugh. 'I just can't seem to think of the right words.'

Rose took him by the hand and pulled him to the couch where they both sat, facing each other.

'I don't even know how to thank you for what you did for me. For Roshaven. I wish I'd never had to ask you,' she said.

'I am your champion,' Ned replied, gazing in her eyes. They were still holding hands. He could feel the heat of her body, smell her perfume. She was so close. He leaned in and kissed her.

There was a loud knock on the door and they sprang apart as Jenni and Willow came in.

'Awright, Boss. Sleep well?' Jenni cocked her head at Ned, assessing him.

'It's good to see you up and about. Do you need anything, Boss?' asked Willow.

Ned cleared his throat and hoped he wasn't blushing

too much. He dare not look at Rose.

'Jenni, Willow. I'm fine. I was just bringing the empress Griff's last item,' explained Ned.

'Oh, wot was it then?' asked Jenni.

'The Pillow of Peace, apparently.'

'Never 'eard of it,' Jenni said cheerfully. 'You staying? Only I didn't fink you was meant to be 'ere.'

Ned frowned and looked at Rose quizzically. She smothered a giggle.

'I'm afraid we ladies have an important delivery today.' She softened her voice. 'But if you need me, I can cancel things. Whatever you want.' She touched his arm, sending shivers down his spine.

Ignoring the delighted stares of Jenni and Willow, Ned leaned in and kissed Rose on the cheek before standing, becoming more and more awkward under their scrutiny.

'No, it's fine. I've got to go to the Runners Office. Ladies' He swept a mock bow at them all, which made them laugh before he left them to their important delivery. He wondered idly for a few moments what it might be, but figured he'd find out soon enough and he bent his thoughts back on what he was going to tell his parents. His heart singing despite the grim task ahead.

The Runners Office was up on Shifters Street and used to be accommodation for fast boys, and girls, who would deliver your message as quickly as possible, for a fee. Nowadays most of the messaging was done through wires and complex tapping. Letters and parcels went on the express coaches and were delivered to the Runners Office for collection or delivery. Ned didn't understand how the tapping worked but it would be the fastest way to get a message to his parents. Short of using magic, of course. Ned didn't want to use magic.

'Good morning! How may we help?' came the cheerful greeting as Ned pushed open the Runners Office door.

'I want to send a message...' Ned began, but he never finished as a very excited clerk bustled around the counter with a large envelope in his hands.

'Here is your message, my lord.'

Lord? Ned narrowed his eyes and gingerly took the letter. It was thick and weighty, but he didn't recognise the handwriting. Tearing it open, he let the envelope fall to the floor in surprise as he read the contents.

From: The Official Records Office
To: Lord Edward de Silverthorpe, Ruler of Fidelia and Roshaven's Chief Thief-Catcher

Greetings and Salutations. Here at the ORO we are delighted to be the first to congratulate you on your new position. We can confirm that the nobility ledgers are being updated as we speak and that your new title of Lord of Fidelia has been legally confirmed.

We wish you a very pleasant day. *Don't forget, it's your generous contributions that keep our offices afloat. So don't delay - order your copy of The Lords and Ladies of Our Land with full colour portraits and pull out, gold-embossed family trees. Just 999 gold bits. Get your copy today!*

Ned snorted at that. The whole thing looked like it was trying way too hard. It must be a fake. A scam to cheat naïve people out of their money.

'Everything alright, my lord?'

'Don't call me that,' Ned muttered, then he glared at the clerk. 'When did you get this?'

'It came on the overnight express, my lord.'

'Were there any other copies?'

'No, my lord. But an updated Lords and Ladies Announcement pamphlet was delivered to the Imperial Palace. Oh, and one to the Thief-Catchers office and of course one to the ruling council in Fidelia.' The clerk readjusted his glasses. 'May I offer our congratulations, my lord?'

'No, you may not.' Ned was confused. Why had he been made the new lord? Surely his father would have been next in line? Then again, Theo had bought the title, no doubt using nefarious ways. There were probably pages of fine print.

Ned left the Runners Office without sending his message. His parents would already be aware of what had happened. His relationship with them was strained at the best of times. He was going to have to sit down and figure out what to say to them. 'Dammit it!' Ned stalked to thief-catcher HQ.

Joe was the only catcher there. He was wrapping elastic bands around an elastic band ball. There were several snapped bands on the floor beside him, as well as a daisy-chain of paperclips.

'Busy, are we?' Ned commented as he shifted a few stacks of paperwork on his desk.

Joe had scrambled to his feet.

'Sorry, Boss. We wasn't expecting you on account of...' He trailed off. 'Congratulations on the er... position.'

Ned breathed out of nose, doing his best to keep his cool and not take his building ire out on the lad.

'Where's Sparks?'

'Um, Sparks is patrolling. He prefers to zip on his own. Something to do with casting shadows. And Willow and Jenni have gone to the Imperial Palace.'

Ned didn't reply, he already knew where they were.

'They had an appointment. They didn't just go, Boss. It's on the planner.' Joe pointed to the wall.

The planner was another of Joe's bright ideas. Along with the clipboard, he had explained to the others that sticking the year up on the wall and writing in the impossibly small boxes what you were doing months in advance was an important, effective work tool. Ned was of the opinion that if you didn't know what you were doing tomorrow, then there was little chance you'd know in six months' time and a piece of paper on the wall would be no help whatsoever. Consequently, his row was defiantly empty. Jenni had decorated hers with colourful phrases whilst Willow had drawn various flora. Only Joe had taken it very seriously and even gone as far as helpfully filling in other people's dates for them. Sure enough, there was *Appointment at the Palace* written in his clear hand.

'Yes, I saw them this morning,' said Ned. 'Have you seen a pen?'

Joe hurried over to his filing cabinet. He'd been insistent he got one. It only had two drawers, but Ned knew it was his pride and joy.

'Here you go, Boss. Some paper too.'

Ned nodded his thanks and sat down expertly on his chair. He had to be an expert to sit on his chair because there were multiple ways it could break and collapse, spilling him out to the floor. Much like his clapped-out boots, the chair was a comfort to him. Ned believed it kept his nerves sharp and his mind keen.

Joe went back to his rubber bands as Ned bent to his task. He needed to write a letter that would tell his parents what happened in the gentlest way possible. It took him several minutes before he could think of how to start. *Hi Mum and Dad* felt too casual, *My Beloved*

Parents too emotional and just writing out their names too weird.

'That your folks, Boss?' Joe had wandered over to Ned and was peering over his shoulder at the note.

'Yes. I have to speak with them about... what happened.'

'How are you going to manage that then?' Joe asked.

Ned frowned up at him. 'What do you mean?'

'Well, it takes a few days to get there, doesn't it? And then a few days to get back. Everyone is talking about what happened. You missed yesterday's express coach already. And then your family will probably want to talk to you about... things.'

'Yes, thank you, Joe. I shall use today's express coach.'

Joe looked out the window. The sun was climbing in the sky, nearing midday.

'You'd better hurry, Boss. It leaves soon.'

Scowling, Ned rummaged in his desk drawer and retrieved the emergency cash box. Thankfully, he'd remembered to refill it after the last emergency.

'Joe, stay alert.' He felt bad for the lad, as if he were leaving him in the lurch. Ned clapped a hand on Joe's shoulder. 'Look after yourself. I'll be back before you know it.'

Joe nodded in bemusement.

Chapter 53

The Imperial Palace was buzzing. Jenni and Willow were amongst the excited gaggle in the courtyard as a huge white box arrived for the Empress. Everyone volunteered to help carry the parcel to the official dressing room, which was fine in theory, but because there were far too many hands for bodily space, both Jenni and Willow had to resort to sharp elbows, or in Willow's case–thorns, in order to keep their spot.

Rose was pacing. Her eyes lit up when the package arrived. She shooed out most of the excitable women, leaving just Jenni, Willow and her maid.

'I can't believe we did this. Let's open the box.' Rose's voice was filled with excitement and the others needed no further urging.

A little while later they stood admiring the dress. It was raw silk in the palest pink. A full skirt and train that pinned up to a small bustle was set beneath a fitted bodice with tiny crystals winking across the fabric. A delicate floor length veil accompanied the dress with crystals at its hem.

'It's so beautiful,' breathed Rose.

'Not bad at all,' offered Jenni. 'You gonna try it on?'

Rose wrung her hands a little.

'Do you think I should? Isn't it a bit... presumptuous?'

With everyone's reassurance, Rose let herself be led behind her changing screen by her maid. So began the painstaking process of trying on the dress.

'It's not bad luck, is it?' Rose overheard Willow

whisper to Jenni.

'Nah. It's only bad luck if the groom sees it afore the day. And e's dead.'

Rose shivered. It was true that her wedding was going to be to Theo, but she'd chosen the dress in the vain hope that would never happen and she would be allowed to marry who she wanted to.

Eventually, she emerged–a vision in pink. Willow gasped and blossomed in delight whilst Jenni gave an appreciative whistle.

'Do you like it?' asked Willow as Rose approached the full-length mirror.

Rose twirled a little in front of the mirror. 'It's wonderful. Do you think he'll like it? Ned, I mean.'

'Oh yeah, 'e loves pink.' Jenni's expression drew serious. 'Was 'e alright when you spoke to 'im?'

Rose's face fell into sadness.

'He said he was, but I don't think he's really processed everything yet. Weren't you with him last night, Jenni?'

'Nah. I fawt I'd give 'im some space and stuff. Figured e'd 'ave fings to work out and that. I didn't want to make 'im feel like 'e had to be alright wiv it. You know?'

The others nodded. Apart from the maid who, like all household staff, had blended into the background and was listening intently ready to report back all the gossip at the supper table later. Rose knew the staff would gossip either way and preferred them to get their scandal directly from the horses' mouth, so to speak.

There was a loud knocking and one of the Highs called through.

'I have pressing news, my liege.'

Rose nodded permission at her maid to let the High

in. He bustled through the door, puffed up with self-importance, and stopped dead at the sight of Rose in her wedding gown.

'Oh, my empress. You look wonderful.'

'Thank you. The message?' Rose smoothed her hands over the dress, luxuriating in the feel of the fabric, as she waited for the news.

'Ahem. We have had an urgent missive from Fidelia. They have declared Edmund de Silverthorpe, also known as Ned Spinks, as their new lord. He is officially ruling nobility. An important... distinction, my liege.'

Rose knew instantly what the High was getting at. Ned was marriageable. As a legally recognised member of the ruling nobility, she could wed him.

'Does he know?' asked Rose.

'We haven't been able to find him yet, my liege. But it's only a matter of time. I've got my best men on the case.'

Rose could see Jenni frowning out of the corner of her eye.

'Perhaps Jenni and Willow could assist the search?' suggested Rose.

The High sniffed and pursed his lips.

'We have one more patrol to send out. You can accompany Palace Guard Fred if you wish.'

'On it.' Jenni presented a semi-passable curtsey to Rose and grabbed Willow by the arm to go scoop up Fred from the courtyard, but someone else knocking at the door stopped her.

It was Fred, accompanied by Joe.

'Wot you doing 'ere?' asked Jenni.

Joe ducked a bow to everyone in the room.

'Um... Ned's gone, or at least, about to go to Fidelia. On the Midday coach. I wasn't sure if it was an emergency or not, so I came here,' he said.

'He's leaving? How much time do we have?' Rose asked urgently.

'Not a lot. 'Ow fast can yer run?' Jenni replied.

'Fast enough.'

And so it was that the first Empress of Roshaven led an unusual bunch of subjects down the cobbled streets as quickly as a woman can run in a silken wedding gown. Naturally, the streets filled with onlookers cheering her on. Rose, Jenni, Willow, Joe and Fred careered around the final corner to the coach park. The coach was getting ready to pull away.

'Wait! I command you to wait!' At least that's what Rose tried to say, but she was so winded, it came out as little more than a whispered croak. She had to put her hands on her knees and try to get her breath back.

Both Fred and Joe had taken a firm hold of the situation, grabbed initiative by the short and curlies and were now banging on the coach doors, scaring the life out of the passengers inside.

'What the bloody hell is going on?' asked Ned, coming out from behind the coach.

Chapter 54

Ned tried to take in the scene before him. Fred and Joe were leaning against each other and gasping whilst Willow was wilted. Jenni was attempting to appear casual propped up against a nearby wall, but Ned knew she was only pretending everything was peachy. He could see her breathing heavily, like she'd just run for her life. They all did. Even Rose, who was wearing the most beautiful outfit he'd ever seen.

'Don't look at me!' screeched Rose.

Ned shut his eyes instantly.

'Will someone please tell me what's going on?' he asked. 'And when I can open my eyes?'

'In a minute,' said Rose before entering an intense bout of whispering.

Ned dithered. He really wanted to know what was happening, but he also needed to give the Coachmaster his urgent letter otherwise he'd have to wait until tomorrow before he could send it to Fidelia.

'Okay, you can look now,' said Rose.

'I um…' Ned looked for Rose but couldn't see her, just lots of ivy covering the wall where Jenni had stood.

There was a clatter of hooves and the imperial coach rolled into the coach yard. Being a relatively small town, the imperial palace wasn't that far away from anywhere in Roshaven, and one of the Highs had clearly had the presence of mind to send the coach after the runners. The ivy moved and got into the imperial coach. Rose's voice called out again.

'Ned, please don't leave for Fidelia yet. I need to

talk to you.'

The Coachmaster grimaced at Ned and tipped his head at the waiting coach, indicating they needed to go but could not counter orders from the empress.

Ned passed his letter up to the Coachmaster who placed it inside his express mail bag. With a piercing whistle, he urged his team of horses to spring into action. Ned coughed at being in the middle of the leaving dust swirl.

'Ned, I know this is odd but don't look in the carriage. Please,' begged Rose.

'Fine.' He stood with his back to the window.

'Will you come to the palace?' asked Rose.

'Am I allowed to look at you when I get there?' Ned replied waspishly.

Rose tinkled with laughter.

'Of course. As long as you let me get changed first.'

'Fine. I'll meet you there.' Ned moved away from the carriage, allowing the imperial horses to turn and clatter back to the palace.

'Boss.' Jenni had recovered sufficiently to stand on her own two feet.

'What was all that about?' asked Ned.

'Why wos you leaving wivout saying nuffink?' countered Jenni.

'I wasn't leaving. I was sending a letter to my parents on the express coach. Why did you think I was leaving?'

'Cos Joe said.'

Ned shook his head in exasperation.

'No, I told him I was writing to my parents, and he said it would take a few days to get there and they'd probably want to talk to me about it.' He frowned. 'Huh, I suppose I can see how he might have thought I was physically going. But I'm not, I was just trying to explain to them what happened.'

'Ow you gonna do that?' Jenni sniffed. 'You gonna write 'allo, I killed me bruvver, how's fings? That ain't gonna work out very well, is it?'

'Well, no. Obviously, I didn't put it quite like that, but I had to say something.'

Jenni shrugged.

'Pends if you want yor parents in yor life or not, I guess.'

They began walking towards the palace, the other catchers and Fred falling in behind.

'I feel like I at least owe them an explanation,' Ned said at last.

'Mebbe. And mebbe fighting for yor city, and for yor love, is summink they can understand. By now they'll already know it 'appened. There's a chance for a bit of 'appiness 'ere for you. If you wants it. 'ear wot Rose's got to say afore you do anyfink else. That's all I'm saying.'

By the time they returned to the palace, both Highs had obviously been briefed to meet them, because they stood waiting with enormous smiles on their faces. Ned was instantly nervous.

'Welcome, welcome my Lord. It is an honour to receive you. The empress will join you in her study momentarily,' said the High Left.

Ned blinked at that. Not the study part, he'd been there before, but the honour part. Essentially, he was exactly the same person he'd been last time they'd seen him. It seemed the addition of a title, no matter how you got one, made all the difference.

Rose wasn't there yet and after Ned, Jenni, Willow, Joe and Fred came in, the study was definitely a bit on the cosy side.

'Fred?'

The young palace guard sprang to attention.

'Yes, Mr Spinks, Sir? I mean, my Lord, Sir?'

'Thank you. I think I can take it from here. Willow, Joe, get back to HQ, would you? You too, Jenni.'

A chorus of embarrassed affirmatives were murmured as they left, and the study was now a lot bigger. Even Jenni had left without a fuss.

There was a loud pop from the direction of the fireplace. Ned turned to see if anything was on fire. There were no flames. Instead, Griff stood in front of him.

Chapter 55

'Ned, my boy!' roared Griff and swept him into a bear hug.

'What?' Ned pushed him away and tried to process what was happening. 'You're supposed to be dead.'

Griff held his arms out and puffed his chest out.

'Are you a ghost?' Ned was having trouble getting past the *meant to be dead* aspect.

'No. I am here and you need to catch me up. What's been going on? Why aren't you dressed to get married?' Griff peered around, looking for a bride that might be stashed away in a corner.

'Get married? Why would I be getting married?'

'Because of the gifts. They were all designed to give you a little push into her arms. And then I would appear at the end–we'd laugh, we'd cry, we'd dance, we'd feast and you and Fourteen would wed. Happy days.'

'Rose. Her name is Rose now.' Ned rubbed a hand over his face. 'Mr Simms said if I didn't deliver the items there would be dire consequences. You played me.'

Griff gave a little shrug.

'Who says the consequences wouldn't have been dire, eh? You two should be together, everyone can see it.'

Ned stared at the smuggler in disbelief. After everything he'd been through with delivering the magical gifts, it turned out that nothing bad would've happened if he'd not even bothered. Ned was too gobsmacked to marshal a suitable response, so he decided to focus on the other issue.

'Can we get back to the part where you're not dead, please?' He flopped down into a chair and gestured for Griff to sit on the couch.

Griff sat, his usual jolly demeanour absent. Ned waited for him to speak.

'I got shot, that much is true. Theo's men have wicked aim, but I haven't sailed around the four seas, visited the Forgotten Isles and learnt the mysterious ways of the N'ka N'ka people without picking up a few tricks. My body has safeguards against things like death. For now.'

Ned knew he was going to have to find out about the travelling to far-flung places another day.

'Where did you go?' he asked instead.

'A physical shell remained, but my essence went into a sort of stasis. It's hard to explain, but it involved ancient forces. I made sacrifices.' Griff's face turned sombre. 'It's not an easy path to travel.'

'We burnt your body. We gave you a state funeral. How have you got another body?'

'I told you, ancient forces and sacrifices. I'm no expert on the mechanics. But a state funeral you say? Who came? No, never mind that. Who shot the arrow? Did they have to do it several times?' Griff leaned forward eagerly.

Ned was getting annoyed.

'Everyone came, and I shot the ruddy arrow. We mourned you, the whole city. And then we found out your utter lack of business sense. Whatever possessed you to not leave details on the trade agreements you set up? Or not put a second in place to run things while you were in bloody stasis.' Ned was about to let Griff answer when he remembered something else. 'And why the gods did you curse us with that bean drink? Do you know how addictive that stuff is?'

'I left a second. And a third. They were both killed by your brother when he killed me. He has big ambitions, Ned, my boy. We have to stop him before he gets any more silly ideas in his head. But don't worry, I have a plan,' Griff settled back into the couch, his smile back on his face. 'As for the bean, create a little demand and people will be begging for more, my lad. It's simple commerce.'

'Tell that to the bean addicts. There is no more, and your fancy little shop has gone out of business.' Ned jabbed a finger in Griff's direction. 'And don't bother planning anything. Theo's already dead. And we've already renegotiated all our trade deals. You don't need to do anything.' Ned had a twinge of guilt for being harsh, but he was angry at being manipulated.

'Okay, you can fill me in on those details later.' Griff looked ruffled. 'What about the gifts? And why the imperial name change?'

'Oh, I delivered your gifts. Except for the pillow, I forgot about that one. But now I see it was all some elaborate game of yours. And she changed her name because Rose is Empress of Roshaven, formally crowned and almost married off to my brother because of some fake ancient scroll which you better not have had anything to do with.' Ned pointed a finger at Griff, who put his hands up in denial. 'What was the big idea with them, anyway?' Ned gestured at the pillow, which was looking a little forlorn.

'When I saw you and Rose together in Fidelia, I knew you were meant for each other. So, I thought I would help you get past the red tape. I spelled the magical items to speak to the inner desires of you both. I would reappear at the delivery of the pillow, ready to marry you. After all, a Captain has that right.'

'We're not about to get married! We've barely spent any time together, what with everything going on. You can't force two people together because you think we're meant to be. You don't get to make that decision. You're not my father.'

'Actually, I need to talk to you about that…'

Ned stared at Griff in disbelief.

'You have to understand, I was a dashing, swashbuckling smuggler and pirate whilst your mother was facing a loveless marriage to a crime lord who cared more about making money than anything else,' said Griff. 'It was a dalliance of passion, a few snatched nights, and then fate intervened and you were created.'

Ned's mouth hung open. It was like the disparate aspects of his life had slotted into place. Why he'd never had a connection to his father—why his father had never cared a jot what he did—why he never felt close to Theo.

'You're my father?'

Again Griff stood and opened his arms wide. This time Ned hugged him back fiercely. A thousand questions were whirling through his head at what this meant. It meant he wasn't legally Lord of Fidelia. Abruptly his elation died.

Ned stepped away from Griff and slumped back into his chair.

'So my question to you, is why aren't you dressed in your finest as per my instruction?' asked Griff.

'What's the point?'

'What's the point? We're going to have a wedding, my boy. You and Rose, all our friends. I have been looking forward to this party.' Griff winked at his son.

'I can't marry her. If I'm not Theo's brother, then

I'm not Lord of Fidelia anymore.'

'Pfft. Who wants to be Lord of Fidelia? Did you pay no attention to the titles in my will?' Griff was grinning widely.

Ned frowned, then remembered Mr Simms reading them at the Imperial Palace. His smile grew.

'Are you really the Duke of Kinglass?' he asked.

'Of course, I am. And more besides. You don't get to be as heroic and dashing as me without earning rich rewards. Makes you a Marquess, my boy.'

Ned laughed.

'One day you're going to have to tell me all about it, but right now, I'm waiting for Rose. We're in her study. She will be so pleased to see you. I never knew you two were so close.'

Griff was still grinning from ear to ear.

'She was always my favourite emperorling,' he said indulgently.

There was a knock and a High poked his head around the door.

'Have you spoken with the Empress yet, my Lord?' asked the High Right.

'No, she hasn't arrived yet,' replied Ned.

The High flicked a glance at Griff, then did a double take.

'You're supposed to be dead.'

'What can I say?' Griff winked at the High.

'Yes, well, never mind that right now. My lord, your new status means that marriage to our Empress can be looked upon favourably but there is still the matter of, how shall I put it, liquidity?' The High Right raised both his eyebrows at Ned.

Ned had absolutely no idea what he was talking about.

'I hear our Chief Thief-Catcher is about to come into a considerable amount of coin.' Griff pointed to the pillow. 'He has fulfilled all the requirements of my last will and testament.'

'Is that even legit now?' muttered Ned to Griff.

'As legit as it needs to be,' the smuggler muttered back.

The High Right twitched a smile, bowed his head and left them alone in the study.

'Why was he asking about liquid? And why did you mention the inheritance? And why am I still getting that?'

'I expect the imperial crown is broke. Most royalty is. So a suitable match must have wealth and title. Liquidity is a measure of wealth, you either flow or you don't. And you, my boy, will flow. I've got plenty more where that came from.'

'I'm not taking dirty coin.' Ned looked Griff in the eye. 'I will not bring blood money to Rose.'

'Son, I'm a smuggler. It's tarnished but a little. I promise.'

Not feeling entirely satisfied, Ned decided he would talk to Griff about this in more detail. Now that their relationship had changed, it was time for a little more honesty on Griff's part and a little less blind eye on Ned's.

Chapter 56

Ned and Griff stood up as Rose came into the study.

'I'm sorry it took me such a long time to change.' She looked at the two men in the room and her mouth gaped open in surprise. 'Griff? But you're dead? What are you doing here?'

'I am born again my liege, much like yourself I hear, eh?' Griff winked at the Empress who did not smile.

'Do you have any idea what we've been through? The city nearly lost everything and you think you can just waltz in and announce you're not actually dead? Who do you think you are?' asked Rose.

'Yeah, Griff. You could have sent us a message. Letting people who care about you think you're dead is pretty low, even for a smuggler,' added Ned.

Griff flinched a little at the venom in Ned's voice whilst Rose picked up the Pillow of Peace and hugged it to her stomach.

'I'm sure Griff did what he thought was best,' she said with a smile for the older man.

Ned frowned.

'You were blazing angry a minute ago, what's going on?' He touched the pillow and his frown faded. He felt calmer and happier.

Ned and Rose smiled at each other, both touching the pillow.

'The Pillow of Peace. Should come in handy when the two of you are wed, don't you think?' Griff had moved over to where a brandy decanter stood and helped himself to a tumbler full.

'Married?' asked Rose, letting go of the pillow as Ned did the same. It fell with a soft plop on the floor.

'Why not? I bet you've got a dress.' Griff knocked back the drink. 'I can marry you right now if you want.'

Ned and Rose looked at each other. He knew it was what he wanted.

'Rose… I want to marry you more than anything else in the world.' Ned stopped talking, his eyes searching her face anxiously.

She stepped closer to him, smiling.

'Me too. Want to marry you, I mean,' she said.

They were holding hands and gazing at each other adoringly.

'Are we doing this now then kids?' Griff broke the spell.

The two of them leaned into each other and turned their gaze on him.

'I'll need at least a day to get everything ready, but yes, we're doing this. Tomorrow?' suggested Rose.

'Tomorrow,' agreed Ned and Griff clapped his hands in delight.

'On behalf of the empire of Roshaven, let me officially welcome you back to the land of the living, as long as you promise not to fake your own death again,' said Rose, straight-faced.

'I can't promise that, but I will try to give you a heads-up next time. Best I can do, eh? How does that sound, son?' Griff looked to Ned and beamed.

'Son?' Rose queried.

'Empress Rose, meet my father, Griffin Bartholomew the Third, Duke of Kinglass.'

Rose stepped away from Ned and looked first at Griff, then Ned, and then back again.

'But that means… you're not officially the Lord of

Fidelia,' she said in a small voice.

'Nope. Thank the gods for that, but it means I'm a Marquess and apparently very watery,' said Ned in triumph.

'Liquid. He means he has plenty of capital,' corrected Griff.

Understanding dawned on Rose's face, and Ned could see her disappointment fade away.

'So, we really can get married?' she asked him.

He grinned back at her, and this time he moved close enough to sweep her into his arms and hug her.

A polite cough from Griff interrupted their embrace.

'I have one other piece of news that I need to bring to your attention. It's to do with the Spice Ghosts,' he said.

'The Spice Ghosts? That's a fae tale to scare children who won't do what they're told,' scoffed Rose. She'd stopped hugging Ned but was still holding his hand.

'I would have thought you'd know by now that most fae tales have some basis in truth, living so close with them as you do here,' replied Griff. His face had lost all its previous mirth. 'They are coming, and they are bent on revenge.'

'Why are they coming here? We haven't done anything,' objected Ned. 'Most of the people here don't even believe in the Spice Ghosts.'

'Someone stole their sacred spirit guide bones, leaving them, and the rest of us, open to unpleasant spirits. They must be returned or else the Spice Ghosts can no longer protect our world from the spirit realm.' Griff had lost his customary mirth and his face was stony serious.

Ned had too many questions. He went for the

obvious one.

‘Who do they think stole them?’

Griff shifted his stance a little and dropped his gaze from Ned as he answered.

‘Jenni.’

The End

Ned and Jenni return in *The Bone Thief*

Get your copy here:
https://books2read.com/u/3LRkgD

The Spice Ghosts have descended on Roshaven accusing Jenni of stealing their sacred bones and are threatening to destroy the city if they are not returned but Jenni the sprite has no idea what they're talking about.

With the help of her boss, Chief Thief-Catcher Ned Spinks, Jenni promises to find and return them however the skeletal trail leads them into the dark and dangerous waters of the dread Sea Witch.

Ned is out of his depth and frantically treading water while Jenni must fight to avoid becoming catch of the day.

Huge Thanks

My thanks go, as always, to my husband Kevin for putting up with me while I ride the writer rollercoaster which has been particularly tough as *The Silk Thief* was written during the Covid-19 pandemic.

Thank you to my brilliant crit group EM Swift-Hook, Darrell Nelson and Scott Tarbet for their valuable input into the first draft and to my wonderful team of beta readers - Donna Tyrrell, Brent A. Harris, Ian Bristow and Martin Frowd. Your fantastic attention to detail and willingness to discuss plot intricacies with me at awkward times of day was invaluable.

Huge additional thanks to Ian Bristow, who created the beautiful cover for The Silk Thief. He captured my empress perfectly. You can find out more about his artwork at www.iancbristow.com

About the Author

Sign up to Claire's newsletter for exclusive content and all the latest writing news: http://eepurl.com/csWd0f

Follow Claire on Twitter: @grasshopper2407
Like Claire on Facebook: facebook.com/busswriter
Visit her website: www.clairebuss.co.uk

Claire Buss is a multi-genre author and poet based in the UK. She wanted to be Lois Lane when she grew up but work experience at her local paper was eye-opening. Instead, Claire went on to work in a variety of admin roles for over a decade but never felt quite at home. An avid reader, baker and Pinterest addict Claire won second place in the Barking and Dagenham Pen to Print writing competition in 2015 with her debut novel, The Gaia Effect, setting her writing career in motion. She continues to write passionately and is hopelessly addicted to cake.

The Interspecies Poker Tournament
Case 27 of The Roshaven Files

Ned Spinks, Chief Thief-Catcher, has a new case. A murderous moustache-wearing cult is killing off members of Roshaven's fae community. At least that's what he's been led to believe by his not-so-trusty sidekick, Jenni the sprite. She has information she's not sharing but plans to get her boss into the Interspecies Poker Tournament so he can catch the bad guy and save the day. If only Ned knew how to play!

The Interspecies Poker Tournament, Case 27 of The Roshaven Files, is a humorous fantasy novella following the adventures of Ned Spinks and Jenni, a prequel to The Rose Thief. If you loved Terry Pratchett's Discworld, you'll love Roshaven.

Get your copy here: https://books2read.com/u/m2Vk0R

www.ingramcontent.com/pod-product-compliance
Lightning Source LLC
Chambersburg PA
CBHW050754190726

48285CB00005B/1653